LAND OF PROFIT

Land of Profit
Copyright © 2010

D.M. Edwards
dmedwardsauthor@gmail.com

LAND OF PROFIT

A Julian Sebasst Novel

By

D.M. EDWARDS

Chapter 1

By midday, *Southern Comfort* was off the coast of Oregon, cutting its way effortlessly through the choppy water. The eight-level maroon and black hybrid ship with its low-profile body and aggressive-looking catamaran hull looked and moved more like a high-speed yacht than a luxurious cruise liner.

Kane was standing on the balcony of his stateroom watching a Coast Guard cutter from Reedsport off in the distance. He couldn't wait to get off the ship as he was sure the same was true for the professor in the room across the hall. Dr. Permullter rarely left his stateroom, choosing to eat most of his meals behind closed doors; the majority which ended back on the tray in the hallway, uneaten. The professor was scared, and he had a reason to be.

Kane came in from the balcony and shut the door. A large panda bear he brought in Panama for Hanna toppled over on the floor. He propped the stuffed animal back on the chair, and called Roth's room, again. There was still no answer. He left another message and hung up—frustrated.

The only thing worse than being on the ship the last six days, was putting up with Erik Roth. Aside from being a narcissist, Roth was a carnivore of women with a pimp attitude, and a psychopath. Women found him irresistible and charming, but he was vicious and enjoyed hurting people. Kane had tried keeping him on a short leash, but it hadn't worked. Roth was uncontrollable. He had killed one of the professors in London, thinking he had the stones, only to discover he was wrong.

* * *

Roth was sunbathing on the promenade deck wearing sunglasses reading a book someone had discarded on a nearby table. He was no more interested in the cheesy romance novel than having his bronzed skin baked further by the hot sun. What he did like was looking good. His naturally sun-bleached hair was cropped on the sides, and tousled on top with a smidge of mousse; his six-pack looking like it was chiseled into his abdomen. It was his bad boy looks and image that the former professional boxer relied on to get women.

Roth reached over and grabbed the bottle of sun block off the chair. He smeared more oil than he needed over his biceps and stomach, then placed the bottle on table next to the empty beer mug.

He got up and went to the outdoor bar for another drink. After he was through, he went to the other side of the ship looking for the blonde he had seen earlier. He found her sleeping on a hammock next to the kid's pool. The woman's white one-piece bathing suit pulled taunt across her flat stomach and arching bosom. One of her long tanned legs dangled off the side of the hammock, and her tussled hair covered most of her face. She was a cougar in waiting—middle-aged, with a body as flawless as her face. Suddenly, she rolled over onto her stomach as though she sensed someone was watching her.

Roth had been on the ship for six days and had slept with just as many women. Tonight was the final night of the cruise and the voluptuous blond would be his last conquest. He thought of waking her, but changed his mind. There was plenty of time.

Roth noticed two mildly attractive women on the other side of the pool watching him. He finished his drink, then slowly strolled over to the diving pool. He climbed the steps to the fifteen-foot-high platform, where he executed a near flawless pike dive. He got out of the water, and took his time drying off his body.

He left the promenade and went down to his stateroom. Despite the last minute reservations and limited space, he had secured a nice room with a balcony. Room service had delivered his pressed tuxedo, which was on the bed. He removed the plastic and inspected the suit. Tonight, a lavish party was being held in the Rotunda by the ship owner and everyone was invited. Roth was determined to be the best dressed man there. He hung the suit in the closet and changed into jogging shorts.

That evening, a crowd of men and women dressed in black suits and gowns, clustered around the staircase leading down into the Rotunda. The circular room was the hub for the 1,300-room ship and the size of a baseball park infield. The white floor sparkled like diamonds in snow from the 1,200-pound crystal chandelier overhead.

White-gloved attendants dressed in tuxes passed out complimentary flutes of champagne to the people coming down the marbled staircase. Elias Kane ignored the drink as he crossed the Rotunda to the dance club. The glass doors were closed, but they couldn't muffle the music from the overhead speakers. People moved like a giant organism dancing on the glass-lit floor. Kane didn't have to go in to know that Roth wasn't there. He went upstairs to the Bay Lounge, which was Roth's favorite after hour's hangout.

The room was a welcomed retreat from the noise and bright strobe lights of the club. The room of plush beige carpet and drapes was comforting to his eyes. White wingback chairs and smoked-glass tables were thoughtfully arranged around an open fireplace and S-shaped bar. Kane estimated eighty to one hundred people in the room, but none were Roth. Roth's three men were drinking at the bar. The three hundred pound South Africans looked ridiculous in their cheap off-the-rack suits that were purchased that day. Everyone was dressed for the occasion, except Kane.

Kane didn't care conformity. He wore the same black three-piece-vested suit every day, along with a white cuff shirt and black tie. His brown hair was slicked back under black-framed glasses. He looked like a 1950's casino pit boss, but he was only forty-two years old.

Kane asked the bartender for water. The South Africans snickered as he wedged his small frame between them to retrieve the glass from the bar. One of the men bumped him, spilling his water. Kane didn't flinch. The men were ignorant, loud, and twice his size, but they weren't going to stop him from completing the job.

He placed the empty glass on the counter and pulled a watch from his vest.

"If Roth doesn't walk in those doors in the next ten minutes, we're going to find him," he said.

Roth was in the shower, letting the hot water pepper his neck. He had overslept, but wasn't in any hurry to get dressed. He knew Kane was looking for him, but he didn't care. Kane was an amateur and he didn't take orders from amateurs—even if he was Cassandra Prophet's man. Kane was preventing him from doing his job. If he had to wait for Kane's plan to work, he'd be waiting forever. Roth needed to be in Johannesburg by the next day in order to pay off a gambling wager; a $30,000 bet he couldn't pay without the money Cassandra Prophet owed him. In order to collect his money he had to complete his contract.

He primped in front of the mirror until his hair was perfect and put on his tux. When finished, he straightened his white bowtie and the matching handkerchief in his breast pocket.

Roth took the elevator down to Level M. He found Permullter's room, which was across the corridor from Kane's stateroom. He pulled a red leather pouch from his coat. When no one was watching, he unzipped the case, and pulled out an electronic key card that was wired to a digital lock decoder. He placed the card in the door's key slot, typed a command into the decoder, and waited. Twenty seconds later, Roth heard the tumbler unlock. He pushed the door open into a dark room.

The professor sat upright on the couch, with the television watching him sleep. Permullter's neck hung over the back of the couch with his mouth wide open, snoring. It took less than ten minutes for Roth to discover that the Alpaca Stones weren't there. He found a letter on the floor next to Permullter's foot, which he read. He slipped the letter into his pants pocket. Permullter sneezed, but didn't wake.

Roth opened the door to leave, but stopped. He changed his mind. He closed the door. A few minutes later, he left the room, went upstairs to the deck, and dropped a bloody knife over the side of the ship.

Chapter 2

Kane saw Roth in the crowd, distracted by a brunette he had met the night before.

Roth whispered in her ear as he caressed her waist. His other hand magically produced a business card, which he slid between her cleavage. The blushing woman smiled, letting him kiss her before he left for the bar.

"Where have you been?" Kane asked.

Roth ignored him as he picked up a flute of Moet from the bar. It was gone in a swallow. "I don't work for you, Kane. Get off my back." He tapped his fingers on the bar to get the bartender's attention. "Give me vodka."

Kane grasped Roth's wrist. "I asked where you were." One of the South African's reached over and squeezed Kane's shoulder like an orange. Kane let go.

Roth frowned. "I was taking care of my business; what you should have done in Florida."

Kane had no idea what he was talking about. "What?"

Roth lifted his drink to his mouth. "Permullter was a waste of our time. He didn't have the stones."

"Of course he doesn't have . . ." Kane suddenly realized what Roth had said.

"What do you mean *didn't* . . . what have you done?"

"He's dead, but you'll probably be happy knowing that you were right. Constantine must have the stones and he's probably waiting for Permullter in Seattle." Kane's mouth opened, but no words came out. Roth laughed. "Don't sweat your little panties, it's all in here," Roth said, handing Kane Permullter's letter.

Kane knocked Roth's hand away. "You killed the only person who knew how to contact Constantine."

"This was supposed to be a two day job that you farted away into almost two weeks. You may not have a life, but I do. Just pay me my money, so I can get the hell out here when we reach Seattle."

"If you think you're getting a dime from us, you're delusional."

Roth's eyes were gunmetal as he came within inches of the short man. His stare was redirected by the woman he saw entering the room.

She wore a vintage Valentino strapless gown with side slits, revealing long tapered legs. Her golden hair was tied in a long fishbone braid, resting on a naked back. Her diamond bracelet and earrings shimmered in the light as she shook hands with several people. It was the blonde.

Kane was talking to Roth, but he wasn't listening. He pushed Kane out of his way. "Save your silly whining for later, and for someone that cares. I've got a date with an Amazon goddess," he said, before walking away.

The blonde sat at a "reserved" table, located in the corner of the room. Roth stood behind her—so close he could see the tiny hairs on the nap of her neck. Her ringlets curled around her ears, and she smelled of jasmine. He sat down in the chair next to her.

"I'm sorry, but that chair is taken," she said.

"Sure it is," Roth said, scooting his chair up to hers.

The woman noticed his eyes centered on her breasts. She flinched backward. "What do you think you're doing?"

"I'd like to talk with you for a minute, that's all. My name is Erik Roth. What's your name?"

"I don't care who you are. I'm married and you're sitting in my husband's chair.

Roth moved his face closer.

She flinched again. "Get away from me."

"Hey, calm down. I just want a chance to talk with you for a minute."

"You don't have a minute. Leave me alone," she said raising her voice.

Roth noticed the couple looking at him from a nearby table. He smiled, waved, and they turned back around. Just as the woman started to say something, Roth slipped his card into her palm and whispered, "If you change your mind, give me a call. My room number is on the back." He winked, and then slid his hand across the tabletop lightly touching her breast.

For a split-second, she sat in shock. Then she slammed her fist into his face.

A collective gasp filled the room as Roth rose off the floor holding a bloody nose. The incident should have been over, but a mixture of embarrassment, anger, and alcohol caused Roth to make the biggest mistake of his life. He slapped her and tore the gown off her body.

Chapter 3

Marcus and Doc had left the men's room when they heard the woman's scream. People were standing, trying to see what was happening in the back of the room.

Marcus pushed an older couple aside and saw his wife clutching her gown to her body. A tall young man taunted her as three fat men stood by ensuring that nobody interfered. Before Doc realized what happened, Marcus was gone.

Marcus broke through the crowd, spearing Roth into the table. One of Roth's men picked Marcus off Roth and tossed him against the wall like he was weightless. Marcus wobbled to his feet and was met with a fist, which sent him down again. Another of the Africans picked him up and stood him to his feet. Before they could hit him again, Doc close-line tackled one of the men. Tables broke and chairs flew as the fight ensued. When security arrived, one of the South Africans was unconscious, and Roth was on his knees reaching for the nearest chair.

Doc covered Caitlin's body with his suit coat. "Are you okay?" he asked.

She trembled. "Yes . . ."

Marcus ran to her. "What the hell happened?" Caitlin didn't have a chance to answer her husband before Roth lunged at him.

"I'm going to kill you . . ." shouted Roth. Marcus sidestepped Roth's clumsy punch and Roth fell to the floor.

Caitlin tugged her husband's sleeve. "Marcus, let's just go."

Doc scooped his friend's wire-framed glasses off the floor. "Marcus, get Caitlin out of here. I'll take care of this," he said, tucking the eyeglasses in Marcus's shirt pocket.

"Naw, Doc, I'm not going anywhere until I bust a cap in this ignorant bastard's head. Who the hell does he think he is coming up in here and putting his hands on my wife?"

Roth sat in a chair wiping the blood from his face with his hanky. When Roth made eye contact with him, Marcus started for him, until Doc pushed him backwards.

"Keep him away from me!" Roth said, struggling to his feet. "I'm going to file criminal charges against your black ass." He spit blood from his mouth. Kane had watched the melee from the bar. As much as he enjoyed seeing Roth get what he deserved, he couldn't afford for Roth to draw any more attention to them. He weaved through the crowd.

Doc pulled Marcus toward the door. "Marcus…I told you to take Caitlin and go!"

"Come on, let's go," Caitlin said, begging her husband. "He's not worth you going to jail for. Let's just go."

Marcus brushed away her tears with his thumbs, holding her tight. "Okay . . . okay," he whispered. He walked her to the door, then turned around and faced Doc. "You better handle this guy, because if you don't, I sure as hell will."

"Let me go!" Roth yelled, while Kane held him down in the chair.

A security guard locked Roth's wrists with handcuffs. "Mister, you aren't going anywhere except jail once we arrive in Seattle."

"Get your hands off me." Roth shook free of the guard's grasp. He reached inside his coat and pulled out his wallet. "I'm with the South African Embassy . . . let me go!" The leader of the security team was uncertain about what to do. He talked to Doc.

After consultation, the guard came back to Roth. "You and your friends will be confined to your staterooms until we reach Seattle tomorrow. After that, we'll let the authorities decide what to do with you."

Roth was livid. Doc stood in the doorway with his hands in his pockets. Until now, Roth hadn't paid much attention to Doc. The black man stood about six-foot-five with a boxer's physique fitted into a Brioni suit.

"I suppose you're a high-priced attorney that told them they could do this to me," Roth said.

12

Doc's squinted. "No. The attorney in the family is the woman you thought it was okay to put your hands on. Get this guy out of my sight." The guards led him out of the room with Doc following.

Kane couldn't help Roth even if he wanted to. The only thing he could do was help diffuse the mess they were in. He waited until things had settled down before approaching the bartender. "I understand that Mr. and Mrs. St. John were celebrating their wedding anniversary tonight. I feel sorry for what happened. I would like to pay for the damages and Mr. St. John's expenses." He gave the man a card from his vest. "Please have the bills forwarded to this address."

The bartender looked at the business card. "Mr. Kane, I'm sure Mr. St. John would appreciate your generosity, but I don't think . . ."

Kane interrupted him. "Please, I insist."

"Okay, I'll let him know, but like I was saying—it's not necessary. Mr. St. John owns this ship."

Chapter 4

Forty minutes later, Doc took the stairs up to his stateroom. He entered and perimeter sensor lights sprang on, flickering against the sandstone-colored vaulted ceiling. He pitched his coat on the bed, and went out on the balcony. It was nearly 2:00 and quiet as an empty church sanctuary, except for the hum of the engines of *Southern Comfort,* slicing through the black water. He sat on the chair and stretched his legs out, resting his feet against the rail. Dark clouds tried to smother the moon, but a beam of light broke through to the water. He reclined, and enjoyed his cigar and the smell of the air.

The ocean made him homesick for his family, who he hadn't seen since leaving St. Croix two weeks ago. His wife and son were waiting for him in Seattle. After Marcus and Caitlin's anniversary party, Doc's plan was to spend a week with his family in Southern California

Doc spent months working on his best friend's anniversary celebration, which included a Panama cruise, ending with a dinner party at the Seattle Legends Hotel. Over one hundred of Marcus's friends and business associates were invited. Tonight's ugly incident spoiled an otherwise perfect week, especially for Caitlin. She didn't deserve the kind of public humiliation she encountered. People like Roth tended to judge her by her looks, rather than her intellect, which was a mistake. She was a partner in a small law firm, and one of the best litigators in San Francisco. More importantly, she was an excellent mother and supportive wife to Marcus.

Doc yawned as his body shuddered from the night chill. It was time to go inside. There was a soft rap on the connecting door to Marcus's suite. Doc unlocked the door and found Caitlin on the other side. She had changed into a crème-colored sweater with matching slacks, and her hair hung loose around her shoulders.

"I thought that was your cigar I smelled," she said.

"I thought you and Marcus were in bed."

"You know how Marcus is when he gets upset. He's downstairs in the gym. I was on my may to have a drink, but I could use some company."

Doc gently touched her bruised cheek. "You sure you feel like being out?"

"Yes, I'm fine—come on."

* * *

On the elevator to the observation deck, Caitlin clutched Doc's hand so tight, he could feel her body trembling. She leaned her head against his shoulder and closed her eyes. She wasn't as fine as she pretended.

The Observation Bar was empty except for a few crewmembers and a bartender. Caitlin went behind the bar and pulled a bottle of Grenadine off the shelf. She mixed the pomegranate-flavored syrup with four ounces of orange juice and pineapple juice, and then poured it into two glasses containing crushed ice. She handed a glass to Doc.

"I can't wait to see Asha and Ellington again. You wouldn't believe how Marcus's eyes light up when he talks about your son. You better keep a watch on my husband, because he has plans for your son to run his 'empire' one day," she said, smiling.

Doc laughed. "Marcus has always been a legend in his own mind. He's never going to quit this business, unless you tell him to. He loves it too much."

"Like he listens to me."

"Yeah, he does; you know that. He would do anything for you." She smiled because she knew he was right.

Caitlin had been with Marcus from the beginning when he barely supported the family working as a security guard for $14,000 a year. She hung with him through the tough times when they worked together to keep his fledging business afloat. Doc helped them through the lean years until the business turned a profit. After years of hard work and sacrifices, Marcus transformed the St. John and Sebasst Security Force into one of the largest privately-owned security companies on the west coast—and Caitlin was a large reason for his success.

"I thought this little vacation I planned for you two would help Marcus see the value of leisure time, but I don't think its working. I always gave him credit for being a smart guy."

"Not smart enough to control that temper of his."

"That's true, but for an old man, he can still move pretty fast."

Caitlin slapped him on the shoulder. "This isn't funny, Julian. You need to talk to him. He could have killed Roth."

"Caitlin, what did you expect him to do? If anyone was out of control it was Roth, not Marcus. He deserved what he got."

Caitlin was surprised by his candidness. Doc was a pastor and university professor by profession, and a pacifist by nature. Rarely did he let emotion interfere with logic.

Doc knew what she was thinking. "There's a time to walk away and a time and place to defend what's yours. Roth crossed the line. I would have done the same if it were Asha."

For a moment she was speechless, not sure of how to respond. She grasped his left hand, running her fingers over his bruised knuckles. "You're a good friend, Julian. Talk to Marcus; he listens to you. Keep him away from Roth."

"Don't worry; I have a call into the Embassy. If I have anything to say about it, Roth will be shipped back home to New York on the first flight leaving Seattle."

"His home isn't New York, and his immunity doesn't give him the privilege of molesting women in our country. I'm going to do everything in my power to see that he gets sent back to whatever hellhole he crawled from. He's not getting another opportunity to humiliate or hurt another woman," Caitlin said.

* * *

Three levels below, Roth was sequestered in one of the crew's quarters, with a security guard posted outside the door. Roth stood in front of the mirror in his blood splattered shirt

16

staring at his face. The ship's doctor had stitched his brow and the deep gash on his cheek caused by Marcus's signet ring. An eye was swollen shut and his lip was split. The damage wasn't as bad as it looked, but that didn't matter. He thought he looked like Quasimodo. He picked the lamp off the table and hurled it at his reflection in the mirror.

Kane came to Roth's room twenty-five minutes later and the guard let him in. Roth was on the balcony, smoking. Kane opened the sliding door.

"What are you doing here?" Roth asked.

"We need to talk."

"Just get me out of here . . . that's what you can do for me."

Kane stepped back into the room. "Please, come inside. What I have to say is for you to hear and not the world."

Roth looked at the smug-looking man, with the blunt nose and thin lips. "This must be the highlight of your life seeing me this way . . . ugly like you. But let me tell you something, Kane," he said, as he came into the room. "I will be out of here tomorrow and the first thing I'm going to do is wipe that smirk off your silly looking lips. Then I'll get St. John for what he's done to my face. He won't get another chance to sucker punch me next time!"

Kane sighed. Roth hadn't learned a thing. "Listen to me. You're not going anywhere near St. John, his wife, or anyone else when you leave this ship. You've already caused us enough problems, and I'm not cleaning up anymore of your messes. You weren't authorized to kill Permullter. Without him we may have lost our chance to get the stones. But of course, you would have known that if your brain could actually conjure thought. And if that wasn't bad enough you decided to publicly humiliate the ship's owner and his wife, and disgrace yourself in the process . . ."

Before Kane said another word, Roth grabbed his neck, shoved his head against the wall and squeezed. Roth froze when he felt cold metal against his nose. He let go when he saw the derringer in Kane's hand.

Kane gripped Roth's hair and shoved the pistol into his nose until it drew blood. "I wasn't finished speaking. You're an idiot. You should have seen that as much as you look at yourself in the mirror. Thanks to you, I had to dispose of Dr. Permullter's body and was forced to notify Ms. Prophet of your stupidity. Your services are no longer required. We take over from here. When we get to Seattle, you will confine yourself to the hotel until I tell you to leave. Is that clear?" Roth nodded his head. "Now, one more thing." Kane twisted Roth's ear, pulling it down to him. He whispered, "If you or one of your friends as much as brush up against me again, I'll kill you." Kane pulled the derringer out of his nose, and wiped the barrel on Roth's shirtsleeve.

Chapter 5

Marcus's secretary, her husband, and another couple joined Caitlin and Doc at their table on the observation deck. Doc excused himself and went downstairs to the private gym. The spacious room looked more like a luxury spa. Nautilus equipment filled the tropical blue and green walls, with a lap pool, recliners, and a widescreen television. Marcus worked on the speed bag in the corner and couldn't hear Doc calling his name over the loud rap music.

Doc turned off the stereo.

Marcus stopped the swinging bag with his hand, and then turned around. "Hey, brother you come to work out?"

"No. How can you stand this music?"

"It makes me work harder," he said, catching his breath.

Marcus's chest glistened with sweat.

"You've been at this for a couple of hours. Why don't you call it a night? Caitlin's waiting for you upstairs."

"I'm not through yet. How about we put on the boxing gloves and go a few rounds. Judging by what I saw tonight, I'd say you could use the work."

"I've had my exercise for the evening, thank you. I would have thought you would have too." Doc sat down on the recliner and pulled out cigar.

Marcus swung at the bag one more time, then picked up the jump rope off the floor and started skipping. "Taking a pound of flesh from Roth wasn't exercise. If anything, he's the reason I'm still here. The boy ought to be glad I didn't kill him." Marcus crossed his arms, propelling the rope faster as his toes barely seemed to touch the floor. "I can't believe this punk would come on my ship . . . disrespects my wife, and I'm footing the bill. Where did that sonofabitch and his three gorillas come from anyway; I sure the hell didn't invite him?"

"Roth works for the Johannesburg Consulate General's Office in New York."

"So, what's he doing in Seattle?"

"Don't know. He and his entourage got on in Panama along with a guy named Kane. He was the one trying to calm Roth down."

"The goofy-looking white guy dressed like a mortician?"

"Yes."

"Well, he needs to be a little more selective in picking his friends," Marcus said, as he continued skipping until Doc grabbed the rope in midair.

"Enough, Qwik! It's three in the morning, I'm tired, and I feel like a bobble-head doll trying to keep up with you. Get some rest or you won't be in any shape for your own party tomorrow night."

"Okay, okay," he said, snatching his towel from the chair. "Can a brother at least take a shower before I leave?"

Doc sighed. "No, you've got a shower as big as the Grand Canyon in your suite, use it."

* * *

Southern Comfort dropped anchor in Seattle the following afternoon on schedule. Maintenance personnel and crewmembers worked getting the vessel ready for its next voyage. A maintenance engineer climbed up a steel platform to conduct a routine inspection of the bilge system. He found a body wedged between the pumps.

Chapter 6

Constantine stood on the pier when two police cars pulled up in front of the *Southern Comfort*. Fifty minutes later, medics carried a covered body down the ship ramp and loaded it into the back of the ambulance. That's when Constantine's deepest fears were confirmed. Permullter hadn't made it.

He walked as fast as his lanky legs would go, and didn't stop until he saw the red-roofed buildings of Pioneer Square. Constantine slipped into a sidewalk cafe and sat in the booth by the window. A waitress handed him a menu, but he passed it back to her and ordered a drink instead. He leaned over the table and looked out the window. A taxi sat at the curb waiting for its fare. Across the street, a group of tourists huddled around a tour guide as she pointed to a historic Seattle landmark. Shoppers lingered in front of a gift shop and art gallery. Constantine fell back against the booth, frustrated. He wouldn't recognize anyone following him unless they had a sign tied around their neck. He was in a hopeless situation—an academic trying to outfox professionals.

He was the last one and by now they knew he was in Seattle.

He had made a big mistake going to the pier to meet Permullter, because he was sure someone was watching for him. Fortunately, he was smart enough not to have brought the stones with him. They were in a safe place where no one could get to them except the person they were intended for.

While cradling his drink, he thought about his options, which were few. He had been running for more than a week and knew it was only a matter of time before they caught him too. He pulled a notebook from his suit coat and asked the waitress for an envelope.

* * *

The lunch crowd swarmed into the Bluepen Pub just as Constantine folded his letter and stuffed it in the envelope. It was time to go. He went to the back of the café towards the men's restroom and slipped out the back door to the alley. Walking east to the Pioneer Square Historic District, he found the Victorian Romanesque building he was looking for in the middle of the block. He opened the door and entered.

The lobby was supported by four marble pillars and emptied into an atrium of terra-cotta tiles and palm trees, resting under hand-carved wooden cornices. On opposite sides of the atrium, were maple staircases spiraling up to the receptionist desk on the second floor. Cornerstone Global Insurance Recovery was etched in white letters on the black marble wall. Constantine approached the desk.

"May I help you?" asked the receptionist.

"I would like to see Mr. St. John."

The woman smiled. "I'm sorry; Mr. St. John doesn't work here. You can contact him at his office in San Francisco. I can give you that number if . . ."

"He has to be here . . . supposed to be here. I saw him get off the ship this afternoon."

Mr. St. John in Seattle? That was highly unlikely. "I'm sorry, but I think you are mistaken. Mr. St. John does not work here. Perhaps one of our agents can help you. Now, if you will give me your name and tell me the nature of your business, I will see who can assist you."

Constantine had a blank stare in his eyes. His fidgety fingers scratched his unkempt silver hair while he mumbled.

"Sir, if I could just have your name, I . . ." she repeated.

He slammed his fists on the desk. "I don't want anyone else. I must see St. John and I must see him now!" He started pacing. "You must get him. He must come here; it is imperative that I speak with him before it is too late," he mumbled. "Do you understand . . . do you?"

22

The receptionist pushed the security button concealed underneath the desk. Two armed guards arrived, but she motioned them to stay back.

Instead of fear, the freckle-faced receptionist felt empathy for the elderly man. He acted a bit crazy, was thin as a rail, and looked like he hadn't slept in days. His white shirt was filthy and his thick mane of hair hung loose to his shoulders. He didn't look much different than the panhandlers in the park. But under closer scrutiny she could tell he wore an expensive suit, and his hair was neatly trimmed. In her mind, she saw an image of him in a clean shirt, tie, and business suit, and determined he wasn't destitute or crazy, just scared. She picked up the telephone and dialed a number.

Three minutes later, a man exited the elevator. "My name is Benno Rood. I understand you want to see Mr. St. John."

Constantine stared at the squat Dutchman, who had a crew-cut, no neck, and looked like he could bench-press 400 pounds. "Yes, it is very important that I speak with him."

"That's not possible, Mr . . .?"

"Constantine. Trevor Constantine."

"Dr. Constantine from Leicester University?"

"Yes, yes," he said impatiently. He grabbed Benno by the hand and pulled him away from the nosey receptionist who was trying to overhear their conversation.

"Mr. St. John was instrumental in recovering some sacred artifacts stolen from the university some time ago. So you see that's why I must see him. He is the only one who can help me," Constantine said.

"Professor, Mr. St. John is no longer active in this company. I am chief of security and acting president of Cornerstone Global and would be happy to assist you with your needs."

Constantine was quiet, confused, and depressed. He couldn't speak. Benno gently coaxed him by the arm toward the door.

"Come on, professor, let's go to my office and maybe you can tell me what this is all about."

Chapter 7

Labor Day weekend in Seattle was unusually sunny and warm. Thousands of tourists flooded the city to attend an array of outdoor activities and celebrations.

A large crowd gathered downtown in front of Westlake Center to listen to the bumping rhythms of a local reggae band performing on the plaza.

A young Jamaican singer spotted a caramel-colored man with speckled silver and black hair, sitting on a planter box bouncing a child on his lap in time with the music. She had a runner deliver a complimentary music CD to him. She winked and threw him a kiss. Marcus bowed in appreciation, as Doc's son pulled the jewel case from Marcus's hand.

"Caitlin should see you now," Doc said, prying his son's fingers off the CD.

"You're just jealous you didn't get one. I can't help it if my popularity precedes me."

"That woman obviously doesn't know you. If she did, she wouldn't have wasted a perfectly good CD on you."

"That's my point. I'm just smooth like that," he said, caressing his wrinkle-free face with his hand. "I attract women like a magnet. I can't help myself."

"Is that right. I don't hear you talking that smack when Caitlin's around your sorry butt."

"That's because she already knows she's got a good, faithful man she can come home to *every* night. She realizes I'm a piece of artwork, and like any fine art, she appreciates that others want a piece of my *essence*. Can you blame them?"

Doc chuckled as he slid a stick of gum into his mouth. "And I thought Toby Jamison had a problem." Marcus laughed. "You planning on sitting here all day or can we go now?"

Marcus frowned. He stubbed out his cigar in the planter. "You sure know how to get on a brother's last nerve. Come on, I know how you get when you're hungry. But I'm warning you," he said, pointing a long finger at him. "Don't take us to some whacked out restaurant for dinner. I'm not in the mood for one of your bohemian experiences tonight." He boosted Ellington up on his shoulders and crossed the plaza to the mall.

They found their wives on the top floor of the pavilion at the food court.

"Mommy, I want some," Ellington said, stretching his arms toward her plate.

"Yeah, me too," Marcus said, staring down at Caitlin's seafood platter. "I hope you two saved room for dinner."

"Dinner? It's only 3:30. We've only been to a couple of shops," Caitlin said as she continued eating.

Marcus looked on the floor and then under the table, but didn't see any shopping bags. "You mean to tell me that you two haven't bought anything yet?"

Asha laughed. "Marcus, shopping is a slow journey to be enjoyed and savored amongst friends. The purpose and joy of the journey is not in the acquisition, but in the journey itself."

Marcus's eye twitched. "Damn, you're even starting to talk like your crazy husband."

Doc sat next to his wife. Ellington pushed some noodles onto the fork, then aimed it at his father's lips.

"Thank you, son—I'm glad someone is looking out for me." Doc opened his mouth wide to receive the food. Asha wrapped an arm around her husband's neck and kissed him. "What's that for?"

"I missed you." She nuzzled up to his shoulder. Doc kissed her on the forehead and then the lips.

"Why don't you two take that someplace else? Some of us are trying to enjoy our food," Marcus said, as he plucked a shrimp off Caitlin's plate.

Caitlin slapped his hand and took her fork back. "Order your own food if you're hungry."

Marcus groaned as he rose to his feet. "Come on, Doc, let's get going. We're not wanted here."

Caitlin stood and gave him a kiss. "Don't pout—just go," she said with a laugh. "I think you guys are on your own for dinner. We'll see you later back at the hotel."

"Okay," Doc said, as he stood up.

"You sure you don't mind?" Asha asked.

"Of course not. Enjoy yourselves."

"What are you two going to do?" Asha asked.

"I don't know. Maybe we'll take the train over to Bumbershoot. What do you think, Qwik?"

"Sounds good to me."

Ellington's eyes bulged. He tugged his mother's pants until he got her attention. "Mommy, can I go with daddy and uncle on the train?"

She patted his head. "Honey, you've been with daddy all day. I think you need to stay with us."

"It's okay. He'll have more fun with us," Doc said.

"Yeah," Marcus said, hoisting the boy back up on his shoulders. Ellington giggled as he playfully drummed on Marcus's head.

The men took the escalator down to Westlake Station and passed through the turnstile. Ellington got excited when he saw the bullet train approaching. A retractable walkway bridged the gap between the platform and the door, transferring the riders into the monorail. The train's bubble windows offered spectacular views of the city's landscape. Ellington begged his father to sit on the other side of the train so he could watch the conductor operate the controls. The monorail glided out of the station on rails elevated and supported on concrete piers that ran over a mile to the Seattle Center. Marcus crooked his neck trying to get a better view out of the bubble window.

"What are you doing?" Doc asked.

"Looking for Cornerstone."

"You'll be standing a long time. Pioneer Square is in the opposite direction. You might have known that had you ever bothered to visit the office."

"Well, I'm here now. Does Benno know we're in town?"

27

"No, I thought we'd surprise him—and Sydney."

Marcus sat down and pulled a sterling silver toothpick from his pocket and stuck it in his mouth. He turned and faced Doc. "Now that you brought her up, let's talk about Sydney."

Doc knew exactly where the conversation was heading. "Let's not go there again."

Marcus's eyes burrowed into Doc as he slowly picked at his teeth. "Naw, man, we're going there. I haven't forgotten what you did. You turned Sydney from me."

"No one turned anyone. I just told her she should consider other options rather than coming back to work for you. If she is going to risk her life for anyone, she should at least be compensated for what she's worth. Besides, she's too smart to be wasting her time as a bodyguard."

"Money is not relevant to her or the issue here. It's a question of ethical behavior, and you overstepped your bounds when you advised her to leave the company. Everything was fine until you opened your big mouth and took advantage of the situation."

Doc started laughing. "And just what situation was that?"

"When she was on her death bed in the hospital."

Marcus had a flair for stretching the truth. "First of all she wasn't dying and secondly—what better time to consider other career options than when you're laid up in bed with stab wounds in your body? Working with you tends to give a person a different perspective on life."

"That's beside the point, Doc. You should have talked it over with me first before you filled her head with all that nonsense. The next thing I know, she and Jordan are out on their own, and I've got a hole in my organization the size of a moon crater that I can't fill. If she was tired of her job, all she had to do was tell me. Hell, I would have given her Cornerstone to run."

Doc sighed. "Qwik, Sydney isn't corporate minded or your personal possession. She's almost forty—old enough to make her own decisions, and she decided it was time to go her own way. I don't know what you're complaining about anyway. It's not like she left the family. She just moved to a new address, that's all. She still does jobs for you and Benno on occasion, so stop complaining. She's doing what makes her happy so you should be happy for her."

"Well, I'm not."

* * *

Constantine woke up in a dark and empty room, with a fleece blanket draped over his body and a pillow stuck under his head. He took another look at his watch, not believing he had slept that long. He rolled over and saw Benno Rood working in his office. Constantine got up and went across the hallway.

"It was very thoughtful of you to let me rest. I did not intend to be a bother to you," Constantine said, as he entered the office.

Benno got up from the desk. "Not a problem, Dr. Constantine. I had some paperwork to do anyway. Are you feeling better?"

He nodded his head. Constantine was embarrassed. He suffered from narcolepsy and often fell into a deep slumber while in the middle of a conversation, like he had today. He lost four hours. "There is no point in me staying here any longer if I can't see Mr. St. John. I should leave now."

Benno came around to the front of the desk. "With all due respect Dr. Constantine, I don't understand your reluctance to tell me your problem. Perhaps our company can assist you as we have in the past."

"I do not wish to put you and others at risk."

"Aren't I already at risk by you being here? If what you told me earlier is true—that someone is following you, they know you're with me right now."

The logic of the statement painted a nervous expression on Constantine's face. His lips twitched as he sat down in a chair. He found it hard to trust anyone—even the sincere looking man standing in front of him. But he didn't have any other choice.

Reluctantly, he pulled an envelope out of his pants pocket and handed it to Benno. "Can you deliver this letter for me?"

Benno looked at the non-stamped envelope. "You want this hand delivered?"

"Yes."

Benno thought as he slapped the envelope against his palm. Why the man didn't simply put a stamp on the envelope and mail it made no sense to him. It was obvious that he was eccentric and paranoid, but Benno felt compelled to help him. The problem was he didn't have any people who could deliver the package. All of his couriers were out for the long weekend. He thought about outsourcing the job to another company, but suddenly came up with a better idea.

He handed the letter back to him. "Hold this for a moment. I'll be right back."

Constantine watched him as he walked down the long hallway and disappeared around the corner.

* * *

Light streamed through the opaque window of the inner office stenciled: *Belleshota and Bloodstone Investigations*. Benno opened the door to find a willowy redhead sitting at her computer. "I was hoping you were in," he said.

The tall woman turned away from the monitor. "Benno, what in the world are you doing here so late?"

"I could ask you the same question. Aren't you supposed to be on vacation?"

"I am—when I finish this report. What's your excuse?" she asked, easing back against the chair.

"Too much work." He sat on the corner of her desk. "Can we talk?"

The Dutchman jangled loose change in his pants pocket, a nervous habit Sydney had grown accustomed to hearing.

She slid her reading glasses below the bridge of her nose. "Before you ask, no."

30

"Sydney, I don't have anyone else. All of my people are gone until Tuesday. I . . ."

"No. Nothing can be that important that can't wait until then. I've been gone for sixteen days. I'm tired and I'm going home."

Benno sighed. He saw the determined look in her eyes. "Sydney, this is important."

She got up and walked over to retrieve some papers from the filing cabinet in the corner.

"Remember Dr. Constantine from Leicester University?"

She slammed the drawer closed. "I still have a scar on my body to remind me every day. I hope he's enjoying retirement in England."

"He's in my office, and he needs your help again."

She placed the papers on her desk and spoke slowly. "Benno, I'm on vacation."

"Just hear me out. If after what I tell you, you decide not to do this, I'll understand. All I ask is that you listen to his story."

* * *

Constantine paced the floor waiting for Benno to return. He had been gone twenty minutes. Outside, the streets were brimming with activity. The siren from a police car drowned out the soft music he heard from the tavern across the street. He turned away from the window when he heard footsteps coming toward the office.

A fair-skinned woman with a bob hairdo, dressed in a white pantsuit and high heels, entered the room. At first he didn't recognize Marcus St. John's associate because her hair was shorter and she seemed taller. "Miss Belleshota?"

Sydney gave him a warm smile and extended her hand. "Nice to see you again, professor."

"I had no idea you were here. I thought you . . . your injuries . . ." He sat down.

She sat on the couch beside him. "My wound was not serious," she said, holding the man's fragile-looking hand. "I

31

understand you have a problem that I may be able to help you with."

Benno interjected. "Ms. Belleshota has agreed to deliver your letter for you. She will see that it arrives safely."

"You will deliver it personally?" Constantine asked.

Sydney looked at Benno and with reluctance said, "Yes . . . I'm leaving for San Diego in the morning. I can drop it off on the way. Can you tell me what this is about—why it's so important?"

"I . . . I just can't," he said, almost on the verge of tears. "Please, you must promise me that you will not open it. You must promise!"

Sydney caressed his hand. "Of course I won't, but you must give me assurances that what I carry can in no way be in violation of the law, or contain anything that puts someone's life at risk. Can you promise me that?"

Constantine relaxed. "Yes, yes. I would not do anything that foolish. The only one at risk is me." Sydney and Benno exchanged furtive glances.

Sydney wrote him a receipt, then placed the letter in a metal briefcase and locked it. "Are you sure there isn't anything else we can help you with? Do you have family here—where are you staying?"

He patted her hand. "Please, have no concern for me. I will be fine now that the letter is safely in your possession. Benno and Sydney walked him downstairs and watched him get in the taxi and drive away.

"Strange man," Benno said.

"That's an understatement. You owe me big time."

Chapter 8

After Erik Roth's arraignment, Kane paid his bail and stuck Roth in a hotel room. Roth was slouched on the couch in a polo shirt and jeans watching a boxing match on ESPN. Kane sat at the table playing solitaire. He hadn't left Roth's side since they had gotten off the ship, and he didn't intend to let him out of his sight again. Roth's stupidity had almost cost them their only opportunity to find Constantine and the Alpaca Stones.

The stones were a little known legend that few knew about and even fewer actually believed existed. The first time Kane heard about them was nearly two weeks ago when his boss received a call from an overseas contact that the stones had been located. The next thing he knew, he was headed to South Africa.

Cassandra Prophet had hired Roth to help him retrieve the stones in Cape Town. Kane quickly discovered that the part-time contract killer was short on patience and brains. He had already killed two archeologists, and now Permullter. The blunders cost them valuable time, but more importantly, the murders brought unwanted attention to Kane that he couldn't afford.

"Kane! Get your head out of those cards and answer my question," Roth shouted.

Kane's mind returned to the task at hand. "What do you want?"

"I asked you when the hell she is getting here. I don't have all night."

Kane stopped flipping the cards onto the table. "You aren't going anywhere until she arrives. If she said she's coming, she'll be here."

"I don't know what you told her, but she better have my money with her. I did my job."

"Your job was to help me get the stones, and follow my orders, not go on a killing spree."

33

Roth turned off the television. "My contract was to terminate them all, not play nursemaid. You changed the plans, and you have to live with the consequences," he said, smugly. "I did my job, you didn't do yours."

"Make sure you tell her that when she arrives." Kane turned his attention back to the cards.

Twenty minutes later, there was a knock on the door. Roth answered and found himself staring at a tall, thin brunette woman with a long neck and pageboy hairdo. Her skin was as white as alabaster and her brown eyes were dead.

"You must be Prophet," he said, leaving her standing at the door as he went back to the couch. She entered the room, ignoring Kane, which didn't go unnoticed by Roth. She removed her trench coat, neatly folding and placing it over the arm of a chair. Underneath the coat she wore form-fitting slacks, boots, a black blazer, and a starched blouse with a collar broach.

Despite her butch looks and bad perfume, Roth thought he saw a glimmer of beauty beneath the rough exterior. He poured himself a drink. "I don't know what your boy over there has been telling you about me, but he screwed up, not me. We had a chance in London to kill them all *and* get the stones, but Kane got squeamish."

Roth waited for her response, but she just stood staring at him like a therapist waiting for patient to reveal more. The longer she remained silent the more nervous he became. Roth got up off the couch, and ran his fingers through his hair.

"Now look, Ms. Prophet, I've done several jobs for you. You know my work. This whole fiasco is Kane's fault."

"Sit back down," she ordered, in a husky voice. He sat. She placed a foot on the armrest. "Do you know who I am?"

"Of course, you're Cassandra Prophet," he said, taking a drink.

"How do you know that?"

"Well, ahh . . . who else could you be. You're here . . ."

"Have you and I ever met before?"

"No."

"Have you ever seen Cassandra Prophet?"

"No."

She leaned over him. "Then I will repeat my question. How do you know who I am?"

Roth flashed a nervous smile, then a look of bewilderment. "I . . . I don't know what's going on here, but I'm in no mood to play games here."

The woman sighed. "You assumed I was Cassandra Prophet because Elias Kane told you she was coming here."

He looked into her dark eyes. They were as cold as any he had seen, but he refused to be intimidated by them. "What's your point?"

Her eyebrow arched. "My *point* is, you also assumed that Robinson and Opperfield had the Alpaca Stones in their possession when you killed them—and then Permullter. Three wrong assumptions on your part. You seem to have the propensity to act before you think. We didn't pay you good money to think. That's Elias's job. Your job was to follow his instructions, and not kill anyone until the stones were retrieved."

Roth's face turned red. He hated being humbled by a woman, especially in front of Kane. He glanced at Kane, who was still engrossed in his card game. Roth was sweating.

He loosened his collar. Despite the drink in his hand, his mouth was suddenly dry. "Okay, maybe I overreacted a little. But at least we now know that Constantine has the stones. I can make this right by Ms. Prophet."

"She isn't interested in hearing your excuses." The woman put on her coat and tied the waist belt.

Roth panicked. The conversation was over and she was about to leave. "Tell Ms. Prophet to give me twenty-four hours. That's all the time I need to find Constantine and get the stones. If I don't have them in twenty-four hours, she doesn't owe me a cent."

With the scornful look of a betrayed woman she said, "I already know where Constantine is." She stuck her hands in the coat pockets. "Elias told me you were as dumb as an onion. I'm afraid he was right." She pulled a gun out and shot him in the center of his head. Roth reeled backwards and fell over the back of the couch. The dumbfounded look of surprise was frozen to his face.

Kane looked up from the table. He slid the deck of cards into his vest pocket and went over to the body. "How do you want me to dispose of him?"

She twisted the silencer from the barrel as they watched the blood pooling around Roth's head. "Leave it. We don't have the time. Besides—he's not worth cleaning up after."

Chapter 9

Ellington was sleeping on his father's shoulders. Doc put the child to bed, kissed him goodnight, and closed the door on the way out.

Asha was in the other bedroom, asleep. Even sleeping, the former Cuban model struck a pose. She lay on top of the white comforter with her black curls fanned around her head, and her hands crossed on her breasts. Doc leaned over and turned the television off.

She stirred and then opened her eyes. "El okay?" she moaned.

"Fine. I just put him to bed."

"How'd it go?"

"We had a great time." He patted her hips. "Come on, you need to get undressed and get in the bed."

She stretched her arms out to him. He kissed her. "I missed you," she said, stroking his shaven head. "What's on the agenda for tomorrow?"

"What do you want to do?"

Asha propped herself up on an elbow. "Drop by and surprise Sydney if she's back in town yet. Maybe she can find the time to join us in Anaheim."

"Somehow I don't think Disneyland is Sydney's kind of place."

"Why?"

"She's a workaholic. A day off for her is taking her Beretta to a pistol range."

"My girl is not that bad."

"Yeah—she is." He lifted her foot, placed it on his lap, and massaged her instep. "You've never worked with her like I have. Now, if you ask her to go shooting sea turtles off the coast of St. John she might find time for that, but not Disneyland."

"You're bad," she said, drawing her foot back. "I'm going to tell her what you've been saying about her."

"Go ahead, she can't deny the truth." He gave her a peck on the forehead. "Get some sleep. I'll be in after I shower."

She knew what that meant. He'd be lucky to make it to bed before 1:00. Even when he didn't have anything to do, he never seemed to settle down until after midnight. His nightly ritual included a little television, a shave and shower, and reading. He kissed her again and turned off the light.

Asha fluffed her pillow and rolled over onto her side. "Julian, don't stay up too late."

Doc found a movie on the television, muted the volume, and settled back to work. He turned on his laptop. He had several e-mail messages from the University of St. Croix, most of which were general information, but six required responses. By the time he finished, the movie was off and it was past 1:00. He looked for his newspaper, and then realized he had left it in the taxi earlier.

He slipped on his shoes and took the stairs down to the hotel lobby. Red and blue lights flashed from the circular driveway in front of the hotel. A uniformed police officer stood by the door, and three more were in the lobby along with two Seattle detectives. Doc picked up a complimentary copy of the USA Today off the front desk. Just as he was leaving, the doors to the freight elevator opened, and the paramedics exited carrying a covered body on a gurney. One of the detectives in the lobby was interrogating a hotel clerk by the elevator. She cuffed a hand over her mouth and rushed over to the desk next to Doc, trembling.

"Are you okay?" Doc asked.

The girl cried. "A man was murdered in the hotel."

Doc pulled a handkerchief from his pocket and handed it to her.

"Thank you," she whimpered.

A shabbily dressed detective came over with a glass of water. "Here, drink this. I still have a few more questions for you before I let you go."

38

She refused the drink. "Please, can't I just go home now? I've told you everything I know."

He ignored her tears. "So, when Mr. Roth didn't answer the door you used your passkey to let yourself in. Why would you do that?"

The girl looked at Doc, who was trying his best not to get involved. Instead of making eye contact with her, he focused on the headline of the newspaper.

"I already told you. He asked me to meet him in his room when I got off work," she said.

The detective grabbed her arm. "So, you're trying to tell me that a man you just met tonight invited you to his room and you went?" She broke down again. The detective sighed. "The sooner you answer my questions, the sooner you can go home. Now quit crying so we can get on with it," he said as he jammed a stick of chewing gum in his mouth.

The man had the personality and face of a bulldog, with a double chin that seemed to sway every time he spoke.

Doc knew it was none of his business, but the detective had crossed the line. "Detective, can't this wait until morning? She's in no condition to help you right now."

The girl latched on to Doc's arm.

The detective looked at him. "Don't I know you?"

"I don't think so," Doc said.

"What's your name?"

"Julian Sebasst."

He smacked his gum as he studied Doc's face, then moved his eyes back to the girl. "You two know each other?" he asked waving his pencil at them.

"I just came down to get a newspaper," Doc said.

"Then that's a no?"

Doc sighed. "No, I don't know the young woman."

"Then I suggest you mind your own business and return to your room or wherever you came from. Unless you're a witness or have something useful to add—beat it," he said, as he began scribbling in his notepad. Doc started to leave, but the girl's eyes pleaded with him to stay. The detective saw what was happening and stopped writing. "Mister, you have two seconds to move your ass out of here, or you and I are going to have a little one-on-one time at the station."

Again, Doc wanted to leave, but found himself rooted in place. "Didn't you tell me I could stay if I had something useful to say?"

The detective's eyes narrowed. "What is it?"

Doc faced the girl. "Miss, I would advise you to seek counsel before answering any more of this officer's questions." The detective's face was flushed.

"You mean an attorney?" she asked.

"Do you have one?"

"No."

"If you like, I can give you the name of an excellent one staying at this hotel. I'm sure she would be happy to represent you. Would you like her name and room number?"

The detective closed his notepad. "Okay, you can go for now," he said to the girl. "But, first thing in the morning I want you in my office." He gave her his card. "And you . . . " He looked at Doc. "Pray you don't see me again."

"Thank you," the girl said, as they watched the detective walking off to join his partner.

Doc saw the detective looking back at them. "No problem." Doc wrote Caitlin's name and room number on the back of the detective's card. "If you need help, call her."

"I will. Thank you again."

Doc started toward the stairs. "By the way, the dead man, Roth—was his first name Erik?"

There was surprised look on the girl's face. "Yes . . . you know him?"

* * *

Constantine stepped one foot out of the shower stall onto the cold wooden floor, then looked around. The room was empty—to his relief. He wasn't accustomed to communal bathing facilities. The rundown motel was filthy, but it was the least likely

40

place anyone would expect him to stay. He looked under the toilet stalls to make sure he was alone before coming out of the shower. He put on a robe, brushed his teeth, and gathered up his toilet items. Fortunately for him it was almost daylight and the halls were empty, but still dark. A single light burned at the bottom of each staircase. On the way to his room, he passed a pregnant teenager in the hallway who avoided eye contact.

Constantine unlocked his door and entered the stuffy room. He opened the window for ventilation, but the air outside was as foul as the garbage dumpster in the ally below.

"Good morning, Professor."

Constantine jumped, smacking his head against the window frame as he turned around and saw a woman in a green trench coat sitting on his bed. A man dressed in black stood behind the door.

"Who are you?" Constantine asked.

"My name is Samantha, but the more appropriate question is what do I want from you. The answer would be the stones. Where are they?"

Constantine was nervous, but surprisingly full of courage. The stones were safe now and that's all that mattered. "You will never get your hands on them." He crossed his arms so they couldn't see his hands shaking.

"Oh, I wouldn't be too sure of that, professor." She got off the bed. Constantine flinched. She laughed as she withdrew her gun and slowly attached the silencer. "I think you'll tell me everything I want to know before I'm through with you." Constantine tried not to show fear. "I'm going to ask you again." She took a step forward. Kane cracked the door to make sure the hallway was empty.

Constantine didn't move from his spot. "Even if I chose to disclose the whereabouts of the Alpaca Stones, it would be of no avail to you without a key."

The woman's face contorted. She lowered the gun. "What are you talking about?" Constantine didn't answer. She lunged at him, cracking the gun barrel against his forehead. The blow knocked him backwards. She whacked him again, slicing a gorge across his cheek. His hand trembled as he tried stopping the flow of blood with his fingers. "Tell me what I want and it will stop!" Constantine stumbled back up against the window and his body slumped down on the sill. His face was covered in blood. Samantha flipped the gun over in her hand, catching it by the barrel, then swung the gun butt against his head. Constantine's limp body folded like an accordion, and fell backwards out of the window.

Chapter 10

Doc got a surprise wakeup call from Marcus. The police wanted to talk to them about Roth's death and a Professor Adam Permullter, who was found dead on the cruise ship.

Doc got dressed and met Marcus and Caitlin outside the hotel at the cab stop. When they arrived at Seattle Metro, the desk sergeant told them to wait in the lobby.

Detective Holloway drank coffee while he and his partner observed the trio from the doorway. Marcus sat next to the water cooler fidgeting with the zipper on his suede jacket.

"I knew that bastard looked familiar last night," said Holloway, eyeing the two black men.

"You mean St. John?" asked his partner.

"No, Sebasst—the one in the cargo shorts. He's a cocky sonofabitch. He interfered when I was trying to get the chick's statement about her relationship with Roth." Holloway's eyes lingered on the attractive blonde in white shorts and tank top sitting between the men. "Who's the hot looking chick?"

"Their attorney."

"Figures. They never use their own people when the chips are down."

His partner spun him around. "Keep your racist views to yourself, Holloway. The captain is looking for a reason to get you out of here. Don't give him one."

Holloway wrestled his arm free. "I don't give a damn about him. Bring them in." Holloway took another sip of coffee, then sat down at the table. He disliked Sebasst, and hated St. John. He remembered seeing their faces plastered across the local newspaper a few years ago when they were involved in a shooting in Evergreen. Several men died, including a rogue cop. The story made big news, but didn't sit well with veteran police officers like Holloway. The shootings were ruled justifiable self-defense, but Holloway still considered them cop killers—especially St. John.

43

St. John had a long history of defiance against police authority. He had a gangster mentality, and used violence to solve his problems. The fact that he was black and rich made Holloway hate him even more. As far as he was concerned, St. John was a prime suspect in Roth's murder.

When they entered the room, Doc immediately recognized the fat-cheeked detective sitting at the end of the rectangle steel table, dabbling in his notepad. Doc couldn't help but worry if the detective would make good on the promise he made to him last night.

Holloway's partner pointed to the two empty chairs at the table. "Please—have a seat." Marcus and Doc took the seats, while Caitlin occupied the chair against the wall.

"My name is Detective Carson Smith and this is Detective Herman Holloway."

Halfway through his introductory remarks, Holloway interrupted him. "Carson, let's just get on with this so these good people can enjoy the rest of their day." The words were just as hollow and disingenuous as they sounded. He turned the tape recorder on. "We can begin. I think everyone knows why we're here today."

Marcus didn't like the police in general, and had a strong dislike for Holloway in particular, after what Doc had told him about the man.

"You know why you called us in here, but I sure the hell don't," Marcus said.

"Weren't you involved in an altercation with Erik Roth, two nights ago on board the *Southern Comfort?*" Holloway asked.

Marcus snickered. "It wasn't an altercation, it was a fight."

"And according to witnesses, you threatened to kill him," Smith said.

"If I wanted him dead, I would have done it then."

Holloway interrupted. "Oh, I have no doubt you would have, if someone hadn't stopped you. Maybe you decided to wait until you had no witnesses around to finish the job. Maybe you

44

found out where he was staying and decided to check into the same hotel and wait for your opportunity."

Marcus tried remaining calm. "We booked our rooms at the Legends Hotel months ago. You would have known that if you bothered to check it out. I suppose it doesn't matter either that I didn't get back to the hotel until after 10:00."

"Yeah, we know you were out with a kid last night. We also know you got back around 10:30. Roth was killed between 10:00 and midnight, which would give you and your friend, *Seebass,* plenty of time to cap Roth and still have time to read a story to the boy before putting him down for the night."

Doc chuckled, shaking his head at the obvious insult. Holloway was baiting him, hoping he would lose his composure.

Caitlin wasn't as tolerant or forgiving. "This is the most outrageous display of police protocol I have ever witnessed, and you are the most pathetic excuse for a detective I've ever seen." She jumped out of her chair and went over to the one-way mirror where she knew they were being watched. "If this is the way you people up here conduct your interrogations, I'm surprised the ACLU hasn't closed this place down. We are not going to sit here one more minute and listen to this idiot. If you want our cooperation, you better have someone with a higher I.Q. than ten in here. My husband hasn't done anything to warrant this kind of treatment!"

"Your husband?" Holloway shouted. The revelation suddenly re-opened an old wound, which he couldn't mask. A twisted sneer appeared on his face as he leaned back in his chair, looking at her. "Maybe you should do a better job in picking your next monkey."

Marcus bolted out of the chair and charged at Holloway. Holloway's chair tipped over backwards as he barely avoided Marcus's fist. The chair crashed against the wall, and Holloway scrambled off the floor waving his gun. Doc held Marcus back.

The captain couldn't believe what he was witnessing through the mirror. He switched on the speaker box. "Smith, pull Holloway out of there, *now!"*

45

A few moments later, the captain had replaced Holloway at the head of the table and tried to restore order. "I apologize for the behavior of Detective Holloway. He has been under a lot of stress lately. I want to make it clear that you are here for questioning, only in hopes that you can shed some information on the deaths of Mr. Roth and Dr. Permullter. We would appreciate your cooperation with our investigation."

"As long as your people conduct themselves in a civil matter, we will cooperate," Caitlin said.

"Thank you. I appreciate that." He opened the file on the desk. "The statement we have from witnesses and security personnel said that Erik Roth provoked the incident by assaulting your wife. Had you or your wife met him before?"

"No," Caitlin said.

"Was he an invited guest on the ship?"

"What do you think?" Marcus snapped.

"Did you see him after you left the ship—in the hotel?"

"No."

"For the record, where were you last night between 10:00 and midnight?"

"He was with me at Bumbershoot most of the evening. We got back to our rooms around 10:15," Doc interjected.

"Were you both in your rooms all night?"

Marcus crossed his legs. "I went to exercise around 11:00."

"Where?"

"The fitness center at the hotel."

"How long were you there?"

"An hour or so."

"Did anyone see you there?"

Marcus smirked. "How many people do you know that go to the gym at midnight?"

The captain smiled. "I take that as a no?"

"Yeah, man—no. I suppose that's what you guys have been waiting to hear. No one saw me—not my wife or Doc, or anyone else that I know. But if you think I'm stupid enough to risk all that I have, including losing my family and my wife's respect over

Roth or anyone else, you're crazy. I was mad enough to kill him for what he did to my wife, but I didn't. He was a poor excuse for a human being, and I'm not going to sit here and tell you I'm sorry that he's dead. The boy was out of control. Diplomat or not, I'm surprised someone didn't cap his ass a long time ago."

"Roth's father is the diplomat, not Roth. He was a former national boxing champion from Johannesburg. A small celebrity in his country, but he didn't work with the embassy in any official capacity. Our preliminary investigation revealed that he was a man with a lot of enemies—any of whom would have gladly killed him given the chance."

"So my husband isn't the only suspect?" Caitlin said.

The captain sat back in the chair. "Mr. St. John was never a suspect, and again, I apologize for the way this whole thing was handled. The reason you were asked to come here is because you may be the only person who knew the two victims. What can you tell me about Dr. Adam Permullter?"

"Not a thing. I never heard of the man, or if I did, I don't remember him," Marcus pulled a toothpick from his shirt pocket.

The captain seemed surprised. He opened another file, and handed Marcus a black and white photo. "Do you recognize him?"

Marcus examined the picture of the corpse on a table and handed it to Doc. "No, I've never seen the man before."

The captain shuffled through some papers and pulled out a black and maroon-colored embossed card. "Isn't this one of the personal invitations you gave to your friends for your anniversary party?"

Doc looked at the card. "I sent these out, but this could belong to anyone. Each guest I invited received two invitations, in case they wanted to bring a guest. The invitation also doubled as their passenger ticket."

"So this was a free ticket to get on the ship. How many did you give out?"

"One hundred and sixty-two, but I don't know how many actually made the trip."

The captain pulled out the passenger list and did some quick math. "It looks like about eleven or so tickets aren't accounted for."

"Who was Permullter?" Marcus asked.

"A retired archeologist from Pennsylvania. He was supposed to be on sabbatical in South Africa. How he ended up in Seattle is a big question."

"That's all you know?" Marcus asked.

"That's all we know about him so far." The Captain scooted his chair away from the table. "How long are you going to be in the city?"

"We're leaving for L.A. tomorrow. That is if we are allowed to leave town," Caitlin said, as she rose from her chair. "Of course you can leave anytime. I would ask that you go through the passenger list and see if you can determine who may have given Dr. Permullter that invitation."

"Do you think Roth and Permullter were killed by the same person?"

"So far we've found no connection between the two men. Both seemed to be traveling alone." The captain gathered the files off the table. He noticed Doc looking curiously at the floor. "Dr. Sebasst, are you okay?"

Doc's eyes narrowed. "Roth wasn't traveling by himself." Marcus looked at Doc, then his eyes lit up. "Yeah, that's right. How about the three gorillas on steroids that tried to paint the wall with my face?"

"Those would be the Krueger brothers. They used to be part of Roth's training team. Unlike Roth, they are employed with the South African Embassy. Roth called them from Panama and invited them to join him on the trip. We checked their story out and they were telling the truth."

"How about Elias Kane?" Doc asked.

"Who?"

"Elias Kane."

The captain opened the file and ran his fingers down the alphabetized list of names. "I don't see his name. Who is he?"

48

Doc pulled out the business card given to him by the ship's bartender and handed it to the captain. "He gave us this card and offered to pay for damages."

The captain turned the card over in his hand. "Cassandra Prophet, Architect. We'll check it out. Meanwhile, I'd appreciate your room number at the hotel just in case we have some more questions."

* * *

By late afternoon the weather pattern had changed. The clouds had moved in off the lake, blocking what little sunlight remained over the downtown. Kane watched from the window as the traffic light swayed from the brisk wind. The holiday was ending just as it had begun—with rain.

Kane was alone in the office, but he didn't mind. In fact, it was a luxury he relished. The only sound in the building came from the radio and the infrequent hum of the fax machine. He reached across the desk and lifted the latest fax from the tray. It was *The Lebanese's* confirmation that he was coming. Kane stacked it neatly with the others on his desk. He glanced at the clock on the wall. Ten minutes to the deadline. At 6:00, no more confirmations would be accepted, no matter how much they offered to get in. Cassandra Prophet was a fanatic for rules, and she paid Kane to make sure they were all enforced.

Kane's job was to schedule the auctions, notify clients, and confirm receipt of the good faith deposits of $250,000. Once the funds were successfully transferred into Cassandra's Swiss bank account, Kane gave the clients the location, date, and time of the auction.

The auctions were never held in the same city twice, and never in Seattle, Cassandra's hometown. However, due to a scheduling conflict, Cassandra had no choice but to host the next auction at her estate, which was in two days.

Tomorrow she would return from Europe, and Kane knew he had better have everything ready by the time she arrived. He

49

wasn't worried—at least not about the auction. But Constantine's accidental death was another matter. Constantine had taken his secret to the grave, and Kane was stuck with the unenviable task of telling his boss they had failed.

He dragged a map of Seattle off the drafting table and spread it over his desk. He marked four X's on the map where Constantine had spent the final hours of his life. One was his motel room. The others were a Café, bookstore, and office building; all of them were in Pioneer Square. The stones had to be in one of those locations, and Kane was betting it was the office building, Houston Spitzer. Constantine was spotted going into the building yesterday afternoon, and hadn't reappeared until late evening. *What was he doing in there for six hours?* Kane chewed on the pencil. A CPA and a civil engineering firm occupied the first floor of the building, but it was the two companies on the second floor that grabbed his interest – *Cornerstone Global Insurance Recovery, and Belleshota and Bloodstone Investigations.*

The fax came alive again. Kane looked at the clock; it was two minutes to six. He looked at the fax. "Jai-Robson Priest." Kane placed it with the others, then waited. At 6:00 sharp, he sent receipts to the bidders, along with a set of instructions. He placed the faxes in a special folder, then took them to the vault and laid them on a silver tray.

Everything was ready. He left the building wondering how Cassandra Prophet would handle the news that Jai-Robson Priest was coming to town.

Chapter 11

The anniversary party was held in the Vegas Ballroom on the second floor of the Legends. The room of translucent panel walls showered the room of white-linen tables and orchids with mosaic purple and yellow light.

Doc had just taken his seat at the head table when he saw Kathleen St. John enter. Her plane had been late arriving from Boulder. She was the oldest daughter, and a second year cadet at the Air Force Academy. As she weaved her way through the maze of tables, Doc was stunned by how much she had changed over the years. She always had her mother's beauty, but now she had acquired her father's magnetic and charismatic smile. She offered the first toast.

"On my flight here, I thought about what I wanted to tell you about my parents and what they mean to me. My father and mother have lived the values they've taught us. My mother taught me that integrity and character matter more than race and gender, and that I could accomplish anything in life without compromising my ethics or soul." She looked over at her father. "And my dad, who I love with all my heart—taught me the importance of loyalty and friendship. Many of you in this room have been the direct beneficiaries of my father's generosity and love. He is my personal hero—the man I most admire, and the best friend any of you could ever hope to have. Happy Anniversary, mom and dad." The crowd applauded as she kissed her parents and took her seat beside Doc. Marcus sat with a Cheshire grin on his face.

Doc leaned over and whispered in Katherine's ear. "You know your father is going to be impossible to live with after all the lies you've just told."

She laughed.

After dinner the crowd was entertained by vintage soul music from a seventeen-piece orchestra dressed in tuxedos, complete with a circular bandstand. As guests settled into an evening of drinking and dancing, Doc and Marcus took the opportunity to go outside for fresh air. They sat under the awning in front of the hotel watching the valets parking cars.

Doc lit his friend's cigar, then his. "I've got a little something for you in my room."

"Man, I told you we didn't want any gifts."

"Yeah, I know. But you say a lot of things you don't mean. Anyway, it's something I wanted to do."

Marcus hugged him. "I love you, bro'; what did you get me?"

Doc laughed. "You're worse than a kid on Christmas day when it comes to gifts. Let me finish this first," he said, lifting the cigar in his hand. They sat silent for a while, both absorbed in their own thoughts.

"You know, Doc, these last two weeks have been the best two weeks of my life. The cruise, the dinner party, and you and your family. It doesn't get much better than this, man. You knocked yourself out on this one and I just want to let you know how much Caitlin and I appreciate it."

"My pleasure. I just wish I had booked the cruise for a different city other than Seattle. If I had, the Roth incident could have been avoided."

"Fate is fate, Doc. Stop beating yourself up over this. You know I need to have some drama in my life from time to time. It makes me feel alive. Everything is cool," he said, as he slapped Doc's leg.

"Yeah, that's the kind of talk that worries me about you, Qwik. You start talking crazy and the next thing . . ."

"Hey, you know I'm not out there looking for trouble. But it's hard to be cool when fools like Roth and that cop, Holloway, get in my face. I have to get ignorant on them; especially when they start messing with my family."

"Well, you can still tone it down a bit. You can't go around taking swings at the police."

"Yeah, I know, but the guy was pissing me off. He's a damn racist."

"Even more reason not to provoke idiots like that, because you never know what they're capable of doing."

One of the valets approached them. "Excuse me, gentlemen."

Marcus tossed his unfinished cigar on the pavement and rubbed it out with his foot. "Sorry, is the smoke bothering you?"

"No sir, that's fine. You are Mr. St. John, aren't you?"

"Yes."

"The hotel concierge would like to speak with you if you have a moment." Doc and Marcus followed the woman into the hotel and waited at the front desk.

A gray-haired man in a striped tuxedo vest and bowtie came out of a back room carrying a briefcase. "I was instructed to give this to you, Mr. St. John," the man said, placing the case on the counter.

Marcus looked curiously at the weather-beaten leather. "Are you sure this is for me?"

"Oh, quite sure." He removed a card from his vest and handed it to Marcus. "The gentleman asked me to personally give this to you." The concierge excused himself and left the men alone so they could have privacy.

"Professor Constantine?" Marcus said, handing Doc the card. Marcus picked up the bag off the counter, then quickly set it down. "What's he got in here, rocks? This thing is heavy." He tilted the briefcase on its side and pulled out several objects that were wrapped in cloth. He removed the linen.

Doc laughed when he saw the oddly shaped stone. Marcus unwrapped another one, then the rest. In total, there were thirty-one irregular shaped stones of different sizes. The largest was twenty inches long and looked hand-carved. Marcus turned it over in his hand, almost dropping it.

"Careful, it looks fragile," Doc said.

"Is this a joke, what am I supposed to do with these?"

Doc inspected the stone. "It looks like a petroglyph."

"What?"

"An ancient stone writing, except these don't look that old." Doc spread a few of the stones out on the counter.

"Do you think they're valuable?"

"I guess you'll have to ask the man that gave them to you. What did you say his name was again?"

"Dr. Trevor Constantine. You know, the professor that hired me to recover the Hebrew document stolen from Leicester University two years ago."

Doc thought there was something familiar about the name. Then he remembered. "I'm almost certain Constantine was on the invitational list for your party."

"Well, if he was, I didn't see him on the ship, and he's definitely not inside at the party either." Marcus went over to the concierge, who was writing in an appointment register. "Do you know what room Constantine is in?"

"He checked out earlier. His only instructions were for me to give you the briefcase if he didn't return by morning."

Marcus exchanged looks with Doc. "That doesn't make sense. If he was planning on coming to the party, why would he leave? What does he expect me to do with this stuff? There's got to be more to this." He turned the briefcase upside down and an envelope fell out, along with a scrap of paper. Doc picked up the paper off the floor, while Marcus opened the envelope, and read the letter.

Mr. St. John,

> *It is because I hold you in the highest regard that I ask you to safeguard the contents of this bag until such time that an acquaintance of mine contacts you. Please give him the contents if he can correctly tell you the burial site of my father, which I pray you will remember from our travels together. You and he are the only two individuals I have shared this information with. For reasons of my own, I cannot divulge the person's identity—for fear that this letter may be intercepted.*

*If it is fate that we shall not see each other again, I wish to
again personally thank you for the immeasurable service
you provided the University.*

> *Your friend,*
> *Trevor Constantine*

Marcus handed the letter to Doc, which he read.

"Does this make any sense to you?" Doc asked.

"No. This is pretty weird stuff. I'm supposed to hang on to these until some guy shows up in a trench coat, dark hat, and shades?"

"I suppose. It doesn't seem like you have any other choice." Doc helped him stuff the stones back in the bag. "Do you know where Constantine's father was buried?"

Marcus leaned against the desk. "Yeah. When I was in London, Constantine and I flew to Romania to negotiate with a middleman for the return of the stolen documents; he told me that his father drowned in a fishing accident in the Black Sea. His body was never recovered."

Doc handed Constantine's letter back to Marcus.

Marcus saw the crumbled piece of paper that Doc was holding. "What's that?"

"It fell out of the briefcase with the letter." Doc unfurled the yellow slip. "It's Constantine's motel receipt."

Marcus folded the letter and put it in his pocket, then buttoned his coat. "How do you feel about taking a break from the party for a while?"

* * *

The taxi dropped them off on Aurora next to a sleazy motel that looked more like a depression-era flophouse than a place someone would pay money to stay at. The Cameroon's weather-beaten exterior was as black as the age-old dirt on the windows. Its guardrails bowed away from the building as if someone had tried to rip them from the foundation.

The entrance was through a side door in the alley, and up a long staircase that led to the desk. The overweight proprietor in the caged office smelled as bad as his pee-stained walls. He told them that Constantine's room was on the third floor.

"I sure want to know why Dr. Constantine is staying in this rat hole," Marcus said as they made their way up the stairs. Three men sat in the lobby on a broken down sofa, staring at a television that didn't work. They eyed Doc and Marcus in their tuxedos as they passed through to the corridor. "We must be crazy to come up in here," Marcus said, noticing the menacing stare from one of the men. Marcus's eyes glared back, warning the men they weren't easy prey.

"Come on," Doc said, tugging him by the sleeve.

When they reached the hallway, Marcus cupped his hand over his mouth. "This place stinks!" he muffled, as Doc searched for Constantine's room number. The wail of a baby crying was heard through the paper-thin walls. An old man opened the door, but quickly shut it again, when he saw them. Doc found Constantine's door and knocked. There was no answer. He knocked again, louder. Another baby cried.

A teenager across the hall opened the door. "I don't think he's there. A man and a woman came here last night and it sounded like there was a fight. I think he's gone, or . . ." He paused as if he just realized the alternative. "Or he could still be there." A girl with a swollen belly joined him at the door, clutching his arm.

Doc turned the doorknob, but it was locked.

"Did you see what his visitors looked like?" Doc asked.

"A short man—maybe my height, in a black suit and tie. There was a tall skinny woman with him, but I couldn't see her face," the girl said.

Marcus pushed Doc aside. "We've got to get in there." He kicked the door, and the doorjamb splintered into pieces. The sparsely lit room was empty, except for a bed, table, and chair. There were no clothes, papers, or anything else to suggest that someone had been there. But something was wrong.

"You smell that?" Doc asked.

"Yeah, butt farts. This whole place smells like it." Marcus knelt to look under the bed.

"No, I mean the fragrance."

Marcus sniffed the air like a puppy. "Yeah, I do smell something. Citrus?"

"Tangerines," Doc said, taking another whiff to confirm his conclusion.

Marcus stood with his hands on his hips. "So, where is the good professor?"

Doc stuck his head into the kitchenette and then as if by default, walked over to the closed window. Droplets of dried blood were on the window sash. He lifted the window open and stuck his head out. Below was an alley, but it was too dark to see anything. "We can start by looking down here."

* * *

They took the stairs down and exited out the side door to the alley. Directly beneath Constantine's window, Doc found more traces of blood on top of the garbage dumpster. Marcus rousted a homeless drunk from his sleep. Two wallets fell from the man's ragtag coat as he turned over and tried to go back to sleep.

Marcus picked them up off the ground. He opened the first one and tossed it back to the ground. The second one he kept. "Hey, Doc, over here; I found something." Marcus nudged the man with his foot. "Hey, where did you get this?"

The man stirred, and tried to focus his eyes on the wallet in front of him. "Hey, mister, that's mine," he said, trying to grab it from Marcus's hand.

"I asked you where you got this." Marcus said, brushing the man's hand away.

"Over there by the dumpster, after it was emptied this morning."

Marcus pulled Constantine's driver's license from the billfold. "Have you seen this man?"

"Mister, I ain't seen no one," he said, without looking at the photo. "I only come back here to sleep. Can I have my wallet back now?"

"Does this photo look like you?"

The man squinted through one eye as he looked at the license again. "No, it don't."

"Then it's not yours." Marcus walked over to Doc. "Take a look at this," he said, handing Doc the small slip of paper that was folded in Constantine's wallet.

Doc held it toward the streetlight. "This is a courier receipt from Sydney and it's dated yesterday. "It looks like Constantine gave her a package to deliver." He looked at Marcus. "I thought you told me she was on vacation."

"She's supposed to be in California." Marcus opened his cell phone and called Sydney's ranch. Ten seconds later he flipped it closed. "The caretaker says she hasn't arrived yet."

"Try her cell."

Marcus punched the number, waited, then closed the phone. "Her cell is not in service. I don't get this. What's going on here?"

"I don't know, but Constantine does."

"Well, judging by what we've found so far, I'd say a good place to start looking for him is in the obituaries."

Chapter 12

The Nevada desert was tranquil and still until nightfall when a strong southwestern breeze moved across the desert, rippling through the sand like a creepy caterpillar trying to consume the unconquerable desert. Sand shifted, forming strange mounds around Yuccas straining to survive in the desolate arid ground.

A pair of kit foxes ran aimlessly in search of lizards and other rodents brave enough to surface the desert night. They fled back into hiding when the bright lights from a Land Rover pulled over in the soft sand.

Sydney turned on the overhead lights and checked her map again. As she suspected, she was definitely lost. Somehow during the night she had gotten off SR 95 and had been driving the last ninety miles on some isolated two-lane road that wasn't on her map. The navigation map on her SUV wasn't any better. She was about two hundred and sixty miles from Las Vegas and still headed south. Worse yet, she had less than a quarter tank of gas and had to use the bathroom. Judging by the long flat stretch of road in front of her, she could be miles from civilization and the nearest gas station.

Eight miles down the highway, she found a gas station and diner that had long been abandoned. She drove around to the side of the dilapidated building, hoping to find a restroom. As she got out of the vehicle, a strong gust of wind blew her against the hood. To the south, a large cloud of sand rolled across the plains. The impending sandstorm was headed straight for her, and she didn't want any part of it. She had the misfortune of being in Lubbock during the sandstorm of 2001 that sent the town into total darkness for two hours and tossed cars in the air like juggling pins. She had to find high ground, fast.

Visibility was poor as she sped along the road, looking for a cutoff to the mountains. After a quarter of a mile, a painted sign on the side of the road read *Poison Springs.* She veered the Rover onto the rutted gravel road.

The road meandered through scrub grass and boulders for three miles before emptying onto a graded dirt road that led to a plateau. Out of the driver's window she saw the desert being swallowed by the mushrooming sand as it blew toward the mountains. She drove five miles before she saw a water tower at the top of the hill. There was an oak-carved sign on the tower that read: Entering Poison Springs - Population 519.

Main Street was three blocks long with intersecting streets at the end of each block. Poison Springs looked far different than its sinister name implied. The town had eighty-foot-wide paved streets, brick storefronts, a modern grocery store, and a town square complete with a garden gazebo. It struck her as being almost too urbane for a small town stuck out in the middle of the Nevada desert. The only store open was the twenty-four hour mini-mart and gas station, located next to the bank. She made a U-turn on the empty street and pulled into the station.

* * *

The young clerk stood at the window watching Sydney pumping gas. When she entered the store, the clerk stashed her magazine under the counter.

"Hi, can I help you?" asked the girl.

"You have a restroom?" Sydney asked.

"Sure, it's in the back."

Sydney eyed some leftover chicken and potatoes baking underneath the heat lamp. "Can you wrap up a few pieces of chicken and jojos for me?"

"Sure, any particular pieces?"

"White meat only—please. Which way is the restroom?"

The girl pointed to the beer cooler in the back corner. "I'll have this for you when you're ready."

Sydney re-emerged a few minutes later, looking refreshed, but she was still tired.

The girl watched her grab three bottles of flavored water from the cooler and set them on the counter.

"How much do I owe you?" Sydney asked.

"Four ninety-three for the water. I threw in the chicken for free. It's been sitting here awhile, and there is no other place open this time of night to eat."

"Thanks. Are there any motels in town?"

"The Roadster Inn on Pine Street—one block down, turn right and go to the end of the street. You can't miss it. It's right next to the park. I'm afraid it's not the best looking place in town, but it's the only one within sixty miles. We don't get too many visitors coming through here," she said with a nervous giggle.

"That's fine, as long it has a bed."

"Where are you coming from?" she asked, as she placed the items in a bag.

"Seattle."

"I knew you were from a big city!" she gushed and then realized how childish she must have sounded. "I mean—the way you dress, your hair, and car—I'd love to have those leather pants and high-heeled boots."

Sydney smiled as she took her change. "Thanks, they may be a little long for you," she joked.

"Even if they sold stuff like that here, there's no place to wear it. It's too hot. This place really sucks."

Sydney laughed. "Why don't you leave, then?"

"I will once I'm finished with school. Me and my best friend are going to Las Vegas and get jobs. Then after awhile, maybe I can save enough money and move to a bigger city like Seattle or Los Angeles."

"From what I've seen thus far, you could be doing a lot worse than being in this town. Poison Springs seems quaint—almost idyllic." The teenager hadn't heard a word she said. Her eyes were riveted on Sydney's teardrop diamond bracelet. Sydney removed her sunglasses. "What's your name?"

"Paulette Eagleton, but my friends call me Paula."

"Then I'll call you Paula." The girl beamed. "Paula, the city is not all it's cracked up to be. Don't believe all the hype you read or see on television. I know people who would trade lives with you in a second to live in a quiet place like this."

The overweight girl with the freckled face frowned. "This place is boring; trust me. There's nothing to do."

"What about school activities like dances?"

"We don't have a school."

"You don't have a school?"

She frowned. "No. There are only about seventy or eighty kids here, so several of our moms home school us. I guess no one ever saw the need to build any . . ." Her voice trailed off.

Sydney felt sorry for her, but she was too tired to be drawn into a long conversation. "Well, young lady, if you ever make it to Vegas or Seattle, give me a call. I'll see what I can do about hooking you up with some *city* clothes." Sydney handed her a business card.

Paula stared at the black embossed card. Her mouth dropped open. "You're a private investigator?"

"Just investigator. I do a lot of different things."

"My uncle is the Sheriff. Wait until I tell him I met you," she grinned.

Sydney felt awkward and a little guilty for wanting to leave the personable girl. She slid the sunglasses back on her face and extended her hand. "Paula, it was a pleasure meeting you. I hope you make it to Las Vegas."

Paula clasped Sydney's hand as though she had just met a celebrity. "I will, I will—and I'm going to call you when I do."

"Good. Now the Roadster is down the next block . . ."

"Next intersection, take a right. You'll see it by the park."

"Thanks." Sydney started out the door and then remembered something. "Paula, you wouldn't by any chance know where the Joshua McCain farm is?"

"Oh, sure. Straight out the back road for fifteen miles or so by the draw. You'll see it; there's nothing else out there. Are you a friend of Joshua's?"

"I'm just delivering a package to him. Thanks again."

Paula waited at the door until Sydney's SUV disappeared around the corner. She went back to the counter and retrieved the magazine from underneath the register. Suddenly, she cursed to herself. She had forgotten that Joshua didn't live at the farmhouse.

* * *

Paula hadn't overstated the Roadster Inn's lack of aesthetic appeal. The log cabin motel looked out of place situated next door to the pristine park with a manicured lawn. The cramped rustic room of checkered floor tile and pinewood walls reminded her of summer camp. And of course, there was no television or radio. At that point she didn't much care. She was just thankful to have a place to stay for the night. She ate at the Formica table with her legs propped up on one of the vinyl chairs. She had lost a day of vacation getting to this place. First thing in the morning she would deliver Constantine's letter to Joshua McCain. With some luck, he could tell her a shortcut to get back to the main highway, and she'd be home by nightfall.

The bed sheets secreted the pungent odor of pine, like the walls. Sydney decided to sleep on top of the covers—and in her clothes. A half-hour later, she was still wide-awake, staring at the yellowed ceiling tiles. This was a waste of time. She couldn't get to sleep. She tossed the blanket on the floor, and then slipped on her boots.

She went to her vehicle and followed Paula's directions to McCain's farm and quickly discovered that math wasn't one of the girl's strengths. Fifteen miles turned out to be thirty-five. Sydney was expecting a sprawling farm filled with livestock, buildings, and farm machinery. What she found instead were two crumbling structures on the verge of collapse, rotting on weed-infested parched land. She parked at the front door of the cabin that was without a porch or windows. The sky was as dark as the inside of a coffin, and she never saw the "No Trespassing" signs posted on the corner of the house.

Sydney kept the headlights on so she could see. She pushed on the front door and it swung open on one rusty hinge. Was this Constantine's idea of a joke? This place hadn't been inhabited in years. She got back in her vehicle and drove around back to the barn, which was also abandoned.

She was tired; too tired to risk driving back to Poison Springs in the dark. Besides, the barn offered a loft full of hay and a lamp half-full of kerosene, which seemed infinitely more appealing than her motel room. Sydney felt safe, but decided not to take any risk with Constantine's letter.

She went outside to the rear of her vehicle, knelt down and flipped the switch that was hidden underneath the bumper. The switch disengaged the passenger seat lock. She opened the door, slid the passenger seat back, exposing a large cavity in the floorboard. Sydney dropped Constantine's letter in the floor safe and locked the seat back in place.

In the morning she would try again to find McCain, but she wasn't hopeful. Constantine was clearly confused if he thought anyone still lived at the farm.

The night air smelled of dust. Another storm was brewing. She grabbed a blanket from the back of her Rover, locked the doors, and went into the barn. Ten minutes later she was fast asleep.

* * *

The shrill of the car alarm startled her from a deep sleep. Sydney stumbled to her feet, blinded and disoriented. She saw blinking lights outside, underneath the barn doors. She jumped down from the loft onto a bale of hay. Suddenly, the barn doors burst open, followed by a cloud of sand that blew in like it had been shot from a smoke machine. Bright lights hit her eyes, which she tried shielding with a hand. She pulled a gun out with the other.

"Who's there?" she shouted, as the sand tried suffocating her. A man grabbed her from behind, picked her up, and flung her to the ground. She raised herself up on all fours, and caught her breath. The large man's silhouette bent over her, and she swung her fist into his groin. He groaned and fell back. Sydney picked up her gun off the ground and wobbled to her feet. Before she could say anything, another man smashed his fist against her face,

64

sending her crashing against the wall. His powerful forearm pinned her head against the rotting boards, while he twisted her arm. She yelled, and dropped the gun. She opened her eyes, but was blinded by the high beam lights of the vehicle outside.

"Who are you—what do you want?" she mumbled.

"Stay where you are . . . perfectly still or I'll break this pretty little neck of yours." His breath stunk of tobacco and tequila. He moved his hands down the sides of her legs, while using his feet to spread them wider. "I got to check to see if you have any more deadly weapons," he said with a coarse laugh. He slid a slow hand between her legs, letting them linger. Sydney snapped her shoulder back, then smashed an elbow into his face. The last thing she saw was his fist.

When she awoke, she found herself behind the steel cage in the back seat of a Sahara staring at the driver. The thick man's neck was full of red pimples with yellow puss, and unruly blond hair curled from underneath a giant cowboy hat. The man was alone. She looked out the back window and saw the lights of her Land Rover following behind.

"Looks to me like you're ready to talk," he said. Sydney turned around. The side of the big man's face was puffy and his nose was red with blood. His sunglasses couldn't hide the hollows around the eyes of his parchment skin.

Sydney winced as she tried to speak. Her lower lip was split. She touched the swelling under her eye. "Who the hell are you and where are we going?"

"Deputy Sheriff Poole at your service, ma'am. That must be a trick question. I don't know where you come from lady, but it must have been from under a rock. You can't go around assaulting officers with a gun and think you can get away with it." Sydney spit blood from her mouth. She didn't know what to say. The man was a moron, but if she wanted to get out of this she needed to keep her poise until she had a chance to talk to the person in charge.

Poole glanced at her in the mirror again. "You gonna tell me what you were doing trespassing on federal property?"

"No."

"What?" he asked, tilting his head back against the cage as though he didn't understand her answer. "What did you say?" he asked, raising his voice.

"No. The word is in the English dictionary. It's the opposite of yes. Look it up. I don't have to answer your questions or talk with you. I prefer you keep your questions and thoughts to yourself until we get to wherever the hell you're taking me."

Poole's huge biceps contracted as he gripped the steering wheel tighter. "Lady, I'm taking your pretty little ass to jail. You're going to be sorry you ever came to Poison Springs."

She was already sorry. She stared out the window for the remainder of the ride and didn't say a word.

Chapter 13

Poole parallel parked in front of the town hall and sheriff's office. His partner pulled Sydney's vehicle into the adjacent stall. They opened the back door and dragged her out. Even in the light, Poole wasn't anything pretty to look at. He had an acne-scared face, bulbous chin, and weighed two hundred and eighty pounds. His partner, Stephenson, was just as big. Sydney kept her eyes focused straight ahead, avoiding eye contact with Poole, as Stephenson unlocked her ankle shackles.

Chief Deputy T.J. Eagleton was at his desk when he saw the reluctant prisoner coming in. Poole unlocked the cell door, released her cuffs, and pushed her in.

"I want to talk to however is in charge," Sydney said.

"Yeah, and I want to win the lottery and retire. Shut the hell up—go to sleep. You'll have plenty of time to talk in the morning," Poole said, walking away.

"What's going on?" T.J. asked.

"This crazy woman attacked us out at McCain's. Look at what she did to my face."

Eagleton ignored the man's crooked nose. "What was she doing out there?"

"Who knows; we found her camping out in the barn—and she ain't talking."

"Was she alone?"

"Yeah, as near as we could tell. Her rig was parked out front, and we searched the place, but she was the only one we saw."

"Who is she?"

Poole put his handkerchief to his nose. "Her license and registration says Sydney Belleshota. And she had this—pulled it on us when we tried to talk with her."

T.J. ran his hand across the gold-leafed barrel of the expensive Beretta. He took the wallet from Poole and studied the

67

license photo. Faces came and went, but not names. "The name is familiar. Run a check for me."

"T.J., this is bull, I need to have my nose looked at. It's damn near 4:00 a.m., can't this wait 'til morning? She ain't going nowhere," Poole said.

"It is morning. Get on it now." Poole hesitated, and then went into the other room.

Sydney sat on the cot wondering how she was going to get out of this mess. She could see the sandy-haired man watching her from his desk. He was stocky and muscular, with a face as rough and sun-beaten as the other deputies. He had the same soft blue eyes and freckled face of Paula Eagleton, but the nervous expression on his face told her he wasn't going to be any more understanding than the other two deputies. He stood up and came over to the cell door.

Sydney jumped up off the cot. "Are you the person in charge here?"

"Yes, ma'am. I'm Chief Deputy T.J. Eagleton."

"Why am I being held?"

"Trespassing and resisting arrest."

"When is it a crime to seek refuge on abandoned property in the middle of a sand storm?"

"Trespassing and resisting arrest are serious offences. You clearly aren't from here and you had no business being out at that farm that time of night. Endangering the lives of my men with this gun of yours only complicates your situation. You know how much trouble you are in?"

"I have a right to defend myself against troglodytes who don't bother identifying themselves and think its okay to wedge their hands in my crotch."

Eagleton's face turned crimson. She had a feeling this was not the first time something like this had happened.

"Who did that, Poole?" he asked.

"I suggest you find him a wall socket to play with," Sydney said.

For a moment, there was an uncomfortable silence.

"I apologize for what he did, but what were you doing there?"

She sensed that the apology was sincere. "Trying to deliver a letter to Joshua McCain. I was told he lived there."

"Josh hasn't lived there in years. Who told you he did?"

"The girl working at the convenience store—Paula."

"Well, my cousin should have known better. The McCains haven't owned that property for more than thirty years."

"And I was supposed to know that?" she asked, raising her voice.

Eagleton sighed. "Yes, there are notices posted everywhere on that property to stay out, including you. You had no authority to set up camp out there. My men said you . . ."

Sydney clasped the cell bars. "Are you as thickheaded as those two dopes you have working for you? I told you, I needed a place to stay for the night. I checked into the Roadster late last night. I tried sleeping on the bedrock they called a mattress and that didn't work, so I thought I could at least get my business with McCain out of the way so I could leave in the morning. As it has been my misfortune since leaving Seattle, I've had nothing but bad luck. It didn't change any tonight when another sandstorm blew through here. I'll be damned if I was going to kill myself trying to drive back to town when I'm tired and in the middle of a storm. So, if you want to make an issue of the trespassing charge—fine. I'll pay whatever fine you want. Just let me out of here so I can go on my way."

Eagleton folded his arms. He didn't like her attitude or arrogance, and he particularly didn't like the idea that she was out at the farm. "You say you were out there to deliver a letter to Josh. If that's the truth, where is the letter? My men didn't find anything but this gun, which by the way, you better have a permit for."

"The permit is in the plastic sleeve of my shoulder holster."

Eagleton looked inside the leather holster and pulled out the paper and read it. "You're an insurance investigator?"

"And a bonded courier. That's why I'm trying to locate Joshua McCain."

69

Eagleton gave her a suspicious glance. "Like I said, if you have a package, where is it?"

"It's a letter."

Eagleton sighed. "Okay, a letter. Where is it and who is it from?"

The inflection of his voice and cold eyes told her the chief deputy was no trust worthier than the others. "Who it's from is immaterial. It's in my possession until I turn it over to Joshua McCain in person. If he wants to divulge the source, that's his business. I can't. No offence, but that's the way I work."

Eagleton's jaw tightened. "Well, this is the way I work. Until I find out who you are and what you're up to, you aren't going anywhere."

"Fine, then at least let me make a telephone call."

"You decide to be more cooperative, and then I might let you make a call. Until that happens, this is your home." Eagleton turned and left the room.

Sydney kicked the cot, but wanted to scream. She felt as helpless as a victim in a horror movie; there was nothing she could say or do that was going to change her situation.

Something strange was going on and it was more than just some simple trespassing offense. The deputies were too interested in the letter. So interested, that she was beginning to wonder if they'd release her even if she gave it to them. Another thing struck her as odd. She had counted over ten Sahara Jeeps outside when they brought her in. Towns twice the size of Poison Springs didn't have a police force as large.

Sydney's head ached and she was tired. She fluffed the flat pillow and tucked it under her head. That's when she noticed the diamond bracelet missing from her wrist. "Damn." She must have lost it in the barn.

* * *

Eagleton looked over Poole's shoulder as he sat at the computer screen. "Anything yet?"

"Yeah." He passed him the printout.

70

Eagleton read it and cursed. "I knew her name sounded familiar."

Poole spun around in his chair. "You know her?"

"She's the daughter of that dead billionaire, Devin Leon-Francis, who died a few years ago. Get my dad on the phone. Poole hesitated. "Now, Poole!" The fat man jumped up and ran to his desk. Stephenson was taking a nap on the couch. Eagleton kicked his feet. "Stephenson, get out to that woman's car and see if she's hiding anything in there."

"Boss, we checked it clean before we brought it in. All she had was some food, drinks, and some toilet items," he said, laying his head back down on the armrest.

"Get your butt up and do as I say. I'm looking for a letter addressed to McCain!"

* * *

The steady stream of deputies through the door kept Sydney awake. By her count, at least eight deputies had paraded past her cell. For a town that shut down at dusk, she couldn't understand all the activity. The last man that entered the office was Sheriff Eagleton. He was in his sixties, but was lean and tempered like his son. Sydney heard the men whispering as they huddled in the back of the office.

Sheriff Eagleton propped a stogie in his mouth as he listened intently to his son's argument.

"I don't think we can afford to take any chances. We need for her to disappear," T.J. said.

Poole sat in the chair across from the sheriff nodding his head. "I second that. We have no idea what she's up to."

"Killing her would only worsen the situation," the sheriff said.

"So, what do we do?" T.J. asked.

Eagleton blew a thick cloud of smoke in their faces. "Release her."

"You're not serious, are you?" T.J. asked.

Eagleton picked up the faxed report off his desk. "You read the report on her. She's got too much money and influential friends. The last thing I need is an investigation or people coming down here looking for her. We don't have any other options. Let her go."

T.J. sat on the corner of his father's desk. "What about the letter she says she has for McCain?"

Eagleton turned to Poole. "Did you find anything in her truck?" Eagleton asked.

"No, there's nothing there. We checked it twice."

"She may have left it in McCain's barn," T.J. said.

"Hell, even if there is a letter for Josh, I don't see what's the big deal," Poole said.

"That's why you're still a deputy, and I'm the sheriff. You may not get concerned when strangers come looking for Josh McCain and are snooping around his farm, but I do. Especially when she's carrying a letter that's so important it has to be delivered by private courier. Now, if the letter is insignificant, there would be no need to hide it, which I believe Belleshota has done—probably somewhere in McCain's barn. I want you to go back out there and look for it," Eagleton said. "And I want Stephenson to follow her once she's released and make sure she leaves town and doesn't double back to the barn."

Poole didn't like that plan. "Send Stephenson to cover the barn. I'll tail her for you."

"You stay away from her, Poole. You're in enough trouble as it is. We wouldn't be doing all this if you hadn't tried to cop a feel. I've warned you about this before. Keep your damn hands to yourself or your wife. I want you at McCain's farm, and I want you to stay on patrol out there until I tell you to come back."

* * *

Sydney had just fallen asleep when Sheriff Eagleton unlocked the cell door. "Sorry for the mix up, you can go. All of your personal belongings have been returned to your vehicle, which is parked out front." He handed her the keys.

For a moment, Sydney thought she was dreaming. She couldn't believe they had released her. "Did you find a woman's bracelet?" she asked.

"A bracelet?"

"Yes, I lost my diamond bracelet. It could have been in Joshua McCain's barn." Eagleton looked at Poole and Stephenson who stood against the back wall. They both shrugged their shoulders.

"No, we didn't find anything like that, Chief," Stephenson said.

Sydney tried reading their faces, but couldn't tell if they were lying. "Well, I'm sure that's where I lost it."

"I'll have one of my men comb the area. If it's there, they'll find it. I have your business card and phone number. If I find something I'll call you." Eagleton gave her his card. "Give me a day or two and call me if you haven't heard from us by then." He guided her by the elbow toward the door. "Anything else?"

He wanted her out of town, and now. Asking for permission to go back to the barn to look for her bracelet was pointless, and would only raise his suspicion. It was clear no one wanted her near the farmhouse again. "My gun, please," she said, staring at Poole.

Eagleton cut his eyes at Poole. "Hand it over, Elan." The deputy slowly pulled the Beretta from his waistband. He handed it to the sheriff. Eagleton discharged the clip from the handle. "Don't load it until you've reached the highway," he warned.

It was 7:10 in the morning when Sydney walked out of the jail. The streets were empty except for two men standing on the corner watching her get in the SUV. She smelled the lingering odor of cigarette smoke on the leather seats, but was relieved to see that the passenger seat was still intact, which meant they hadn't discovered her floorboard safe. Deputy Stephenson came outside, followed by T.J. Stephenson got into a Jeep and backed out of the stall, while Eagleton stood on the corner watching her. That's when she noticed something peculiar. Other than the sheriff's men, she hadn't seen anybody else on the streets since arriving.

Sydney turned onto Main Street and headed toward the highway, with Stephenson close behind. As she passed the mini-mart, she saw Paula Eagleton in the parking lot getting out of her truck. Sydney swerved across the lane and pulled into the lot.

The exhilaration of seeing Sydney's Land Rover disappeared when the tinted window lowered and she saw Sydney's face. "What happened to you?"

"I had a little accident last night at Joshua McCain's, no thanks to you. Why didn't you tell me he wasn't living there? You could have saved me a lot of trouble." Almost immediately, Sydney regretted her harsh words. Tears formed in the corner of the girl's eyes. "I'm sorry Paula, I don't mean to take it out on you. I've had a rough night."

Paula saw Stephenson parked at the corner. She stuck her head through the window. "I should have warned you to stay away from there. That place is dangerous. A few years ago a couple of prospectors fell in one of the abandoned wells out there and died."

"Prospectors?"

"Yeah, these hills are loaded with old guys running around looking for gold."

"So, how can I get in touch with Joshua McCain?"

"His girlfriend is the town clerk in Weavilwood."

"Is there anyone here that knows where he lives?"

"I don't know, a few people maybe. But most everyone around here is gone during the day. They work over at the air force base or the White River Copper Mine in Weavilwood. I'm really sorry I didn't tell you about Josh."

"You can make it up to me by giving me the directions to Weavilwood."

Chapter 14

Tuesday morning Asha woke to the soft sounds of jazz playing on the radio and the smell of herbal tea streaming to the bedroom. She rolled over and saw the other side of the bed empty. She got up and went into the living room.

Ellington was watching television, while his father sat at the table drawing on a large piece of butcher paper.

Asha tied her robe as she stared at the mosaic collection of stones lying on the floor. She sat down at the table next to him. "I can see what you've been up to all night. Have you figured it out yet?"

"It's a map of some kind, but of what I don't know. There are some missing pieces," he said, pointing at the incomplete jigsaw puzzle on the floor.

The collage of strange markings didn't make any sense to Asha. She pointed to one of the stones. "What are these numbers?"

Doc knelt down on the carpet. "Random alphanumeric numbers—probably coordinates of some kind."

"And you've been trying to solve this since last night?"

"It's been bugging me."

She looked at the large sheet of butcher paper he had stretched across the table. "What's that you're working on?"

"I'm making a copy of the map. There is a professor at the university who may be able to make some sense of this and I don't want to cart around seventy pounds of rocks."

Asha recognized the glint she saw in her husband's eyes. She had seen it many times before when he was about to immerse himself in a project. That didn't make her happy. She gave him a long stare.

"Julian, I hope you're not going to get involved in this. Dr. Constantine will explain why he left these for Marcus when he returns."

"Constantine won't be showing up at our door any time soon. I'm pretty sure of that. As far as we know, these stones are the only thing he left behind, which must have some intrinsic value if he had them locked in the hotel vault."

She had been down this road before with him, and she didn't like where it lead. "Don't do this to me, Julian."

He stood up. Ellington took the opportunity to dive off the sofa into his father's arms. Doc caught him and lifted him to his shoulders. "Asha, you know Marcus. He isn't leaving here until he finds out what happened to Dr. Constantine."

"Okay, what does that have to do with us? We've been planning this trip for over a year." Ellington pinched his father's cheek with his fingers.

"He just wants to know what he's supposed to do with these stones."

"No, this is about Marcus going off half-cocked on another one of his adventures and he's managed to suck you in too. You told him you pieced some of the stones together, didn't you?"

"Yes, he stopped by the room just before you woke up."

"And knowing him, I suppose he thinks this heap of rocks is a treasure map of some kind—right?"

Doc had to smile. "Something like that. But that really is secondary to finding out what happened to Constantine." He placed Ellington back in his chair, and wrapped his arms around his wife's waist. "It really wasn't my intent to ruin this trip, but Marcus is not backing off this thing. If I leave him here by himself there's no telling what will happen. Why don't you and Caitlin go on to California like we planned and we'll meet you there in a couple of days. I promise I'll make this up to you," he said, kissing the side of her neck.

She stood rigid. This was their first real vacation in years, and he had spoiled it.

"You've wanted me to take some time off from school. Let me do this and I promise I won't teach next quarter. We can go and do whatever you want."

"No night classes or lectures either."

"Okay," he said, pulling her closer.

Her arms slowly came to life as she responded to his kisses. "The whole quarter—you promise?"

"Yes," he mumbled as he nibbled on her neck.

"Okay, but I'm still disappointed in you," she said, sliding away from his arms and going back into the bedroom and shutting the door.

Ellington clung to his father's leg with a bemused smile on his face. Suddenly, Doc felt alone.

* * *

Marcus was waiting for Doc when he came out of the hotel. "How did it go?"

"How do you think it went?" Doc snapped.

"Brother, I'll make this up to you. Just tell me what you want and you've got it."

"What I want is for you to turn those stones over to the police and forget about this. Three men are dead, and I have a sneaking suspicion those rocks have something to do with it. Let the police sort this out, so we can get up out of here and be with our families like we're supposed to be."

"Naw, can't do that. Dr. Constantine flew halfway around the world to give this to me and I at least owe it to him to find out why. Even Elizabeth thinks I'm doing the right thing."

"Your daughter is as crazy as you." Doc signaled the taxi on the corner. "I bet Caitlin wasn't as agreeable."

"Yeah, she understood."

"Sure she did," Doc said sarcastically, as he opened the back door of the taxi.

Chapter 15

Elias Kane was double parked at the airport, when a police officer tapped the car window and told him to move the limousine. Kane pulled the car against the curb and parked in front of the baggage terminal. Usually he met Cassandra at the gate, but her flight from Prague arrived late, and she had called to tell him to meet her outside. She sounded tired on the phone, but Kane knew that wouldn't stop her from going directly to the office. She was a workaholic, but that's why she was one of the preeminent experts in cathedral restorations. Her architectural business took her all over the world, but that wasn't the business that took her to Prague.

Cassandra Prophet's other vocation was that as a purveyor of goods and services. Her exclusive clientele consisted of people she knew — all of whom were wealthy and eager to pay for what they wanted. She had the uncanny talent of finding things others couldn't, like the Mesopotamian scroll she was bringing back from Prague. The Iraqi and U.S. governments had spent four years trying to find the ancient manuscript that had been looted from an Iraqi Museum. Somehow Cassandra had tracked down the wealthy Syrian businessman who had bought the ancient scroll from an Iraqi looter. She relied on the resourcefulness of former Russian intelligence officers for most of her information. Once they found what she wanted, people like Kane and Roth were dispatched to get it.

Kane drummed his fingers against the steering wheel as he smiled and waved to the motorcycle policeman who pulled in front of the limo and parked. Anyone else with as much to lose as Kane would not have been so foolish, but Kane had learned a long ago that it was easier to avoid police suspicion if he didn't try avoiding them.

* * *

Kane saw Cassandra in the rearview mirror approaching the car. She was five-five, but looked shorter in her denim jeans outfit and baseball cap that partially obscured a side-swept ponytail.

Behind her was her four-year-old daughter, Hanna, who was desperately trying to keep pace with her.

He took their bags and put them in the trunk. Hanna jumped into his arms and gave him a hug. Like a doting father, he kissed her small face and opened the limo door for them. Hanna screamed and giggled when she saw the giant panda bear sitting across from her. She was so excited; Kane couldn't keep her still long enough to attach the safety strap.

Cassandra snatched the buckle from his hand and pulled the belt taut across her daughter's chest. "Elias, I told you not to coddle her—or spoil her. Every time you do it, you're undermining me. Hanna is spoiled, and I don't intend to reinforce that kind of poor behavior. Taking her with me on this trip was a complete disaster, which won't ever be repeated. For now on, she stays at home with you or Claire. I will not tolerate a child's interference when I am trying to work."

Hanna began crying.

Kane didn't say anything. He closed her door, got in the front seat, and started the engine. Cassandra was brilliant at business, but inept at motherhood. She displayed the behavior of an apathetic and narcissistic mother, who cared more about her own welfare than her child's. He had seen it before.

Like Hanna, he was the product of selfish parents, who was told at the age of nine, that his father had left the family to return to his first wife. It wasn't long afterwards that his mother disappeared with a soldier. He never saw either of them again. The chore of raising him and his two siblings fell to a widowed aunt, who had two children of her own. Every time Kane thought about his childhood, the dual ache of abandonment gnawed at his stomach like a lacerated ulcer.

Kane lowered the privacy glass separating him from Cassandra.

She pulled a Smartphone from her backpack and scribbled notes on the screen with a pen. "Give me an update on where we are, Elias."

"Roth's interference set us back," he said, craning his neck so he could see her face.

"I don't care about Roth. Have we found Constantine yet?" she asked without looking at him.

"We found him, but he's dead. Samantha pushed him too hard when he wouldn't give up the stones. We're still looking for them."

"So you don't know any more than you did yesterday?"

"We know he spent a lot of time in an office building in Pioneer Square last night, and your sister found a connection between him and an insurance company located in the building. A few years ago he hired the company to recover some stolen artifacts for him. Samantha is checking them out now."

"I don't like it. Did Constantine have the stones with him when he entered that building?"

"According to Samantha he didn't, but she lost him a couple of times. He could have passed them to someone in the building."

She stopped writing and looked at him. She was paler than her sister, but they had the same wide mouths and funnel chins.

"Don't ever question my sister's competence again. If Constantine spoke with anyone in that building, Sam will find out. How many are coming for the auction?"

"We have thirteen confirmations."

"Even more than I expected. Is *The Lebanese* coming?"

"He was the first to submit a deposit."

That brought a smile to her face. "As I expected he would be. He will drive the price up. I'm beginning to think the scroll will be our best seller yet."

"Did you have any trouble acquiring it from the owner?"

Cassandra fidgeted with her ponytail. "Let's just say I offered him a reasonable price and he accepted it—after I assured him that the Syrian General Security Department won't be raiding his secret underground vault where he keeps his other stolen war trophies. Now, fill me in on the details for tomorrow night."

"When you get to the office, you'll find all the information in the vault—names, flight arrival times, and hotel reservations. I've made arrangements to have the viewing and auction in the boathouse where security and privacy can be maintained. While it may not be the most suitable environment, it certainly is the safest—particularly since your benefit will be going on at the same time."

"I agree—totally. You have prepared well as usual. I wouldn't know what to do if you weren't looking out for me."

Kane smiled at her through the mirror, even though he didn't believe a word she said. Her compliments were as hollow as she was. He hesitated a minute before hitting her with the bad news. "Jai-Robson Priest is also coming."

The little color she had in her cheeks disappeared. "What did you say?"

"Priest will be there. He followed the rules like everyone else."

"I wrote the rules, you don't need to recite or interpret them for me," she snapped. She leaned forward in the seat. "That barbarian uses every opportunity to try and buy respectability, as if that were possible. Fine, if he wants to waste his money, I will enjoy taking it from him. But I will not tolerate any of his outrageous behavior in my home and around my friends. If indeed he does come, I want him kept on a short leash. The slightest provocation on his part and our business arrangement is over. He'll have to find someone else to get his product for him." She settled back in the seat and turned to look out the window—Kane's cue to start the car.

Kane pulled away from the curb and headed down the airport ramp toward the freeway. Short of Jai-Robson Priest killing someone, Kane knew Cassandra wasn't going to back out of her business arrangement with him. She had worked too long and hard in putting the deal together.

* * *

After dropping Cassandra off at her office, Kane drove Hanna home. When he pulled into the gate, a Seattle detective's

81

car was parked in front of the four-car garage. He backed the limousine into the courtyard as two men came through the garden and approached the car. Kane rolled down the window.

"Are you Elias Kane?" the detective asked.

"Yes. How can I help you?" he asked as he opened the door.

"We'd like to talk with you for a minute."

"Just give me a minute." He opened the back door and unbuckled Hanna from the seat.

"Uncle, I'm hungry," she said as they walked toward the house.

"I'll fix you something." He put her on the ground.

One of the detectives smiled at her as he ran a hand through her curly hair. "And what's your name?"

"Hanna Prophet," she said, boastfully. The men laughed.

Kane smiled. "If you don't mind, can we talk while I make her something?"

The lead detective looked hesitant, almost unsure of the invitation. "Yeah, I guess that will be okay." They followed him to the kitchen, where the detective introduced himself and his partner. They were there to question him about Erik Roth. Kane tried to act surprised, all the while wondering why it had taken them so long to show up.

In his line of work, Kane was always prepared, which meant having a convenient alibi when he needed one. When on business, he billed everything to Cassandra's name and used one of his six aliases. He always covered his bases, never leaving anything to chance, including this anticipated visit from the police.

They wanted to know what he was doing in Panama City, his relationship with Erik Roth, and how he ended up on the *Southern Comfort*. Kane knew the art of a good liar was to get them to buy the first one. After that, everything else was easy. He told them he had been on vacation visiting friends in Argentina and returned home on the *Southern Comfort* because he always wanted to see Panama. His former employer, Teoni Perguree, who lived in Buena Aires, would corroborate his story.

"I met Erik Roth in Panama. We were staying at the same hotel. Among boxing aficionados, Mr. Roth is a minor legend. Did you know he won an Olympic Gold Medal when he was just seventeen? He is practically a national hero in South Africa," Kane said. After twenty minutes of questioning, the detectives were satisfied.

After they left, Kane went out to the car and got Cassandra's document tube from the trunk. He unscrewed the lid and pulled out a set of blueprints, which he laid on the table. Then, he pried the liner out, and carefully removed the Mesopotamian scroll hidden in the liner. The old Babylonian script was yellowed and soiled, but in excellent condition. He carefully untied the scarlet ribbon binding the document and unfurled it under the light. It was worth $500,000, but would sell for more at the auction. The sisters would make a nice profit, but nothing compared to the money they would make with Jai-Robson Priest.

While Priest would be in town for the auction, Cassandra's multi-million dollar deal with him wasn't scheduled to take place until next week. The date and location were still a mystery, but Kane would find out. He knew he would have to tread carefully, because there would only be one chance. If he got caught, there wasn't a country in the world where he could hide.

Chapter 16

Benno Rood sat in his office chair pondering what to do. The woman who had just left his office was a little too smooth. She told him she was an art dealer looking for help to recover stolen art from her father's collection. Thirty minutes into their conversation she casually mentioned Dr. Constantine's name, and that he had spoken highly of the services Cornerstone Global had provided to Leicester University. Of course she didn't know Dr. Constantine personally, but the recommendation came through a friend of a friend who worked with Constantine.

Ordinarily Benno might have taken the bait, but the woman's arrival was too coincidental with Constantine's arrival. Was this the person Constantine was so afraid of the night they met; the person he was convinced was following him? The more reticent Benno was, the more she pushed to see what he knew. Benno never divulged his meeting with Constantine or anything about the letter he had given Sydney. She left him with a warm smile and firm handshake. He watched her take the elevator down to the lobby. What he didn't see was that she stopped at the front desk and questioned the receptionist.

Benno decided the events of the last forty-eight hours were important enough to interrupt his boss's vacation. He picked up the telephone and called his secretary. "Get me Mr. St. John's office in San Francisco."

Chapter 17

Professor Knudson was head of the Department of Geography at the university, but he was stupefied by the mysterious map he was studying. "Gentlemen, I don't have any idea of what you have here. This isn't much to go on. The coordinates you have listed here are for property boundaries, but without the other stones, there is no way to determine the proper context. I'm afraid I can't help you." He neatly folded Doc's map and handed it back to him.

"Is there anyone who can?" Doc asked.

"Professor Shengatti. He's a mathematician and an expert in cartography and geographic information systems. He may be of some help to you."

Fall classes at UW had not begun, and Shengatti wasn't on campus. His administrative assistant contacted him at home, and to her surprise he agreed to come in and meet with Doc and Marcus.

Shengatti was a bearded short robust man filled with the same youthful exuberance of an eager student.

"This is fascinating," he said, as he carefully examined Doc's map. "And you say these carved stones are made of gypsum?"

"Yes."

"Well, that may help localize the area." Shengatti pulled an engineering tool from his desk and took some measurements.

Marcus watched him taking notes as he carefully inspected every line and symbol on the map. "Do you know what kind of map this is?"

"It appears to be a cadastral survey, or should I say, a crude facsimile of one. The rectangular lines are territorial or property boundaries. The heavy line here," he said pointing with his pencil "represents a large body of water—perhaps a tributary or even a river."

"What's a cadastral survey?" Marcus asked.

"A way of measuring and mapping property boundaries for establishing ownership. It could be an individual tract, but I believe it defines a territory."

"A territory? How old do you think it is?"

"Probably 1800's. I'm just sorry this is all you have. The missing stones must have the boundary corners, which is critical to determine the exact parcel and location."

Doc stood over the professor's shoulder. "Is it that accurate?"

"It may be. Whoever made the map certainly had good knowledge of surveying, or had access to a cadastral map of the area. Many of them weren't entirely accurate during that period. The slightest error in just one digit deviation could throw the exact location off by a few hundred feet. Of course, multiple errors can have an exponential effect."

"You mean miles?" Marcus asked.

"Hundreds of miles."

"So, you're saying that without knowing the exact corner of a boundary there's no way to identify the location of this property?" Doc asked.

Shengatti sat at his desk and grabbed a piece of paper. He drew a large circle, covering the whole page. "Imagine this is a two hundred acre corn field, and you get dropped down into the middle of it with a set of directions to find a one-foot square box in the field. Now, imagine that it is night and you have no moon or stars to guide you. That's how hard it is," he said, dropping the pencil on the desk.

"You didn't say it was impossible," Doc said.

Shengatti smiled. "That's correct, I didn't, but it will take some time."

"We have the time if you do," Marcus said.

* * *

Doc went to the water fountain in the hallway. He checked his phone and saw that Asha had called four times. When he called her back she sounded anxious.

"Julian, I've been trying to get in touch with you. Where are you?"

"We're still at the university. Is everything okay?"

"Benno has been trying to get in touch with Marcus. Is he still there with you?"

"Yeah. What's up?"

"He has information about Dr. Constantine. He said it's very important, and he wants Marcus to call him right away. I have his number for you."

After writing down the number, Doc told her he and Marcus were running late.

"You're not going to make it back before we leave for the airport, are you?"

"Asha, I'm right in the middle . . ."

"I don't need your explanation. I'm married to you, remember. Do whatever you have to do, but you better be in L.A. in time to fly back home with us. If you're not, I will never forgive you."

"I don't know how you endure my irresponsibility."

The qualities she loved about him were often the same ones that caused her pain. He could be tenacious as a bulldog, and couldn't leave things unfinished—just like Marcus. "You're not irresponsible; your priorities are just clouded sometimes. I don't want to be a mom and surrogate father too. Just remember that the next time."

"This won't happen again."

"As long as Marcus draws breath, it will. You two are joined at the hip. Remind him that he has a wife too, and that she needs to hear from him. Promise me that you will be careful."

"I'll be okay, and I promise you that I will be in Los Angeles in a couple of days."

Marcus came out into the hallway as Doc closed his phone. "Everything okay?"

"Fine. You need to call Caitlin before they leave for the airport. How's the professor doing?"

"I'll say one thing for him, he doesn't give up very easily."

"Where's your cell phone?"

"I left it back at the hotel—why?"

Doc handed him his phone and Benno's telephone number. "Benno needs to talk to you about Constantine. I'll check on the professor."

Doc found Shengatti riveted to his desk watching the computer monitor screen.

"Ah, my friend, you are just in time," Shengatti said.

"You found something?"

"Nothing conclusive yet, but we are perhaps on the right trail. The inverted 'W's' are mountain ranges. The smaller indentations or impressions between the 'W's' I believe represent a valley or the low lands. Again, the circle is the desert, a rather large desert. I calculate that the size of the area is over 300 square miles, and probably much larger than that if we included the missing pieces. The arrows, I believe, are meaningless, perhaps included more to confuse rather than to elucidate. The line running diagonally across the stones I believe to be a river—a rather large river. With those as my assumptions, I ran some computer models utilizing the coordinates shown on the map in hopes they could identify the river source."

"What did you find?"

"Nothing. None of the coordinates are anywhere near a water source. However, after careful study of the terrain, I am almost certain this area can only be in the southwest—near the Mojave Desert in California or Southeast Nevada."

"But no river?"

"Nothing like what you have drawn here. If this is an accurate portrayal of the carving on the rock, this has to be an enormous river. There's nothing like this in the deserts of California, much less in Nevada. My original theory was that it was the Colorado River, but it flows to the west, emptying into the Gulf of Mexico. Without the ability to identify the water source, I cannot establish any boundary corners and therefore can't with any degree of accuracy, narrow down the location."

"That's as much as you can tell me?"

Shengatti stood up from the stool and stretched his back. "I'm afraid so. You know, this may all be some elaborate hoax—someone's idea of a bad joke."

Doc looked at the various computer monitors displaying GIS satellite images of the Southwestern United States. Maybe Shengatti's theory about the Colorado wasn't wrong.

"Did you look at any of the historical maps of the area?"

Shengatti flashed a row of crooked teeth, and sat back down at the computer. In seconds he produced a set of territorial maps of the 1800's. He studied them. "You would have done well in one of my classes, Dr. Sebasst," he said, as his fingers pounded away at the keyboard. "There seems to have been two tributaries that once ran further west off the Colorado. It's possible one or both could have once flowed as far as the desert."

After spending several more minutes inputting data, he sat back and waited for the results. Within five minutes, the database produced two topography maps for the territories of California and Nevada. He dragged the computer mouse slowly across the screen, inspecting each quadrant of the maps. "The survey lines and markings are very similar," he said. He printed the images to the large GIS color plotter.

Marcus came back in the room as the plotter finished printing. Shengatti tore off the oversized map and laid it on a lighted map table, where he inspected it with a magnifying glass in one hand and Doc's drawing in the other. "Yes, very similar terrain indeed. I believe this could be the area . . . right here," he said, circling the spot with his pencil.

Doc leaned over the table. "Crazy Flats?"

"But it probably doesn't exist anymore. The map shows that it was a mining town, and like most mining towns after the gold rush era in Nevada and California, it simply vanished," Shengatti said.

"So what's there now?" Marcus asked.

Shengatti reached across the table and grabbed a set of map transparencies. He found the one he was looking for and placed it on top of the old map.

"A town called Poison Springs."

A chill swept over Marcus's body. "Nevada?"

"Yes," Shengatti said.

"Damn, that's where Sydney went," Marcus said.

Doc looked up. "What?"

"Benno just told me she left yesterday morning headed to Poison Springs, Nevada to deliver a letter for Constantine."

"Benno saw Dr. Constantine?"

"Yeah, the night we arrived in Seattle. He came to the office to see me. Benno said he was acting strange—thought he was being followed. He left after Sydney agreed to personally deliver a letter for him.

"To who?"

"A man named Joshua McCain."

"Has Benno been in touch with Sydney?"

"No—he's been trying for hours, but her phone is still out of service."

Doc unwrapped a stick of gun and put it in his mouth. "I don't like this."

Marcus took a seat beside him. "It gets worse. A woman came by the office today asking questions about Constantine and Sydney. Benno didn't tell her anything, but the receptionist did. She told her that Sydney was out of town on an assignment. From the description he gave me, I think it could be the same woman that paid a visit to Constantine's motel. She left her business card with Benno. Her name is Samantha Prophet."

"Any relation to Cassandra Prophet?" Doc asked.

Shengatti had been sitting quietly listening to the conversation until he heard her name.

"Samantha Prophet is the older sister," he said.

"Who are they?" Marcus asked.

"Cassandra Prophet is a Seattle architect and public education advocate. She's one of the university's most avid boosters. She hosts an annual fundraiser for Seattle schools, which I believe is tomorrow night at her home in Medina."

"Is it a public event?" Marcus asked.

"No, it is by invitation only."

Doc scratched his chin. This was the second time Cassandra Prophet's name popped up, and now her sister's name. Doc wanted to talk with them, and the auction might be his best chance for that. He needed an invitation. "I think we need to talk with Toby Jamison."

* * *

The cabby that dropped them off at the university two hours ago picked them up in front of the UW medical center. "Back to the hotel," he said.

"No, Shaft's Men's Store on First Avenue," Marcus said, as he rested back against the seat. "You know Constantine was probably killed for those stones. If the Prophet woman is involved in any of this, she may think Sydney is in possession of them. We have to find a way to contact her."

"Isn't she meeting Jordan?" Doc asked.

"Yeah, but Jordan is still in New York, and won't be getting in until later tonight. They weren't scheduled to leave for Baja until the morning."

The taxi turned off 45th Street and took the freeway south.

"How much do you know about Constantine?" Doc asked.

Marcus paused. "He's a likable enough guy. A little on the eccentric side, but so are most brainiacs. The way I see it, these stones were important enough for him to fly all the way over here to see me. Thinking that someone had him popped, doesn't settle very easy with me. Not only may Sydney be in danger, so are we—and we don't even know what the hell for. But I bet it has something to do with that letter she's carrying."

The taxi exited the freeway and went up Fourth Avenue.

Doc looked at his watch. "It's after 6:00, you sure Toby is still at work?"

"Toby is always at work. He'd stay open 24-7 if he could." Marcus scooted forward and tapped the cabby on the shoulder. "Drop me off at the hotel, first."

"What's up?" Doc asked.

91

"I'm going to have Benno send some people to pick up the stones for safe keeping. I'll meet you back at Jamison's when I'm through." The cab dropped Marcus off in the Legends driveway.

* * *

Doc got out on the corner next to the expensive men's store. The sign said it was closed, but the door was unlocked. A large black man wearing a white pinstripe suit with baggy pants, blue tie, and matching shoes was in the back of the store busy rearranging a suit rack. Doc slipped up quietly behind him.

"Shaft—can you dig it?" Doc said, startling the former semi-pro football player.

The 330-pound man with no neck flinched and turned around. "Doc Sebasst! I can't believe my eyes." He gave Doc a bear hug, easily lifting him off the ground. Doc felt the air leave his lungs. He patted the man's gargantuan arms for him to let go. Toby Jamison towered over his old friend like a grizzly bear with a grin on his fat face.

"You're still as strong as an ox," Doc said.

"Man, when did you blow into town?"

"A couple of days ago. I'm staying up the street at the Legends Hotel."

"Why didn't you let me know you were coming? You could have stayed at my place."

"You still staying in that dump you call a house?"

"Yeah, you know it. I'm not going anywhere, man. I own everything on the block now, including a car wash and beauty salon. I'm diversified, Doc! The hood has been good to me, man," he said, laughing.

"Yeah, I can see that." Doc rubbed the big man's belly. "You must own a few rib joints too."

"Ah, man, can't stay buff forever." He slapped Doc's flat stomach. "You'll find that out one day. Now, tell me why you're in town."

"Taking care of some business—and I need your help."

Toby pulled a tape measure from his pocket and placed it around Doc's waist. "You know you came to the right place."

92

"Brother, I don't need any clothes."

Toby stepped back, assessing Doc's wardrobe. He shook his head. "Yeah, you do. You need to come up out of them loafers and Dockers. I've got some fine Italian slacks, and those athletic cut suits you love. I've got a few rags in the back I think you'll like."

Doc snatched the tape measure from Toby's hand. "Toby, I don't need any new threads."

"Then what you come here for, man?" he asked, as though he were insulted. He turned to put the suit back.

"You still have juice in this city to get me anything I need?"

"Depends," he said.

"On what?"

Toby faced him with his arms folded. "On whether you want to buy some clothes."

"You mean to tell me that . . ."

"Hey, Doc, I'm just another black entrepreneur trying to make it in the white man's world. You know how tough it is out here? No, you wouldn't know, because you're living on some paradise island in the South Pacific or someplace, while I'm still struggling in the hood trying to make a dime and . . ."

Doc laughed. "I'll buy a suit as long as you agree to keep your big mouth shut."

Toby flashed a wide grin. "Now you're talking, brother. I'm also thinking you need a shirt, maybe a nice tie, shoes . . ."

"Yes, all that too. Now, can we get to my business?"

"Sure, what you need, brother?" Toby measured Doc's inseam.

Doc pulled a newspaper clipping out of his pocket and gave it to him. "I need two official invitations to this event, and I need them by tomorrow."

Toby didn't stop what he was doing or look up. "Done. That's all?"

"I'll need directions to the hostess's house. A woman named Cassandra Prophet."

"I got it," he said as he continued working.

"You going to write this down?"

"I told you, I got it. How are you going to get there?"

"We can catch a cab."

Toby stood to his feet, giggling. "Man, you can't be going to some highbrow affair in a yellow cab. People will think you're whack."

"What do you suggest?"

"I can hook you up with something sweet," he said with a wink.

"Fine—as long as it runs."

"Done. I'll have it dropped off for you at the hotel in the morning along with the invitations."

Marcus tapped on the front window.

Toby motioned for him to enter. "I should've known if Doc was here, you'd be close behind. How the hell you doing, Marcus?" He gave Marcus the same ritualistic hug he had given Doc. "Those are some nice rags you got on your back," he said, stroking Marcus's Italian trench coat. "Yeah, really nice rags," he said as if in a trance.

Marcus frowned. "Hey, let go of my coat, man."

"This here is a designer, huh; where'd you get it?"

"Forget it, I'm not telling you jack. Besides, you couldn't afford it."

"Ahh man, don't be like that. We being blood and all, why you trying to treat me this way?"

Marcus arched an eyebrow. "Because even your momma knows you would charge her a dime to borrow a nickel."

Toby draped his arm over Marcus's shoulder. "Naw, man it ain't like that. I'm just trying to stay on top of my game, and one step ahead of the man. Just look at my pitiful inventory over here, and you'll see why I need a brother's help like you to spruce up my line."

Doc sat down in the chair, laughing. Toby pulled Marcus over toward the overcoats and suits. They were going to be here awhile.

* * *

An hour and a half later, with bags under their arms and dusk settling in, Doc and Marcus left Shafts and went to *Paupers*, a 14th century Renaissance-theme restaurant in the middle of downtown. They were seated in "the arena," a tiered dining room circled around a concrete pit, which served as a graveyard repository for pheasant, turkey and Cornish hen bones. Marcus watched in disgust as a man threw his freshly gnawed bones down to the pit.

"I should have known better than to trust you. You do this every time we go out together. I could have stayed in my hotel room and chucked rib bones in the corner if that kind of stuff appealed to me. I can't believe you brought me to this Neanderthal haven. This isn't funny, Doc—stop laughing!"

"Forget the atmosphere; they've got the best Cornish hens in town.

* * *

Two hours later, the noise was deafening. A man sitting at the table next to Marcus slammed his empty goblet on the rustic table, and a bodice-wearing maiden was dispatched to pour more of the frothy brew.

Marcus raised his goblet for a refill. "We've got to get one of these places in the bay area!" he said, as he tossed the gnawed turkey leg down to the pit. He picked up the roasted Cornish hen and sank his teeth into the juicy bird. When he finished, the hostess brought the bill. Marcus handed the receipt back to the hostess. "Please put their bill on mine," he said, pointing to the octogenarian couple sitting next to him. They were celebrating their forty-fifth wedding anniversary. Marcus gave the waitress a fifty dollar tip.

"Yes, sir. Thank you, sir," she said.

Doc smiled at Marcus. "You *must* be having a good time."

"I'm glad I let you talk me into coming."

"Had I known you'd embarrass me like you did, I would have left you at home."

95

The men took the stairs to the lower level and exited on the street. Cold air hit their faces.

"Damn, this is the only thing about this city I hate. A few degrees drop in temperature, a little night breeze, and you have to bring out a snowsuit to stay warm." Marcus buttoned his coat, and rubbed his hands together to keep warm. He noticed something peculiar across the street, next to the tower clock that wasn't working.

"What are you staring at?" Doc asked.

"Nothing man, just checking the time on that clock. I think it's a little fast. Let's go." Marcus headed east.

"Where are you going?"

"It's still early; I thought we could walk over to the waterfront."

"Are you kidding—that's in the opposite direction of our hotel. Why do you want to go there?"

"I like to watch the ferries at night. Come on," he said, tugging Doc's arm.

Doc pulled his arm away and stopped. "Wait a minute; you want to go way back over there just to see some stupid boats docking at the pier?"

"Look, bro', humor me. Let me check out one or two ferries and we can call it a night. We can catch some hot chocolate to get this chill off our butts, have a cigar, and talk. It'll be just like old times."

"I've never enjoyed talking with you, Qwik."

"Come on, man," he said, slinging his arm around Doc. "Don't be like this, you know you love me."

"I can't stand your whining butt, and get your hands off me."

* * *

It was even chillier on the ferry dock. The men huddled over the railing, looking at the incoming jumbo ferry.

"Do you think we're wasting our time fooling with Constantine's map? I mean, we could be chasing a big goose egg here. Not to mention the possibility of running into some pretty nasty people," Marcus said.

"When has that ever bothered you?" Doc asked as he lit a cigar.

"When I'm not getting paid for it. I'd like to believe the stones are valuable, but I'm not feeling it. I sure don't see the value in them."

"I'm sure Dr. Constantine knows."

Marcus blew his breath into cold hands, then suddenly walked off.

"I thought you wanted to watch the ferries from here," Doc asked.

"Nope, we can get a better view from over here," Marcus said speeding around the corner to a pier.

Doc tried to catch up, but when he reached the pier, Marcus was nowhere in sight. "Marcus . . ."

Two hands grabbed his jacket and yanked him behind a dumpster. "You're slipping, brother. Someone's been tailing us," Marcus whispered. Footsteps hurried along the pier, turned, and ran away. The men came out of hiding.

Marcus poked his head up. "He's gone."

Doc dusted off his slacks. "Who?"

"I don't know, but he's been following us since we left the restaurant."

Chapter 18

It was past midnight when Samantha Prophet arrived at her sister's office. She used an electronic key to open the underground garage doors, then took the elevator up to the top floor.

Cassandra's office was a cantilevered glass bubble, jutting out from the side of the building, with a hundred and eighty-degree view of Fifth Avenue. Deco artwork and chrome furnishings blended nicely together with the butterscotch area rug. Cassandra sat at her desk working. Her Chinese dinner sat untouched after two hours.

Samantha hung her coat on the rack and picked up the box of uneaten food. "I figured you'd be here. When did you get in?"

"This afternoon," Cassandra said.

"Where's Elias?"

"At the house watching Hanna," Cassandra looked up at her sister, who was using her fingers as a fork. Cassandra opened the desk drawer and tossed her some chopsticks.

"Thanks, what are you working on?" Samantha asked.

"The program for tomorrow night. Elias has everything ready, but I need you to handle security and the auction if the benefit isn't over by midnight."

"Where's Kane going to be?"

"Keeping an eye on Jai-Robson Priest. He's coming to bid on the scroll."

Samantha almost spit up her food. "You can't let that man in our house. He's uncouth, ignorant, and a complete fool."

"True, but he's our best customer and I can't afford to alienate him."

"You can't afford to let him humiliate you either. He needs us more than we need him."

"That's why we need to keep him happy—within certain limits." Samantha leaned back against the wall with her legs crossed, attacking the Chinese noodles with chopsticks. Cassandra used her foot to push a chair over to her. "Sam, sit down, before you drop food on my rug." Samantha sat on the credenza.

"What did you find out?" Cassandra asked.

"After Constantine left the ship, he went to a company called Cornerstone Global Insurance Recovery, hoping to see the owner—a man named Marcus St. John. The same man Roth had the fight with on the ship."

"I've heard of him."

Samantha pulled a marijuana joint from her sister's desk. "Constantine hired him a few years ago to recover some stolen . . ."

"Elias already told me all that. What else?"

"A woman named Belleshota, who used to work for St. John, is now an investigator who still has ties with St. John and Cornerstone. She saved Constantine's life. If Constantine was looking for someone to trust—someone to hold the stones for him, she's the most likely person he'd pick. The receptionist says she postponed a vacation she's had planned for months, to do a favor for Constantine."

"Where is she now?"

"Don't know yet. She's supposed to be at her ranch outside San Diego, but the caretaker says she hasn't arrived yet. That tells me she must have made a stop."

Cassandra leaned back in the chair, twiddling her fingers, and in deep thought. "Or is taking a detour. I'll give Eagleton a call to see if she knows anything."

* * *

Detective Holloway's truck bumped the garage door as he tried to park. He had been drinking, which had become a common occurrence.

He had started on the bottle of Jack Daniels earlier, while waiting for St. John outside Shafts. He followed the men to the restaurant, and later to the   waterfront. He was certain St. John had seen him on the pier, but equally sure he hadn't been recognized. Nevertheless, he had to be more careful, which meant no more booze.

Holloway was a time bomb waiting to explode. His wife had left him a year ago with his house and half his pension and he hadn't spoken to his daughter ever since she married a black man four years ago. After nearly twenty-three years on the force, all he had to show for his hard work and dedication was an over-mortgaged home with payments he couldn't afford. He had been suspended earlier this year for using excessive force against an informer. Now he was on suspension again; this time for getting out of line with St. John and his wife. The captain had taken his badge and gun. He sealed his fate when he lost his temper and called the captain St. John's pimp.

It didn't matter if St. John was a murderer or not. Holloway hated him and what he represented. St. John used money and power to buy respectability. It was because of him that he was probably going to lose his badge, and the little dignity he had left. It was easy to convince himself how much better he could sleep if St. John weren't around.

Chapter 19

After leaving Poison Springs, Sydney stopped at the first motel she saw and slept for six hours. It wasn't until she woke that she discovered her cell phone was missing. She had lost it along with her diamond bracelet out at McCain's farm. A cool shower cleansed the grit and sand from her body, but didn't cool her anger. A Poison Spring deputy had followed her as far as the highway to ensure that she left town, which was a waste of his time. There was no way she was ever setting foot in that town again. Her only regrets were that she hadn't found Joshua McCain, and that her bracelet was gone, probably forever. The thought of that made her sick. It was clear that Sheriff Eagleton and his deputies were more interested in finding out what she wanted with McCain, than in helping her, which made her more determined to find him. She finished showering and got dressed.

When she stepped outside the motel, the heat consumed her like a furnace. Her black Land Rover was layered in the champagne-colored dust of the desert sand. The motel diner next door and flat desert were the only things visible for miles.

She hadn't had a decent meal since leaving Seattle, and she didn't have any faith that her luck was about to change, after looking into the window of the greasy spoon diner. Nevertheless, she was starving. She slipped on her sunglasses and went inside.

The diner's interior was no better looking than the exterior, but the people were cordial and the food was surprisingly good. Sydney shared space at the counter with a biker from Weavilwood, who told her the best way to contact Joshua McCain was through his girlfriend at town hall—a woman named Gretchen Anderson.

Sydney reached Weavilwood just before dusk, but the town was void of any life. What she did see was a collection of boarded up clapboard buildings, wooden sidewalks, and dirt streets. It was a ghost town.

An elderly woman driver pulled up beside her and lowered the window.

"Miss, if you're looking for Weavilwood, its six miles down the road. This is old town."

"Thank you. Do you know Gretchen Anderson?"

"Sure, she's the town clerk, but she's out of town visiting her sons. Are you a friend of hers?"

"No, I thought she could help me find a man named Joshua McCain. Do you know him?"

"Everyone knows Josh. He comes in and out of the valley all the time."

"How I can get in touch with him?"

"You might catch him down at the White River Copper Mine. He's a mining equipment engineer for the county, and spends a lot of time down there."

"How do I get to the mine?"

She turned in her seat and pointed. "Go back to the highway, turn right and follow the signs to Bitterwater Junction. Take another right at the junction and you'll see a large sign for Barstool Basin. Follow the road down to the bottom of the basin and you'll see the mine."

Sydney turned around and headed south. She drove for forty-five minutes before reaching the junction. She couldn't have missed Barstool Basin if she had been blind. The excavated crater in the earth was half a mile in diameter, and seemed just as deep. She followed behind a thick cloud of dust from the slow moving earthmover in front of her as it made its way down in the crater.

The White River Copper Mine was a cluster of four metal buildings, surrounded by razor fence wire, and under the protection of a guard tower. She couldn't see past the black windows of the towers, but she had a feeling she was being watched. She parked in front of a singlewide mobile home that substituted as the job shack.

When she opened the screen door, the suffocating odor of sulfur mixed with body odor nearly made her gag. She rushed past the frail-looking man behind the counter to get to the beverage machine against the wall. Three men sat at a table smoking and playing cards.

Sydney saw them out of the corner of an eye, gawking as she guzzled the bottle of cold water. She went back over to the counter to the old man who was staring at her like he had never seen a woman before.

He wiped his swarthy face with a dirty rag that was as dark as he was, and then removed his soiled railroad cap from his head and smiled. "Can I help you ma'am?"

"I'm looking for a man named Joshua McCain."

"Josh isn't scheduled to be here again until next month. You missed him by a few days."

"Any idea how I can reach him? It's really important."

"I have his office number, but he's not in. He left this weekend to go up in the hills for two weeks."

"Two weeks!"

"Yeah, he's a gold chaser when he's not working for the county. This is the usual time of year he goes on vacation and takes off for the hills. You may be able to contact him through his girlfriend over in Weavilwood. She's . . . "

"Gretchen Anderson and she's out of town too," Sydney said, completing his sentence. "I don't suppose you have his cell phone number?"

The men in the break room had come out of the room. One of them was chuckling. "Lady, those things are worthless out here. Maybe I can help you out until Josh gets back," he said, watching her dab the sweat from her neck."

"Knock it off!" the old man said. "Sorry, ma'am. They're ignorant cave dwellers, not used to seeing ladies around here much."

"My skin is as thick as his head." The men laughed, even the one that was insulted. "I suppose you don't know how I can contact him?"

"McCain could be anywhere between Ely and Las Vegas, which is practically the entire state. He'll pop up in a few days, don't worry."

"I don't have a few days," she said, angrily. "I'm sorry; it's been a long day. Thank you for your help, anyway."

"My pleasure, ma'am," the old man said as she left the office. The smile disappeared from his face. He picked up the phone and called the sheriff's office. "A woman just left here asking for Josh McCain."

* * *

Sheriff Eagleton slammed down the phone. "Where's Poole?" he shouted.

"Still out in East County where you sent him," said one of the deputies.

"Well, get him on the radio. T.J., I want you to go out and find Josh McCain and bring him here."

"What's wrong?" T.J. asked.

"I got a call from the Weavilwood Sheriff. That Belleshota woman has been over at White River asking about him. She's persistent. Whatever she has to tell him must be pretty damn important, and I want to know what it is."

"How am I supposed to find Joshua. He could be anywhere?"

"Check on Hickcut Ridge and Anvil Creek. Some of those old guys he hangs out with will know where he is."

Eagleton's son grabbed his hat. "The woman is a nuisance, but how do we know the letter she's carrying has anything to do with us?"

"We don't, but I'm not willing to take any chances. The sooner you get Josh McCain, the sooner we'll find out what this is all about. On your way out, swing by McCain's place just to make sure everything is okay. I don't trust that woman not to go back there."

* * *

Twenty-two miles from Joshua McCain's farm, on the back road, Elan Poole was lying in bed at Gertie's brothel. He rolled over and reached for his smokes off the table. After lighting a cigarette, he dropped his head back on the pillow, blowing a cloud of smoke at the ceiling. The young woman lying next to him turned away, pulling the covers over her naked body. Poole yanked her long hair, turning her back over. He rubbed his callused hand between her thighs. She cringed and rolled away from him.

He slapped her butt. "Where do you think you're going?"

She gave him a nervous smile. "I need to go to bathroom," she said in broken English.

Poole pushed her out of the bed onto the floor. "Go, but I want you back here, understand?" She nodded and then ran to the room, shut the door, and started crying.

"And you better not be in there all day," Poole shouted. He reached for the telephone and called his wife. He'd be late again for dinner.

He settled back against the pillow and finished his cigarette. The only good thing about being stuck in the east valley was that it made it easier for him to visit Rose. That wasn't her real name. He had changed it just like he changed her. Since her rescue, she was now his property to do with her what he wished. He got her the job at Gerties, and in return used her whenever he wanted to. There was an immense sense of power in dominating her. She was young, beautiful, submissive, and the object of all his sexual fantasies.

The telephone rang. Poole picked it up.

"The sheriff is trying to reach you. Get out to your radio—fast," said Deputy Stephenson.

Poole jumped from the bed, pulling up his pants. "Rose, don't go anywhere, I'll be back in ten minutes," he said as he stuffed his shirttail in his pants. He swung his jacket off the back of the chair, accidentally knocking a picture frame off the table. He didn't see the tiny object that fell from his pocket. He ran to his Jeep in the parking lot and called the office.

"Where are you?" Sheriff Eagleton asked.

"I just grabbed some food at Mary's out on the highway. What's going on?"

"Belleshota may be headed your way. If she is, make sure she takes the cutoff at the junction to the California state line. If she heads towards McCain's farm, call T.J.. He's in route there now."

Poole flipped the radio switch off and cursed. He had lied. He was miles from where he was supposed to be and out of position to cover the junction cutoff. He peeled the Jeep out of the gravel parking lot and headed for the highway.

* * *

When Rose was certain that Poole was gone, she unlocked the bathroom door. She sat at the foot of the bed with a blood-stained towel, and cried with her face buried in her hands. Tonight, Poole's crude lovemaking had been particularly savage. He had bitten her neck like a vampire in heat while grunting out another woman's name—Sydney.

The picture of Rose's daughter lay on the floor by the nightstand. She stooped to pick it up and saw the platinum diamond bracelet under the bed. She blinked several times, then wiped the tears from her eyes and studied it closer. It was the most beautiful piece of jewelry she had ever seen—and it was valuable. It could buy freedom for her and her daughter. She stuffed it under the mattress and got back in the bed like she had been told.

* * *

Sydney's mind was not on the music playing from the car stereo. Her thoughts were on Josh McCain. She wasn't a quitter, but there was no way she was going to wait for McCain to show up in Weavilwood. She had been around danger enough to recognize its smell, and the valley reeked of it. Constantine must have known that too, before he begged her to deliver his message. As far as she was concerned he was out of favors. The first one almost cost her life when she and Marcus rescued him from the thieves that had stolen the university's artifacts. Pressing her luck might cost her a lot more than a week in the hospital; especially since Doc and Marcus weren't around.

She missed working with them. They were like surrogate fathers, who would willingly risk all they had for her. Friendship, loyalty, and honor were just as valuable to them as family, and that's why she admired them. She had loved her father, but he was on the other side of the law. After his death, she sold his multi-billion dollar empire, giving most of the money to charities. The

106

only items of intrinsic value to her were her mother's cello, which was stored at Doc's house in St. Croix, and the platinum diamond bracelet she received from her father.

The junction cutoff was up ahead. Sydney turned left and followed the road to the state highway headed west to California. Two miles from the state border, she jammed the brakes, made a U-turn, and doubled back. She would never forgive herself if she didn't at least try to find her bracelet.

Chapter 20

A man pulled two mules slowly across a dry creek bed and up the hill to the ridge overlooking the McCain farm. He took the familiar path down the steep slope to the draw behind the barn. A fancy truck he'd never seen before was out front. He left the mules in the draw and sneaked around to the back of the barn, where he peeked through a knothole and saw a tall redheaded woman. She was on her knees sifting through the straw.

* * *

Sydney heard the sound of a vehicle coming through the front gate. She dusted the straw off her slacks and went outside. An old brown Dodge truck came to a stop in front of the barn.

A middle-aged man jumped down from the oversized 4x4, dressed in overalls and a mining cap. He had a Paul Bunyan frame with a grisly face and gold tooth. Sydney didn't rattle easily, but she also didn't take unnecessary risks. She put her hand on her gun.

The burly man walked toward her. "Mind telling me what you're doing in my barn?"

"Joshua McCain?"

He gave her a suspicious look. "Do we know each other, lady?"

"I asked you whether you're Joshua McCain."

He frowned. "Yes. Who are you?"

"Sydney Belleshota. I was hired by Dr. Trevor Constantine to find you."

"My brother?"

"You and Constantine are brothers?"

"Half-brothers. What's this about?" he asked in a raised voice.

"First, I need to see some I.D., please."

"I.D.—lady, you're standing on my property asking me for some identification?"

108

Sydney parted her jacket, exposing her gun.

"Hey, I don't know what your problem is, but you're making me nervous," he said.

Sydney pulled the gun halfway out of the holster.

McCain backed away. "Okay, my wallet is in the glove box in my truck. I need to go over and get it, okay? Just take it easy."

She followed him. The dog in the front seat started barking.

"Don't mind Miner, he's harmless," McCain said. He reached in the window and got the wallet. Sydney inspected the license and handed it back to him.

"Sorry, Mr. McCain, I had to make sure it was you. I've been through a lot to find you." She pushed the berretta back in its holster. "Your brother wanted me to give this to you." She reached into her pocket and pulled out the letter.

McCain leaned against the truck and opened the envelope. As he read the letter, the stoic expression on his face turned to a smile, and then a wide grin. "I'll be damned," he said as he kept reading. He slid down onto the fender, his eyes transfixed on the piece of paper. "I can't believe it."

Sydney saw the excitement in his eyes. "If you don't mind, I'd like to know what's so important about that letter that it couldn't have been mailed to you."

"Trevor doesn't have my address. This is the only place he knows, and he hasn't been back here in forty years."

"That figures," Sydney said with disinterest.

"Have you read it?"

"No, I'm just the courier. I tried explaining that to your sheriff, but he was more interested in keeping me away from you. Why are so many people interested in you and your farm?"

"I'm kinda the local expert on lost goldmines in this area. People are always sending me tidbits of information and theories. The Sheriff doesn't have much patience for gold hunters and outsiders, especially those hanging around here. The county condemned this property several years ago, after they found traces of uranium in the water. The EPA has since taken it over. The only reason I still come out here is to visit a few friends in the area, every couple of weeks or so."

Sydney smirked. "The sheriff is more than just a little suspicious, and he seemed particularly interested in your letter. Whatever is in there must be important to someone other than you."

"A lot of people have been trying to find old man Alpaca's gold for years. I just never thought the sheriff was one of them."

"What gold?"

"Trevor says he's found the map to the Alpaca gold mine. My father, rest his soul, and a lot of people around here have spent their lives searching for it. Dad talked about it all the time. So much so, that Trevor got the same bug. He's been obsessed with finding the mine his whole life. After all these years, he says he finally found a map to its location. He says he gave it to a Marcus St. John for safekeeping. Do you know him?"

"Yeah . . ." was all Sydney could manage to say. She was angry. She had lost her bracelet, screwed up her plans, and endured abuse for the last two days just for a silly old map. "Well, I hope you two enjoy it together. If you will sign the form in my car I can finally get out of here."

"Sure." He followed Sydney to her vehicle. "Trevor mentions in his letter that he was in some trouble. How was he when you last saw him?"

Sydney retrieved the clipboard off the front seat of the Rover. "He wasn't looking very good. I suppose if anyone knew he had the map and thought it was valuable, he had probable cause for being paranoid."

McCain scratched his beard. "You may be a skeptic, but believe me, the gold mine exists."

"Then I would stay away from Eagleton and his brood. Sign here." She handed him the clipboard with papers attached.

He barely read the disclosure statements, before scribbling his signature on the receipt.

He passed the clipboard back to her. "They're a quirky bunch, but by and large okay."

"Okay? You would have to be dumb, blind and stupid to see everything isn't okay around here."

"What do you mean?"

"Take that copper mine over by Weavilwood for one. That crater is half the size of Nevada, but I didn't see one truck hauling ore or any miners working."

"Oh, that. You're right. White River doesn't mine nearly the ore it did years ago, but the family who owns it keeps it running to support the town and families. If they ever shut it down, you might as well add Poison Springs and Weavilwood to the growing list of Nevada ghost towns. The Prophets have been very good for the valley."

"Who?"

"The Prophet family. Old man Alpaca's family. They own the mine, the towns, and everything else in this valley."

Sydney was about to ask him another question, but was distracted when they saw the Sheriff's Jeep pull into the farm. T.J. Eagleton stepped out. "Hey Josh."

"T.J., what are you doing here?" McCain's smile disappeared when he noticed the shotgun by T.J's side. Sydney moved away from McCain.

"I got a report that this woman was trespassing again."

McCain relaxed. "Everything is okay now. She just wanted to give me a letter from my brother."

"I didn't know you had a brother."

McCain's throat became dry. "Ahh. . . yes. He says he's coming home in a few weeks to visit—that's all."

T.J. could tell he was lying. "Is that right, anything else?" He raised and cradled the rifle in his arms.

"Yes, that's about it. Says he can't wait to see me."

"That's nice. Why don't you let me see it for myself?" He reached out to get it.

McCain squeezed the letter in his hand. "What's this about, T.J.? I haven't done anything."

"Just let me see it, Josh, and I'll be out of your hair."

McCain's hesitation to hand the letter over was born from fear rather than an act of defiance. "Now, T.J., I don't see how . . ."

T.J. pumped the rifle and fired. McCain's body flew against his truck. Sydney drew her gun and shot T.J. in the shoulder. He managed to pump the rifle again and fired as she dove behind her vehicle. Two more rounds from the shotgun dropped the front of the Land Rover to the ground like a wounded tank in the desert.

Sydney returned fire, sending two bullets to Eagleton's chest. His body slumped against the truck and slid to the ground. McCain's dog barked, clawing at the window.

A yellow Jeep spewed clouds of sand as it swerved through the gate. Sydney knelt beside Josh McCain and felt his pulse. He was dead. She pried the letter from his hand as the jeep came to a stop.

Poole rolled out of his vehicle with his gun in his hand. T.J. was face down in the sand.

"You've really done it this time, bitch. Drop that gun, turn around, and put your hands on top of the truck, now!"

Sydney dropped the gun. "Eagleton killed Joshua McCain . . ."

"Don't say another damn word to me. Keep your mouth shut! Put your hands behind you." He handcuffed her hands. "I told you, you would regret it if you ever came back. When I'm done with you, you'll be begging me to take you to jail. Now, turn around and . . ."

Sydney heard the sound of metal striking bone. Poole groaned, and dropped to his knees.

She turned around and saw a bearded man in cowboy cloths holding an iron skittle in his hand. "Who are you?"

"The name is Gingham, ma'am, but that don't much matter at a time like this. If you got some things in that rig of yours, you best get them now. We ain't got much time, and the sun is fixing to set."

"I'm not going anywhere with you."

112

His knobby, but strong fingers gripped her shoulder like a vice. He turned her toward her vehicle and emitted a heavy sigh.

"Missy, unless them new trucks come with two spares, you ain't got no other choices. This man over here you done killed is Sheriff Eagleton's son, and he's going to be plenty mad. Your life ain't going be worth spit on a cactus bush once this piece of trash over here blabs his mouth." He kicked Poole's unconscious body. "Now, help me grab my provisions out of Josh's truck. We're going to need them for our trip."

"What trip?"

"To my place in the mountains. It's safe up there."

"Where's your car?"

He took his hat off and wiped his brow. "Missy, do I look like someone that would own one of them? All I got and need is over there in the gully behind the barn. Ma and Pa—my mules."

Sydney's mind was spinning. Two dead bodies lay in front of her, and a wild-eyed man dressed in nineteenth century cowboy clothes was offering her the only alternative she had.

"Missy, you planning on rooting in that spot or doing what I told you? Grab them supplies and the dog. We ain't got no more time for reminiscing."

Chapter 21

Cassandra Prophet's home stretched across one hundred and twenty feet of frontage on Lake Washington. A red carpet extended from the walkway, through the house and ballroom, and out the back door down to the garden. Carpenters assembled the stage in the ballroom, while others set up gaming equipment and canopy tents outside.

Kane was in the two-story boathouse playing with Hanna. From the large bay windows, he saw Samantha Prophet coming down the pier. He went out on the upper deck.

Samantha stood on the edge of the pier, looking up at Kane as she shielded her eyes from the sun. "Is Hanna with you?"

"She's inside playing."

"It's time for her to get ready." Kane went inside and brought Hanna out.

"Is everything set for the auction?" she asked as Kane handed her the child.

"Yes, everyone has arrived, except Priest. I have them checked in at the Hamilton. At eleven, I'll be bringing them across the lake to the boathouse."

"Two security teams will be working the lake and grounds around the house. I want you to stay with Priest. Cassie wants him out of here as soon as we auction off the scroll."

Samantha started walking away, then stopped. "Another thing, we're not paying you to be a nursemaid and friend to my niece. She already has a nanny. Don't forget that."

Kane leaned on the rail, watching Samantha tugging the teary-eyed girl behind her.

* * *

Cassandra sat in her bedroom in front of the mirror combing her hair. Samantha gently pushed Hanna toward her mother.

Cassandra saw Hanna in the mirror. "Stop crying!" She slammed the brush down on the vanity. "You've played enough today, now it's time for you to put on your dress and act like a little lady."

"Mommy, I don't want to go. I want to stay and play with uncle." She picked her daughter up and composed herself.

"Hanna, this is a very important night for mother. Put on that pretty dress uncle bought for you, and if you act like a nice little lady tonight, I'll take you to the zoo tomorrow."

The little girl's eyes brightened up as she wiped away the tears. "You will take me to the zoo?"

Cassandra smiled and gave her a kiss on the cheek. "Yes, now hurry downstairs to your room so you can get ready. The little girl hugged her mom and ran out of the room. Cassandra turned back to the mirror and continued with her hair.

Samantha sat on the bed, flipping through a magazine. "You shouldn't make promises to her that you know you won't keep."

"I'll let her go to the zoo, but with Elias. She'd rather be with him than me, anyway."

"And whose fault is that? You're never around her long enough for her to like you. You never should have gotten her. I warned you. Kids require a lot more attention than you're willing to give. It's not too late you know . . ."

Cassandra looked at her older sister's reflection in the mirror. "I'm not sending her off to some school, Sam."

"Suit yourself. It's your life." She tossed the magazine aside and crawled across the bed to retrieve another one off the table.

Cassandra stopped combing her hair. Of course Sam was right; she always was when it came to giving good advice. Cassandra had no desire for marriage, or child bearing, but she wanted to groom an heir who could take over her business one day. What once seemed a logical solution four years ago was now a dismal failure. She didn't have the motherly instinct or even desire to want to have a normal relationship with her daughter. She had made a mistake, but she wasn't giving up yet. Hanna was smart, and Cassandra had the rest of her life to mold her into the type of person she wanted her to be.

She stroked her hair. "How are things going downstairs?"

"The palm tree displays aren't ready and the caterers are late, but everything else is running smoothly," Samantha said.

"And Elias?"

"He's ready." Samantha tossed the magazine on the floor and bounced off the bed. "Cassie, I think we should let him go. He's way too attached to Hanna and she to him."

"That's an excuse, not a reason," Cassandra said, as she sprayed perfume across her flat bosom. "Give me a good reason."

Samantha stood at the window. "We don't need him. I was handling all of your problems before he arrived, and I'm still capable of doing it now."

"We're larger now, and that means even bigger problems. You can't be in two places at the same time, and Elias knows his business. You're not jealous are you?"

Samantha looked over her shoulder at her sister. "Of a man? You must be kidding."

Cassandra laughed, but she knew her sister was serious. Even as a child, Samantha loathed males, though she spent her life trying to emulate them, even down to the way they dressed. Hiring Kane had only magnified her sister's insecurities, because she felt threatened by him. He was a professional expert skilled at quietly getting the job done without drawing attention, while her sister was less discreet. She'd rather kick a door down first before checking to see if it was locked.

Samantha turned her attention back to the window. Three black SUV's circled the water fountain in front of the house and came to a stop. Samantha parted the sheers to have a better look. "Shit."

Cassandra got up and went to the window. "What?" She looked down and saw the Escalades parked in the driveway. A giant African emerged from one of the vehicles wearing a full-length white mink coat, military hat, and carrying an ivory walking stick.

116

"That pig is not supposed to be here!" Cassandra shouted. "Sam, I don't have time to deal with this or him. Go out and straighten this now. I can't believe this," Cassandra mumbled, storming out of the room. Samantha peeked through the curtains again. Jai-Robson Priest's bodyguards began unloading his luggage. She flung the curtains closed and went downstairs.

* * *

Priest was nearly seven feet tall, black as tar, with a mouthful of white teeth stretched across a round face. His huge arms embraced Samantha's body, burying her face in mink. "It is very good to see you again, Sam. Very good!"

"Welcome to our home, minister. We expected you a little later in the evening along with the other bidders."

He saw her plastic smile. "You do not wish that I have come?"

"No, of course not. We are delighted you are here. Unfortunately, you have caught us unprepared. My sister and I were not expecting you until later tonight. Cassandra has a prior engagement to attend before the auction this evening."

Priest noticed the caterers unloading food from the vans, and marching it into the house. "You are having a party?"

"Just a few friends over for a charity benefit."

"Charity?"

"Yes. My sister is hosting a fundraiser to support public schools."

His eyes brightened. "Excellent, yes—very excellent. Education is the key to unlocking the mind's potential. In my country I have done many wonderful things to help my people. I believe that . . ."

Samantha tuned him out as he kept talking. Jai-Robson Priest was like a broken spigot. You couldn't turn him off once he started. The more he talked, the more excited he became, and the louder he got. His deep voice resonated through the halls of the mansion.

Samantha listened to his two-minute diatribe before interrupting. "Minister, you must excuse me, but the time is getting

117

late. I have to help my sister prepare. I have instructed Elias Kane to assist you with whatever you need while you're here. I will have him take you and your party to the hotel where the other bidders are staying."

Priest was big and boisterous, but he wasn't stupid. He looked her squarely in the eyes. "The great prophet, Jesus, said that only in his home town and in his house is the prophet without honor. Like him, I now know the meaning of those words. My good friend, Cassandra Prophet no longer values my friendship."

Cassandra stood in the doorway listening to him. The mere sight of him made her nauseous, but she had to keep him happy, even if it was personally discomforting. She quickly made her way down the steps to the lawn.

"Nonsense, Mr. Minister. You are always welcomed in my home," she said.

"Cassie!" He extended his arms to welcome her. "You are beautiful!" He stood back admiring her red-laced gown and flip hairdo. "You must surely save me a dance tonight at the charity benefit. Of course, after all the other eligible young men have had their turn." He winked and gave her a wide grin. Cassandra forced a smile. He had invited himself to the benefit, and she was helpless to deny him. "Tell me, how does a flower in full bloom continue to be lovelier each day?" he asked as he held her hand.

Cassandra knew he was lying, but she stilled blushed. "Come in, minister. I have a few minutes before my guests arrive."

Priest summoned one of his men to bring the two briefcases from the vehicle. Then in his customary grandiose style, he turned to his five bodyguards. "Stay and protect until I return."

Samantha felt her face melting with embarrassment.

Cassandra took him downstairs to the theater room, where she closed the sound proof doors behind them. Priest sat down on the leather recliner next to her.

"Now, what's on your mind?" Cassandra asked. He waved his finger and his aide placed the opened briefcases on the table between them, then stepped back. The cases were packed with money.

118

"What's this for?"

"I must have the scroll."

"If you want it, you can bid on it tonight. You know the rules."

"I hope to persuade you to suspend the rules. I have brought you a gift of two million dollars, plus the money I already have deposited into your account."

Cassandra ran her fingers over the money. She hoped Priest didn't notice her trembling. He was offering her a lot of money, but she could get more.

"You're offering to pay me two million dollars for the manuscript?"

He grinned. "Yes, a more than fair deal."

He was right, but Cassandra was a good businesswoman. She could barely take her eyes off the stack of money. "You know the rules, Mr. Minister. I don't change them—not even for that amount of money. She closed the briefcase. "With this kind of money, you may easily outbid everyone tonight."

Priest bridged his fingers into a triangle. "Perhaps, but I do not wish to take the risk. *The Lebanese* is determined to own the scroll at any cost."

"I can't help you," she said, rising up from her chair.

"I have no more cash at my disposal. All of it is invested in our other transaction."

"Then I'm sorry. I am a businesswoman. Which of my clients would ever trust or respect me again if I make an exception to the rules for you? My credibility would be ruined, and I'd be out of business. My reputation is worth more than two million dollars."

His eyes narrowed. "How much more?"

"Fifty percent of your overseas market."

* * *

Kane heard Priest's laughter as he opened the door. He took a seat behind Cassandra.

Priest's body shook as he continued laughing.

"Cassie—you are very funny. Your United States Constitution is not even worth that. You are indeed a bright woman, but you are also crazy."

She gave him a stern look. "Crazy? I don't think so. I'm not the one trying to authenticate my lineage back to the great kings of the Babylonian Empire. How crazy is that?"

Priest sat straight in the chair. His cold, steel eyes revealed pure hatred—something his countrymen were well familiar with. "How do you know this?"

"It's my business to know everything about whom I do business with. I know you have plans to someday return to your homeland and reclaim the power you lost. And to achieve that, you intend to claim to be an ancestor of the great Babylonian king—Nebuchadnezzar. In recognition of our long-standing working relationship, I'm willing to lower the cost to twenty-five percent."

He pounded his fist on the armrest. "Never!"

Cassandra flinched, but didn't waver. "Fine, then you can take your chances like everyone else tonight. Perhaps *The Lebanese* will be generous and let you win. Elias will now take you back to the hotel."

Priest's fingers gripped the armrests so tight, Kane thought his fingernails would puncture the leather. Kane eased the derringer out of his vest.

Priest swore as he lifted himself from the chair. "The price you ask is too much. I cannot pay it."

"Then our business is concluded."

"I will give you Thailand and Vietnam, but no more!"

"And Cambodia."

He huffed and puffed. "Yes—Cambodia, but nothing more, and not twenty five percent. Ten percent."

"Fifteen."

"Yes—yes, fifteen percent," he frowned.

"Good, we have a deal."

"Then the manuscript is mine?"

"Yes. Elias will prepare it for transport and will personally deliver it to you, if you like."

Priest flashed a row of teeth. "You are a very shrewd woman. We will do well together."

Cassandra turned to Kane. "Now that our business is concluded, have the minister's luggage brought to one of our guest rooms, and see that he has everything he needs."

Samantha met her sister in the hall after everyone had left. "I can't believe you're letting that fool stay in our house."

"He's a fool, but we've just bought a piece of his seventy million dollar-a- year operation."

Chapter 22

A young black man knocked on Doc's hotel room door and handed him a brown folder. "Mr. Jamison told me to give you this. The car you ordered is waiting for you downstairs." Doc closed the door and opened the folder. Inside were two personalized invitations to the Arabian Nights Casino Charity Benefit. Doc grabbed his coat and unlocked the connecting door to Marcus's suite.

Marcus stood in front of a full-length mirror admiring his new suit. "Are those the invitations?"

"Yes. Toby did a pretty good job."

"I have to hand it to him too; he knows clothes." Marcus turned sideways, pulling on the sleeves of the designer coat. "Yeah, the brother can do at least one thing right."

Doc was getting impatient. "Are you ready to go yet?"

"In a minute, hold your horses. Do you think I need my trench coat?"

"What on earth for? It's a beautiful evening outside."

"I don't know . . ." He turned around in the mirror. "My trench coat would flow nicely with my suit."

"Qwik, you're worse than a bride getting ready for a wedding. Come on, it's getting late."

* * *

The valet brought a white car around to the hotel entrance, and handed Doc the keys to the tricked out sports car with oversized tires, spinners, and tinted glass.

"This is our car?" Doc asked.

"Yes sir, it just arrived. You need to sign here, please." He shoved a piece of paper under Doc's nose. "Mr. Jamison said for you to keep the car as long as you need it. He'll settle your account when you're finished."

"I'm sure he will." Doc passed him a ten dollar bill.

122

"Thank you, sir."

Marcus got in and fastened his seat belt. "Leave it to Toby to give us a pimpmobile instead of a normal sedan."

* * *

The trip to Medina took fifteen minutes. A nine-story hot-air balloon was tethered over Cassandra Prophet's mansion. An attendant parked the car, while two harem girls escorted them to the red carpet.

They were greeted at the door by a sheik who took their invitations. "Dr. Sebasst—Mr. St. John, welcome to the Arabian Nights." He refolded the invitations and handed them back. "Please see one of the gentlemen at the end of the hall." The long hallway stopped in front of a ballroom with three doors—with men at each checking the names of the guest list.

"I didn't count on this," Doc whispered. They walked up to the middle door and handed the invitations to the black doorman.

He flipped though his clipboard of names. "I'm sorry; I can't seem to find either of your names on the list."

Marcus looked around to make sure no one was watching. He slipped some folded paper in the man's palm. "Look a little deeper, brother."

The doorman discreetly counted the hundred dollar bills. He flipped through the pages again. "Of course, they are right here. My mistake. Enjoy yourselves, gentlemen."

When they stepped into the room the waiters were clearing the tables, while others prepared the room for the bachelorette auction. A large group of guests stood admiring the collection of bachelorette photographs prominently displayed on large easels near the stage. Doc and Marcus went out onto the back terrace. The tiered yard was covered in sand, palm trees, and white tents. Bamboo torchlight's lit the pebble walkway weaving down to the lake.

"It must have cost a fortune to haul all that sand in," Marcus said as they stood watching people enter the gaming tents. "You feel like losing some money for a good cause?"

"No, but you can go if you want. I'll find us some place to sit."

"Try to stay out of trouble until I get back." Marcus took the stairs down to the garden and entered the baccarat tent.

* * *

Holloway had followed the men to Cassandra Prophet's house only to discover that he couldn't get past the gate without an invitation. There was no street parking in front, so he circled the block and followed the street up a steep hill to the bluff overlooking the lake. He drove slowly along the street of exclusive homes looking for a good vantage spot. He found a vacant home with a 'for sale' sign in the lawn. The house had a panoramic deck in the back with a perfect view of Cassandra's property. Holloway set up his camera equipment and telescope.

Tailing St. John was becoming more difficult by the hour. He and Sebasst were like conjoined twins. Where one went, the other followed. They spent hours at the university with a professor of cartography, and then an afternoon with Toby Jamison, an ex-con with a long history of larceny. With Sebasst always at St. John's side, it would be risky trying to take out St. John, but Holloway was determined to it. He just needed the right opportunity.

At 11:10 Holloway spotted a large boat of people being escorted across the lake to Cassandra Prophet's backyard. They docked at the boathouse and took the stairs up to the deck, where a small man fitting Sebasst's description of Elias Kane, greeted them before they all entered the boathouse. Two guards were posted at the door.

Holloway trained his telescope at the boathouse window. He saw eight people; seven men and a woman, two of whom he recognized. The woman was Teoni Perguree, the head of an Argentinean cartel, and the other was the wealthy Arab known as *The Lebanese*. Both were arms dealers. Kane spoke to the group for about five minutes, before *The Lebanese* bolted out of his chair, apparently agitated by something Kane had said. Moments later, the group went down to the boat and headed back across the lake. Kane watched them from the deck.

Holloway swung the telescope away from his face. "What the hell is going on over there?"

Chapter 23

Doc was still outside on the terrace when people began moving back into the ballroom. The room's metamorphosis was complete. The dining tables were gone—replaced with five hundred velvet-back chairs. The stage was outfitted with theater lights and fresh-cut flowers. Doc opted to stand in the back of the room against the wall.

In the garden, a eunuch blew a trumpet, announcing that the auction was about to begin. Ten minutes later, all but one of the chairs was occupied. Marcus found Doc standing in the back with the waiters.

The room lights dimmed and an opaque, skinny woman in a dated dress approached the podium and microphone. Suddenly, the center doors sprung open and Jai-Robson Priest made his grand entrance. He was dressed in a white military uniform and hat, covered with embroidered ribbons. He paraded down the center aisle and took a seat in the third row.

Marcus pulled a toothpick from his coat and stuck it in his mouth. "Who is that clown?"

Cassandra cleared her throat. "Ladies and gentlemen, my name is Cassandra Prophet, and welcome to my home. I hope you have enjoyed the festivities tonight and are ready to lose a lot more money. But for a great cause." The audience laughed. "If you need to be reminded . . ." That was Kane's cue to send Hanna out on stage. He whispered in the little girl's ear and nudged her toward her mother. Hanna stopped halfway to the podium and began crying. Cassandra's faced burned with embarrassment. Kane came out from the curtains, grasped Hanna's hand, and walked her to the podium. He lifted her to Cassandra's arms.

Cassandra's hands trembled as she planted an awkward kiss on her daughter's cheek. "This is why we are here tonight. To ensure that our precious children are afforded the best education, and the best teachers possible." Priest was the first to his feet giving her an ovation. Cassandra handed the child back to Kane.

"Isn't that Elias Kane up there?" Doc asked, pointing.

Marcus squinted at the small man with the greasy hair, bad tuxedo, and black and white bowtie. "You sure?"

Doc pulled his camera from his pocket and focused the zoom. He snapped three shots. "It's him."

Marcus took the camera from him. He focused the lens on Kane, then Cassandra, before passing it back. "Well, I hope they're not making babies together, because they would be messed up."

The trumpets sounded. The center doors opened and fourteen women with escorts entered the room. The bachelorettes wore black evening gowns and heels, and ranged in age from eighteen to fifty-one. The statuesque ebony woman caught Priest's attention. His eyes were riveted on her body as she passed.

* * *

Cassandra explained the auction rules. "Bidding will start at $5,000, and subsequent bids will be made in one hundred dollar increments. The highest bidder will receive a night on the town with their date for an evening of dinner and dancing."

The first woman auctioned was a nineteen-year-old college student who went for $9,800. She was followed by a twenty-seven-year-old artist who fetched $8,300. A thirty-four-year-old doctor went for $10,400. The twenty-seven year-old ballet instructor was won by her husband for $12,000. The last woman to be auctioned was the twenty-eight-year-old law clerk from Barbados. Her boyfriend started the bidding with $6,000. Two more bids brought it up to $8,000. Just as it appeared that the bidding was over, Jai-Robson Priest jumped to his feet. "I will pay $20,000 for this magnificent woman."

Cassandra cringed—so did the black woman when she saw the giant.

"Twenty-one thousand dollars," said a voice from the back of the room. Priest and everyone else turned to see the bidder hidden in the shadows.

Embarrassed that he had been upstaged, Priest pulled his wallet from his jacket and pointed it at the woman. "I am prepared to pay $35,000 for this woman!" A loud gasp echoed from the room. Cassandra felt like melting through the floor.

"Fifty thousand dollars," said the voice. Cassandra slammed the gavel down before Priest had a chance to blink.

"Sold to the gentleman in the back! Please come and claim your lady." The audience stood applauding, as Doc came forward. Publicly humiliated, Priest eased out into the aisle to leave—his eyes locking on Doc as they passed each other. Doc walked up the steps to the stage.

Cassandra grabbed his hand and pulled him to the podium. "On behalf of everyone here and our kids, I would like to thank you for your extraordinary act of generosity. Your name, profession—please," she said in her typical efficient manner, shoving the microphone in front of his mouth.

Doc leaned over the podium. "Julian Sebasst." He handed the mike back to her, and went over to his date. He escorted her down the steps and handed her back to her boyfriend. The room erupted in applause. Priest stood at the side door, watching. He turned and left through the door.

Cassandra thanked everyone for coming and gaveled the auction and benefit over. She tossed the gavel to a crew hand and stormed off the stage. Kane was waiting in the wings, holding a very sleepy Hanna in his arms.

"Elias, was that who I think it was?"

"Yes, and the man with him is St. John."

She watched the men as they stood in line at the cashier station. "I want to know what they are doing here and how they got in my house. Get Sam."

* * *

Doc handed his credit card to the cashier.

"I'm sorry sir, we only take cash."

"You expect me to be carrying $50,000 in cash?"

"A personal check will suffice."

"I don't use checks." Doc turned to Marcus. "Pay the man."

Marcus wrote the check and handed it to the cashier. "Why the hell don't you ever have any money?"

"As long as I have you, I don't need any. I think it's time to meet Cassandra Prophet." Doc surveyed the crowd looking for her. A few hundred people were still mingling in the ballroom, but Cassandra and Kane were nowhere to be found.

Marcus saw a thin woman dressed in a black double-breasted suit working her way through the crowd with a security team close behind. "I have a feeling we aren't wanted here," he whispered. Doc turned around as Samantha Prophet approached the cashier station.

"Gentlemen, may I please see your invitations?" she asked.

They handed her the black and white embossed cards. She inspected them carefully and then handed them to one of the guards. "These invitations are not authentic."

"How do you know that?" Marcus asked.

"Because my sister wrote the invitations and your two names weren't on the list."

Marcus removed his toothpick. "Maybe she's losing her memory." He smiled.

"Maybe you want to tell me why you're here?"

"I thought a friend of mine would be here tonight—Dr. Trevor Constantine. You haven't seen him lately, have you?"

She remained stone-faced. "I don't know what you are after, Mr. St. John, but you would be wise to take my advice. Stay away from my sister."

Doc saw a snicker on Marcus's mouth and knew he was about to say something ignorant, and create a bigger problem than they already had. "Excuse me, are you Samantha Prophet?" Doc asked.

"Yes, I am," she said, turning her attention to him. "My warning applies equally to you also, Dr. Sebasst."

"Ms. Prophet, tell your sister we had a wonderful evening. Perhaps one day we'll have a chance to meet her," Doc said.

"That will never happen."

"Well, that's too bad. I understood she shares a passion for archeology as I do. I guess I was wrong." Doc stepped around the men standing between them and the door. "Come on, let's go."

Marcus smiled and winked at her as they left.

It was raining when they went outside. Doc handed the valet ticket to the man for the car.

"I knew I should have brought my trench coat," Marcus said, buttoning his coat. They walked slowly down the sidewalk toward the driveway.

"Did you get a whiff of what the sister was wearing?" Doc asked.

"Yeah, I almost gagged on it. It's that same citrus funk perfume we smelled in Constantine's hotel room. I think we made her a little nervous."

"It would seem so." The valet pulled their car up in front. As they stepped from the curb, a black Escalade came out of nowhere, screeching to a stop in front of the Jaguar. Two Africans stepped out of the vehicle and approached them.

"Minister Priest wishes to talk with you," said one of the men.

"Isn't that an oxymoron?" chuckled Marcus. The big Nigerian didn't find him humorous.

Doc saw the tinted window of the Cadillac slide open. "I don't have anything to say to him," Doc said.

The Nigerians moved closer.

"Back off our space," Marcus warned. One of the men unbuttoned his coat, revealing the gun on his hip. "You try and put your hand on that and I'll break it off for you," Marcus said.

The other Nigerian stepped toward Marcus until he was stopped by Doc's hand on his chest. "I wouldn't do that if I were you."

The back door of the Cadillac swung open, and Priest got out. A small crowd watched from the lawn.

Priest's hands were tucked in his pockets as he approached Doc. Marcus kept his eyes on the two Nigerians.

"Brothers . . . brothers, there is no need for this. I only want to congratulate my brother here for his splendid victory tonight. Is that too much for me to ask?" He rested his heavy hand on Doc's shoulder. "After all, we are from the same land and people. We are all alike."

Doc shoved Priest's hand off his shoulder. "Thanks for the congratulations, but now will you please move so we can get in our car and leave?"

Priest cocked his head to the side, looking down at the smaller man. "My brother, I don't understand your rudeness toward me. I have done nothing to you, and have come to you in friendship."

"I have enough friends already, thank you."

Priest stepped backwards and gave Doc a glaring stare. He poked his long finger in Doc's face, and whispered, "I forgave you earlier for the disrespect you showed me because you are an ignorant American niggah, too foolish to realize your own stupidity, and who you are dealing with." Then he shouted. "Blessed are ye, when men shall revile you, and persecute you, and shall say all manner of evil against you falsely." His voice turned to a whisper again. "In my country I would have you shot for simply standing on the same hallowed ground with me."

Doc looked him squarely in the eyes. "You don't have a country anymore, and you're wasting your time trying to bully me. I know what you are and no amount of scripture quoting on your part will change that. I showed you no respect tonight, because you don't deserve any. Now, get out of my way."

The size of the crowd had grown. Priest noticed Cassandra and Kane watching from an upstairs window. He was creating too much attention.

"All manner of sin and blasphemy shall be forgiven, but blasphemy against the Holy One will not be forgiven." He stepped aside and let them pass. "Go in peace my brother!" he said, opening the passenger door for Marcus. "Even the greatest must humble themselves for his brother." He gave a fake smile and bow.

Marcus locked the door and watched the giant get back in his vehicle and drive away. "Somewhere in Africa, a village is being deprived of its idiot."

Doc peeled out of the driveway.

"You mind telling me what that was between you two?" Marcus asked.

"I don't like him," Doc said as he punched the gas pedal.

"Hey, I figured that out when you first laid eyes on him, and sucked fifty grand from my wallet to embarrass him in front of 500 folks. Who is he?"

"Jai-Robson Priest—an exiled West African thug and leader of a Nigerian cartel."

"What's his game?"

"Trafficking."

"Drugs or guns?"

"Both—and he's a slaver."

"He sells humans?"

"And kills them."

"Damn." A moment later, Marcus started chuckling.

"What's so funny?"

"I was thinking, you finally picked on someone your own size. If I were you, I'd start sleeping with one eye open."

Chapter 24

Holloway tapped the bottom of his cigarette pack with his fingers until a cigarette dropped into his hand. He leaned against the deck rail thinking as he reached for the lighter in his shirt pocket. He had just witnessed Jai-Robson Priest's confrontation with Sebasst and St. John, all of which made him deliriously happy. There was another person who shared disdain for the men. Holloway was thinking of a way to capitalize on that, even if it meant allying himself with someone as reprehensible as Jai-Robson Priest.

Priest wasn't a wanted criminal in the United States, but his barbaric face and acts of brutality were known worldwide. Holloway was shocked to see him in Seattle, and especially at Cassandra Prophet's home. The purpose, he didn't know, but he was sure it had nothing to do with her charity benefit.

He packed up his equipment and went back to the truck, where he called the precinct. He talked to one of the detectives who owed him a favor. Holloway wanted to know where Priest was staying. His friend called him back with the name of the hotel and a room number.

An hour later, Holloway met with Priest in his room, and left $15,000 richer with a plan set in motion.

Now, all he needed was some information, and he knew the man to talk to—Toby Jamison. Jamison was a known informer, whose only loyalty was to cash. Holloway had the cash. What he wanted was to know what St. John was after.

* * *

Long after the guests had gone, Samantha and Cassandra sat on the terrace drinking and watching the workers dismantling the harem tents in the garden.

"Tonight was the absolute worst night of my life," Cassandra said, as she poured more wine into her glass. "It's taken me years of hard work to establish a reputation in this city only to lose it because of an ego-maniacal despot with a Jesus complex. When reporters get wind of what happened tonight, I'll be ruined. Selling him that scroll wasn't good enough. He had to come out of his room and make an ass of both of us. And then on top of everything else, my own daughter publicly embarrasses me. I'll never be able to show my face in public around here without someone whispering about me."

"It's not that bad, Cassie. Everything can be fixed; I can fix it . . ."

"No you can't, Sam! This is one thing you can't fix," Cassandra said, with tears in her eyes.

Samantha knocked the wine bottle off the table. "One thing I can do is take care of Sebasst and St. John."

"No, we're not going to touch them."

"Why?"

"They're fishing. They want me to know they have the Alpaca Stones in their possession. They're playing with us. They want to know what we know."

"Even more reason for them to die. We can't afford the risk of them finding the mine, especially with your deal with Priest coming up. It's more important than ever to get those stones."

"If they had discovered the secret of the stones, they wouldn't have been here tonight. Killing them accomplishes nothing, because we still won't have the stones. We're going to negotiate to get them."

"Cassie, these guys have money. What can we offer them that they can't buy?"

"The life of a friend—Sydney Belleshota."

"How do you propose we do that? We don't even know where she is?"

"I spoke with Eagleton and he confirmed my suspicions. She's in Poison Springs, and I want you to go down there to get her."

"No, I'm not going anywhere. You need me more than ever to be with you here."

Cassandra reached across the table and took her sister's hand. "I appreciate that you want to help me, but you can best do that by going to Poison Springs."

"You don't need me to get Belleshota. That's what we're paying Eagleton for."

"True, but you're the only I can trust to ensure that everything will be ready when I arrive."

As with most of their disagreements, Cassandra prevailed. Samantha had to admit that her sister made sense. Cassandra was taking them to the next level, and it was Samantha's job to ensure that nothing interfered with their plans.

Kane was under the terrace listening to their conversation. When they finished, he eased back in the room and shut the sliding door.

Chapter 25

The following morning, Kane sat at the kitchen table eating oatmeal while gazing at the lake. Every morning around 8:30, he watched the elderly couple glide their double skull past the house, before disappearing into the morning fog that smothered the lake. Their daily voyage across the water to the university was a familiar sight Kane had grown accustomed to seeing. Sometimes he acknowledged them with a wave, but usually he just watched unobserved from behind the house's leaded-glass windows. The couple represented normalcy to him—something Kane had never known. For most of his adult life, he had been a nomad, moving from country to country.

So many countries were after him that if he were ever caught, they'd have to have a lottery to determine which one got to execute him. His four years with Cassandra had been the longest he had stayed with any employer.

The Prophets were smart, shrewd, and trusted no one but each other. Although he was an integral part of their organization, they never shared their deepest secret with him. A secret he was now convinced could only be unlocked by the Alpaca Stones.

Cassandra had made an error in judgment by not taking her big sister's advice to kill Sebasst and St. John. Keeping them alive was a mistake and a liability for him. They knew he worked for Cassandra and they could tie him to Erik Roth, maybe even Constantine. Kane thought about killing the men, but he couldn't run the risk of Cassandra finding out. But on the other hand, he couldn't just sit back and do nothing. If he did, it wouldn't be long before the police paid him a call. Neither choice was particularly appealing to him.

Kane finished his cereal, washed the bowl, and put it away in the cabinet. He opened the utility closet and pulled out his gardening gloves and pruning shears.

Thirty-five minutes later, Samantha shuffled through the kitchen in a robe, pajama bottoms, and a headband. Barely awake, she yawned as she poured a cup of cappuccino. She sat at the table and kicked a leg up on the chair, and tried to wake up. Kane was in the greenhouse with his back to her, diligently working on his plants. He carefully inspected each miniature fruit tree for disease, cross branches, and root damage. He methodically removed any offending limbs with the precision cut of a surgeon. Samantha thought he looked like a mad doctor, dressed in a white French-cuffed shirt, black vest, gloves, and protective goggles. When he finished, he gathered up the cuttings, wrapped them in linen cloth, and dropped them in the trashcan. He removed his gloves and put on his coat.

Samantha watched him slowly brushing particles of dirt off his pants. Kane was an enigma to her. He lived a minimalistic lifestyle, had a passion for gardening, dressed like a Mississippi gambler, and had the demeanor of an English banker. The only thing he loved more than those damn plants was Hanna.

Kane had previously worked for Teoni Perguree as a transporter in South America before coming to work for Cassandra. At the time, Cassandra had needed someone to safeguard and transport her goods, and Kane had come highly recommended by Teoni Perguree.

In the four years Kane had worked for them, he had proven his loyalty countless times. He was short on words and did everything asked of him, including murder. Best of all, he didn't ask questions. But still, underneath it all, there was something disquieting about him that Samantha didn't like. Until she discovered what that was she would never totally trust him.

Kane entered the kitchen. "You're up early this morning."

"I've got a busy day ahead," said Samantha.

"You need any help?"

"No, but I want you to keep an eye on Cassie while I'm gone. I'll be back in town in a few days after I wrap up some business."

Kane washed his hands in the sink. "You expecting trouble?"

"No, but I don't want Sebasst and St. John bothering her again."

"I understand. If they become an uncomfortable problem I can deal with it."

"Just watch," she said, as she sipped her coffee.

"You don't want me to get the stones from them?"

"I said, just watch. The stones are a lesser priority right now. Just keep those men away from Cassie."

After Samantha left, Kane washed her coffee cup and cleaned the table. As he walked back to his room, he thought of his next move. With Samantha out of town, Cassandra could crumble like a stack of cards under pressure. That's when he realized Sebasst and St. John were more useful to him alive than dead.

Chapter 26

Holloway sat in his truck outside the Spitzer office building waiting for St. John to come out. He had been there since early morning with only a newspaper and warm coffee to keep him company. St. John had been in the building for over three hours.

Holloway grabbed a section of paper off the dashboard and reread the story about the corpse discovered in the local landfill. The police identified the man as Dr. Trevor Constantine. Holloway knew the name. He was the same person St. John and Sebasst had been searching for at the Cameroon Motel.

Constantine's death came as no surprise. Death seemed to follow St. John like a shadow. First, Dr. Permullter, then Erik Roth, and now Constantine. They were all dead, and St. John was somehow connected. He balled up the newspaper and tossed it out of the window. Things weren't going any better for Holloway than they had last night.

First he had a late night encounter with Toby Jamison that turned out to be a waste of time, and then his partner called with bad news. St. John's wife was causing all kinds of hell for the department and the police commissioner because of St. John's treatment. The outcome would not be good for Holloway. He tried not thinking about that as he looked out his side mirror. The black Escalades were still parked across the street, waiting.

Chapter 27

Doc was late getting to the Legends Restaurant. As usual, Alexia was on time. She waved to him from across the room.

The auburn-haired woman with olive skin was in her mid-forties, but looked thirty. She wore a spring dress and heels, with long hair swept behind her ear. The former NATO commander had been friends with Doc for more than twenty years, when they both worked in Europe.

Alexia was devoted to her job, unquestionably loyal to her profession, and uncompromising in character. She worked for the U.S Marshal, and Doc needed her help.

"It's been a long time, Alexia. Good to see you again."

"You look well, Julian. How's your family?"

He sat across the table from her. "Fine. They're in California, vacationing, which is where I'm supposed to be right now." The waitress came over and handed him a menu.

Alexia smiled. "I was surprised to get your telephone call this morning asking me to join you here for breakfast. I wasn't sure whether I should have agreed."

"I don't know if that's good or bad," Doc joked.

She crossed her legs. "Well, let's just say I had second thoughts. The last time I saw you, you asked me for a favor that almost cost me my job."

"That's true, but look at you now. From airport security to the U.S Marshal's Office. That's not too bad."

"I couldn't very well go back to my boring job after my last adventure with you and your friends. How is Mr. St. John doing, anyway? I hope he's staying out of trouble."

"He's always *in* trouble. He's here in Seattle with me. He asked me to extend his apology for not coming, but he had a previous appointment to keep."

She sipped her coffee. "And Sydney?"

Doc leaned back against the chair, tapping his fingers on the table. "Frankly, I don't know. She drove to Nevada a few days ago to do a job, and we haven't heard from her since."

I'm almost afraid to ask, but is there anything I can do to help?"

"Thanks, but I think we've got that covered. There is something I could use your help on." Doc pulled out some photos from his pocket and passed them across the table. "I need you to I.D. the man in these photos. He claims his name is Kane—Elias Kane, but it might be an alias."

Alexia wrote the name on the back of the picture. She stared at Kane's silhouetted oval face. "What makes you think it's an alias?"

"It's just a hunch. There's something odd about him, and he has a habit of popping up when people die—two men on a cruise ship and Dr. Constantine. You may have read about in the Times today."

"I saw the story." She held the photo closer. "What does this have to do with Sydney's disappearance?"

"Maybe nothing, but I need to know who he is. He works for the woman in those photos. Her name is Cassandra Prophet."

"I've heard of her."

"Heard what?"

"She relocated her business here from Santa Fe a few years ago, and that she and her sister donate millions to charities. Other than that, they keep a low profile."

"She makes that kind of money as an architect?"

"She also runs a large foundation."

"What do you know about the sister, Samantha?"

"Nothing. Why?"

"She was asking a lot of questions about Sydney, and may have been involved in Constantine's murder."

Alexia looked at him curiously. "How do you know that?"

"Another hunch. She and Kane fit the descriptions of a couple that paid a visit to Constantine's motel room the night he disappeared."

"Why would they kill him?"

"He had something they wanted." Doc told her about the stones and his encounter with Jai-Robson Priest.

Alexia leaned forward. "The FBI have been monitoring Jai-Robson Priest since he arrived. We'd love to nab him on something—anything, but he hasn't broken any laws yet." She removed her eyeglasses. "Priest is a crazed demagogue with no respect for civilized authority. He's raped and brutalized women all over the African continent, and nothing is sacred to him. He's the last person you want to have as an enemy, Julian, so stay away from him."

Doc grabbed her hand. "Alexia—chill; I get the message. I'll be careful. Just find out what you can about Kane and anything else on the Prophet sisters. Priest didn't come all this way just to attend a fundraiser."

Alexia placed the photos in her purse and stood up. "Julian, I'm not making you any promises. Constantine and the other deaths are a matter for the local police and FBI, not you. I'll do what you asked, but if I discover information vital to the police's investigation or if it falls under my jurisdiction, I will not feel compelled to share the information with you."

"Fair enough."

After she left, Doc took a cab over to Cornerstone Global Insurance Recovery.

Holloway saw him going into the building.

* * *

Marcus was still in a meeting with Benno. Doc sat in the hall and waited.

Not long afterwards, Benno's secretary came through the office. "Dr. Sebasst, Mr. St. John would like you to join them in the conference room." Doc followed her up the stairs and across the glass sky bridge that took them into the conference room.

The room glistened in honey-maple hardwood and yellow high-back leather chairs. Marcus sat at the head of the table with Benno and a gray-haired matronly woman in a black suit.

142

Marcus rolled a chair back for him. "Have a seat, Doc, we're just finishing up here. Did you see the morning article on Constantine?"

"Yes."

"There have been some new developments since this morning. First of all—our fears were right. Sydney is in Poison Springs, Nevada, or at least her Land Rover is. Her anti-theft tracking system puts the exact location about thirty-six miles northwest of the town. We contacted the sheriff of Poison Springs and gave him the coordinates of her vehicle. They'll get back to us if they find anything. We officially have her listed as missing, and have contacted every law enforcement authority between here and L.A. So hopefully, we'll start hearing something soon. Second thing; I sent some people over to the Cameroon Motel with your photos. The manager positively I.D.'d Kane as the man who visited Constantine the night he disappeared. I think it's pretty clear that Samantha Prophet was the woman that was with him."

"Anything on Cassandra Prophet?" Doc asked.

The gray-haired woman answered. "Cassandra and Samantha are thirty-five and thirty-eight years old, respectively. Both are single, but Cassandra has an adopted daughter named Hanna. They were born in Santa Fe, New Mexico, the parents of missionaries."

"Hmm . . . who says apples don't fall far from the tree," Marcus said. "Maybe if the sisters had spent more time in church like their parents they would have turned out to be better humans."

"There may be some truth to that. The parents spent considerable time working in foreign missions overseas, while the sisters were raised by relatives in New Mexico."

"Are their parents still alive?" Doc asked.

"No, they died in 1988 in a bus accident in Chile," Benno said.

The woman interrupted. "But they left them a small inheritance, which allowed Cassandra to finish college."

"And Samantha?"

"She was already practicing law in New Mexico."

"Is she a practicing attorney here?" Doc asked.

"No."

"Then you need to find out what she is doing, other than finding time to whack people. Is that it?" Marcus asked.

"So far. We can't find as much as a traffic ticket on either of them, but we're still working at it," the woman said.

"Good. These people aren't saints, especially if they're hanging around with the likes of someone like Priest," Marcus said, rising out of the chair. "Benno, keep me in the loop on this—and I want a jet ready if I need it. Doc and I have to split."

"Where are we going?" Doc asked, hurrying to catch up.

"Professor Shengatti called from UW. He wants to see us."

* * *

They Jaguar pulled away from the curb. Holloway made a U-turn in the street to follow them, with the two black Escalades close behind.

The car left the city, crossing the bridge over to Redwood. When the Jaguar entered the private gate to the university's research facility, Holloway turned off onto the side road leading to the rear of the facility. He parked under the cover of the evergreen trees.

He dragged a suitcase off the seat as he got out of the truck. He pushed his way through the thick wall of rhododendrons and azaleas to reach the windows on the south side of the building. Opening the case, he assembled the laser rod, pointed it at the window, and placed headphones on his head. When he heard footsteps in the corridor, he turned on the recorder.

* * *

Professor Shengatti's office was housed in a theater-size hall with dozens of wall maps hanging from ceiling racks, like rugs being displayed in a furniture store. The room smelled of old paper, ink, and glue from the hundreds of books and magazines crammed in the bookshelves around the walls.

Shengatti sat behind a mission table large enough to seat twelve. When he saw the men standing in the doorway, he motioned to them. "Gentlemen, down here, please."

"You call this your office?" Marcus asked as they came down the center aisle.

"This is where I come to do my serious work and pursue my passion, which are the historical maps you see above. The university allows me the use of this old lecture hall in lieu of additional compensation they've promised me for years. But poverty and privacy have their rewards," he said with a smile as he waved a lit stogie in his hand. "Now, I have something you and Dr. Sebasst will be interested in seeing." He got up and moved over to the large map at the end of the table. "My interest was piqued by our first conversation, and I decided to do a little research on my own."

He smoothed the corners of the map. "This is a territorial map of Nevada in 1861, and the area I have marked in red is where the town of Poison Springs currently sits. As you can see, the town didn't exist then. In 1859, after the discovery of the Comstock Silver Lode, thousands of fortune hunters and settlers flooded into the territory seeking to get rich. Hundreds of mining camps sprang up across Nevada with prospectors hoping to strike it rich in silver or gold. One of the camps was Crazy Flats, which we know was located right about where Poison Springs stands today. The camp apparently was named after the thirty or so misfits who lived there, and because it was right in the middle of Indian country."

Shengatti sat down on a stool. "In order to protect themselves against Indian raids, the men worked as a team—all except an Englishman the Shoshone Indians called Snowbeard. He was obsessed with the stories he'd heard about the vast deposits of gold in the mountains. He would disappear for weeks in the mountains before returning to camp. When he did, he kept to himself. In August of 1862, a German immigrant named Bonkowski arrived in Crazy Flats. He and Snowbeard became friends and eventually partners. A year later, sometime in September of '63', Snowbeard left the camp with his mules and was never heard from again. Bonkowski showed up eighteen months later in Carson City with saddlebags filled with gold, followed soon after by a mule team loaded with gold. Assay papers claimed that Bonkowski and Snowbeard were joint owners in a goldmine of an undisclosed location. For the next two years, Bonkowski transported monthly shipments of gold with an army of guards protecting it. He died a wealthy man in Carson City at the age of sixty-seven, never divulging the location of the mine. Supposedly, Snowbeard was the only one who knew the directions to the mine. He etched them into the side of the mountain inside a mine shaft somewhere deep in Shoshone territory."

"Whatever happened to Snowbeard?" Doc asked.

"Bonkowski said he had long since left the area with his share of the gold. Snowbeard's real name was Alpaca Uriah Prophet, a surveyor from England. He moved to San Francisco, married, and eventually died a pauper."

"Don't tell me that the Prophet sisters are related to him," Marcus said.

"He's their great-great grandfather."

"Damn. Tell me something, professor. Could the stone tablets I have be the map to the mine?" Marcus asked.

"It's possible, I suppose."

"It would certainly explain why the Prophets are so interested in getting their hands on them. But what doesn't make sense to me is, if Alpaca Prophet died penniless, that tells me there is no more gold in that mine. It's worthless," Marcus said.

Doc had been studying the old map. "If the mine were worthless, people wouldn't be dying trying to get the stone."

"So, what does that leave us with?" Marcus asked.

Doc paused. "I don't know."

Marcus got up from his chair. "Well, I do. The answer is right here in Poison Springs," he said, poking his finger on the map. "And Sydney is right in the middle of it. Doc, we've got to go." Marcus jumped to his feet.

"Professor, thanks for all your help. You've done a helluva job. If you ever want to make some serious money, I could use a man like you on my team."

"Thank you, I'm very flattered, but I would be lost outside academia. However, I would like some time to view the stones, if possible."

"Fine, I'll have one of my people drop them off to you."

* * *

Doc handed his car pass to the guard as they left through the gate. He eased the car around the tight corner and headed down the isolated mountain highway.

"The more we dig around in this mess, the worse it smells," Marcus said, reaching into his pocket and pulling out his silver toothpick.

"You're right, we need to find Sydney and we need to do it fast."

"Well, that's not going to happen if we keep sitting on our butts in Seattle."

Doc thought about Sydney's business partner, Jordan. "We could use Jordan's help. See if you can get her on the phone."

While Marcus was busy searching his phone for Jordan's number, Doc's attention was on the winding road in front of them, and not the scenery. He never saw the vehicle hidden behind the trees as his car zoomed past.

Seconds later, he looked through the rearview mirror. "We've got guests."

Marcus twisted around just as the black Escalade hit their bumper. The small Jaguar swerved across the centerline before Doc regained control.

"I don't think these guys are trying to tell us they want to pass. We can't take another hit like that!" Marcus shouted, looking back at the big SUV. "They're right on our ass again, Doc. "Do something!"

Doc saw the sports utility truck barreling down on them. He pushed the pedal to the floor. The XKR sprang to life and shot down the road. It roared around the corners going sixty miles per hour and jumped to one hundred and ten by the time the road flattened out.

Marcus looked back. The Cadillac was nowhere in sight. He relaxed. "Whoa man, you can ease up. I don't see them anywhere." Doc stomped the brakes, throwing Marcus against the dashboard as the car skidded sideways and stopped.

"What the hell are you doing?" Marcus shouted.

Doc pointed his finger. A hundred yards in front was another Escalade that blocked the road, along with four armed Africans. The Escalade that had been pursuing them came into view and stopped forty-five yards behind the Jaguar.

"We're boxed in. I think your giant friend is more than just a little ticked off with us," Marcus said, pulling two guns from underneath his jacket.

Doc saw him checking his clips. "No guns."

Marcus looked at him like he was crazy. "Okay, you better have a better plan. How do you want to handle this?" Doc studied the situation. Marcus kept his eyes on the SUV's. "These guys aren't going to wait on us all day, Doc."

The Escalade was big, but not long enough to block the entire road. Doc saw a small exposed gap between the truck's bumper and the mountain. He hoped it was large enough for a small car to squeeze between.

"I can get around the roadblock, but I can't do anything about the guys in our rear," Doc said.

"Well, I can." Marcus opened the door and jumped out of the car. A rifle bullet meant for his head, landed short—hitting the car roof. A second bullet shattered the passenger window. The shots weren't coming from the Escalades, but from the hill above. Marcus dropped to the pavement, rolled, and fired three shots into the trees. Seconds later, the Escalade behind them suddenly roared forward. Marcus jumped to his feet and fired at the speeding vehicle until his guns were empty. The bullets hit their marks. The SUV flipped, rolled, and exploded as it went over the embankment.

Doc jumped out of the car, slamming the door. "Marcus!"

"Hey, it's not my fault." He pointed a gun at the clump of trees on the ridge. "There was someone up there on the crest of the hill trying to take my head off. What did you expect me to do?"

"Doc crouched behind the car, but couldn't see anything but trees. "Come on, we've gotta go!" They got back in the car. "Fasten your seat belt."

Marcus cinched the strap tight across his chest as he looked down the road at the men crouched behind the vehicle waiting. "What are you going to do?"

"Get us out of here—hold on!" He punched the pedal and the car rocketed toward the roadblock. When the car was in range, two bullets hit the grill, and one shattered the windshield. Doc and Marcus ducked. Sixty yards from the blockade, Doc swerved off the road into the ditch, and kept his foot pressed to the pedal as the Jaguar shot for the gap.

Marcus clutched the dash, lowered his head, and closed his eyes. The mountain shaved the driver's side of the Jaguar, rocketed past and catapulted back up onto the road. Priest's men continued firing until the car disappeared from view.

* * *

Holloway left a trail of blood as he ran up the hill to his truck, which was parked on the Old Mountain Highway. He flung his rifle and gloves down into the ravine, and jumped in the truck. He didn't think about his wound until he was back on the main highway, and seven miles down the road. He pulled into a truck stop and parked between two semi-trucks.

He reached underneath his seat and found an oil rag, which he used to wrap around his forearm to stop the flow of blood. St. John's bullet had missed the bone, but it was deep and hurt like hell. Reaching for the whiskey bottle from the glove box, he noticed that his hands were still shaking. He had two drinks to medicate the pain and a third to help him forget about his abysmal failure.

Chapter 28

The lobby of the Legends Hotel was as busy as an airport terminal. Lines of people massed together at the registration desk waiting for assistance.

Marcus squeezed through the small crowd blocking the entrance to the lounge. "I need a drink."

"I'm going to the room to check messages and give Jordan a call back. I'll meet you back here in a few minutes," Doc said.

Marcus went into the room and saw Toby Jamison sitting at the bar.

"Toby, what are you doing here?"

"Man . . . I've been looking for you guys for hours. Didn't you get my messages?"

"We've been out all day. What's up?" Marcus signaled the bartender to bring him a beer.

Toby looked around the room. "Where's Doc?"

"He'll be down in a minute." Toby's foot nervously taped against the bar rail. "What's with you, man?" Marcus asked.

Toby's conspiratorial eyes searched the crowd before he whispered. "This dude comes to my house late last night, you know. He's a cop and wants information. He's packing plenty bank. I mean the dude pulls out a roll of cash as big as my hand, and says for every correct answer to his questions I'd get paid. He starts asking me questions about what you and Doc are up to, why you went to that woman's function last night, and lot of other silly questions. Of course, I kept my mouth shut—didn't tell him nothing. Then he starts threatening me—bringing up stuff I ain't done in years. Says if I don't cooperate, I'm going to end up like you."

Marcus spit up the beer he was drinking. "What?"

"Yeah, that's what the dude said—straight up."

"You sure he was a cop?"

"Yeah, he didn't flash a badge, but he talked like one and he knew all about my record, and that I got you and Doc those phony invitations—everything."

"Sounds like it could be Holloway."

Toby's jaw dropped. "You know this cat?"

"Did his face look like a turkey—fat cheeks swaying in the breeze?"

"Yeah that's the dude."

"Then I know him," Marcus took another drink. "I ran into him at the police station."

Toby hit the bar with his fist, drawing attention. "Damn. Had I known that I would have pimp-slapped him silly."

Marcus whispered. "Toby, you don't need to be messing in my stuff. I appreciate the thought, but if you see this guy again, leave him alone. He's a stone racist. Call me and I'll deal with him. The guy is psycho."

When Doc arrived, Toby retold his story.

"Sounds like Holloway has been following us," Doc said.

"Yeah, and he was probably the one stalking us the other night down on the pier," Marcus said.

Toby was still shook up. "Doc, the dude's eyes were on fire like one of those crazy Ahab terrorists."

Marcus laughed. Doc fought to suppress a smile.

Toby looked at the two men, and then bolted off the barstool. "Oh, this is what I get for trying to help my *brothers* out. Forget you uppity Negroes. I'm outta here . . . just give me back my car and pay me what you owe me, then I'm gone!" He downed his drink and slammed the empty mug down on the bar. The man sitting next to him moved out of Toby's way.

"Come on, man. Don't leave. I'm sorry. We appreciate the heads up on this guy," Doc said.

Marcus continued drinking with his back toward the men. "Yeah, especially the part about his *Ahab* eyes," he said as he reached into the bowl of peanuts on the counter and started munching.

"Man, I'm about sick of your ass. That cop called me all out of my name, slapped me around, and this is the thanks I get?"

"Ignore Qwik," Doc said, patting Toby on his shoulder.

"Did Holloway give you his card—tell you how you could get in touch with him?" Marcus asked

Toby glared at him. "Don't you think I would have told you that if he had?"

"Okay, man, I'm sorry. Chill," Marcus said.

"You must think I'm some kind of idiot if . . ."

Marcus spun around on the stool facing Toby. "Man, I said I was sorry. You know me; I was just playing with you. Now, can I get a hug?" Toby looked at the stupid grin on his cousin's face and swatted Marcus's hand away when he tried to shake hands.

"Fine, be that way then. I don't know why you were getting mad at me, anyway. I'm not the one who tried to move a mountain with your car." He turned back around to the bar.

Toby looked at Doc. "What's he talking about?" he asked, sitting back down.

"We encountered some road problems and the car took some damage."

"How much damage?"

Doc grabbed some peanuts from the bowl and popped them in his mouth. "The body got chewed up a little and the windows need replacing, but nothing that can't be fixed."

Toby was off the stool again. "Man, you know how much that car costs?"

"Relax, we'll pay you what it's worth," Doc said.

"Speak for yourself, brother, I wasn't driving, I'm not paying him jack," Marcus said, patting his hair in place, while looking at his reflection in the mirror over the bar.

"Okay, I'll pay for the damages. Send the bill to my house for what I owe you. I'll see that you get paid."

Toby crooked his neck to the side, staring at Doc like he was an alien life form.

"To your home! Naw, man," he said, shaking his head. "I trusted you, Doc, with my *baby* and you wrecked her? And you

152

want me to bill you at your home? You're as crazy as my cousin over here," he said, raising his voice. "This ain't no thirty dollar newspaper subscription I'm trying to collect on, and I ain't no paperboy that's going to wait for my money to come in the mail. You owe me sixty-two grand, *brother.*"

"Sixty-two thousand dollars?" shouted Doc.

Marcus busted out laughing again.

Toby eyes widened. "What did you think you were driving, some turbo Honda or something? That Jag was the top of my fleet—my honey, my money machine. Now I've got to go out and buy another one. Of course that's going to take time, because I gotta do my research to find just the right one," he said, with his hands flying around in the air like he was directing traffic. "And after I order it, I'm going to have to wait at least twelve weeks for delivery, and that's assuming it's already made. There's a lot of down time, which means lost rental revenue to me that I'm not even charging you for. You know how much I could rent that puppy out for? And I haven't even thought about the emotional stress this is going to cause my wife. She loved that car, Doc. There's no way I can go home empty-handed and tell . . ."

Marcus got tired of listening to his rant. He wrote a check and handed it to Toby. "Here, now shut the hell up!" Toby inspected the check as thoroughly as a treasury agent.

"Get that stupid Mayberry grin off your face," Marcus said, as he tried to enjoy the last of his beer.

Toby folded the check and slipped it into his pocket. "Thanks, cuz, I appreciate the way you handle your *business.* What else can I do for you brothers while you're here?"

"We need a lift to the airport," Doc said.

"We do?" Marcus asked.

"Yeah, I just spoke with Jordan. She's going to meet us in Poison Springs."

* * *

Samantha Prophet tossed her bag in the overhead compartment of the airplane and squeezed past the fat woman to get to her window seat. She normally flew first class, but the midnight flight to Las Vegas was full. She fastened the seat belt and gazed out of the window at the rain sprinkling the runway. In two hours she'd be in Vegas where Eagleton had arranged for her to be picked up and flown to Poison Springs. The timing was horrible because she hated leaving her sister alone, but the priority now was to find the mystery letter Belleshota was carrying. If Samantha was right about what she thought was contained in the letter, the sisters stood to lose more than just their multi-million dollar transaction with Priest. They could be out of business for good.

Chapter 29

His name was R.C. Gingham and he was from Ely, Nevada, although he had spent the last twenty-some odd years living on Hickcut Point near Poison Springs. He and Sydney had traveled on foot for a day and a half across the mountain of parched ground and scorching sun. R.C. didn't move any faster than the two mules he dragged behind them. Neither beast nor man seemed in any particular hurry to get to where they were going. The trip had taken its toll on Sydney. Her feet were swollen and she could barely walk. R.C. ripped the high heels off her boots, which made it more comfortable and easier to walk over the sharp rocks. Sydney's silk blouse was matted to her body in sweat, with her sunglasses offering her the only relief from the sun.

They stopped to rest at noon. R.C. collected some wood and made a fire. Sydney wandered a few hundred feet from the campsite, ending up at the edge of a cliff. To the west was the impenetrable Mohave Desert and off to the east were the towns of Poison Springs and Weavilwood. She had no idea where she was. The only thing for certain was that her hope rested in a man that moved slower than his mules, and whose house was as isolated from civilization as he appeared to be. She sat on the rock ledge mopping the sweat from her body with her jacket. What she would give for a nice cool shower and cold drink. So far, the only water she had seen was from the canteens attached to the mules. Sydney couldn't understand why any sane person would choose to live in such a harsh environment.

"I ain't got no boss, can chew and spit my tobacco wherever I want, don't have to worry about some woman telling me I snore too loud—and can run buck naked whenever I want," he had told her. The life of a prospector was in his blood just like his daddy's. "He had a lot of Greyhound in him. Had to be free to run and chase his dreams. I reckon' the same hound's blood runs through me, too."

Sydney tossed a rock over the side of the mountain and watched it bounce off the rocks before disappearing into a cluster of yellow and black creosote bushes.

If only she could get off the mountain as easily. But she knew she couldn't because every law enforcement officer in Poison Springs and Weavilwood was looking for her. She was going to need more help than R.C. could provide if she stood any chance of making it out of the valley alive.

R.C. had a hotplate of red beans, sausages, and bread waiting for her when she returned to camp.

Sydney held the large polish sausage in her hands and bit it. "Umm, this is pretty good." She took another bite. "How do you manage to keep it fresh?"

"Josh slips a couple of frozen packs in my monthly provisions," he said, stirring the beans with his fork. "I figured in this heat and all we best eat them while we can."

"How long before we reach your place?"

"By sunset." He stuffed his mouth with beans and bread. They sat quietly while they ate. Afterwards, R.C. cleaned the plates, fed his mules, and kicked dirt on the fire. "We best go." Sydney dropped into her familiar position alongside him and the mules with the dog trailing behind.

"What does 'R. C.' stand for?"

"Nuthin'—just R.C. My ma was too lazy and too tired poppin' out babies to ever gettin' around to figure it out."

"You have any family or friends living with you?"

"Nope—just me. Met a lot of people, but Josh and Charlie Whitefingers are the only ones I call my friends. The rest ain't worth a mule's fart. I'm gonna really miss that boy."

Sydney noticed the distant look in his eyes. "How long were you and Josh friends?"

"Bout seven years or so. He was the only one that give a damn about me and some of the others living on the mountain. His papa was a prospector, so Josh knowed the life. He'd buy me some provisions out his own. Told me I could pay him back when I struck it rich."

"How did you know he would be at his farm?"

"First Thursday of each month he makes a path by his old farm, on business. He usually leaves me somethin' in the farmhouse. He was a good old boy that way. I can't believe that backstabbin' T.J. Eagleton would shoot him in cold blood. You best be sure that if you hadn't killed T.J., I would have. There was no sense in killing Josh—no sense," he said, his voice trailing off.

He was right. Joshua McCain had been killed for a scrap of paper that didn't mean anything.

"R.C., tell me some more about this Alpaca gold mine."

He spit a line of tobacco juice on the ground as he yanked the mule line for them to keep up. "Pert near told you all there is to say. Old man Alpaca struck it rich somewheres around these parts, all right, but there ain't no more gold here. Me and others been through every inch of territory through these mountains. Believe me missy, any gold out here is fool's gold, exceptin' the few nuggets we find from time to time."

"Whatever happened to Alpaca Prophet?"

"Stayed around these parts for a while raising a family and buying up most of the valley, before scooting off. Don't know what happened after that, but people say he died broker than me. Now, I know that ain't true," he chuckled.

"Josh McCain sure seemed convinced that the mine exists."

R.C. stopped walking. "Never said it don't—just ain't no gold there. Besides, these mountains got hundreds of mine shafts running through them, and I been in every one at least two times."

"How about the White River Copper Mine?"

"Now why would I have cause to go looking for gold in a copper mine?"

"When I was there they certainly weren't bringing out much ore, which struck me as being pretty odd."

He laughed. "Missy, that ain't odd. There ain't enough copper in that mine to make one decent spittoon."

"So what's the deal, why are they still open?"

"Jobs. Without it, this place would dry up faster than snot along with all the jobs around these parts."

157

"That's crazy. No business can stay afloat if they aren't making a profit. You're telling me that the only reason the copper mine is still in existence is to provide employment?"

"Yep—just like the mill, the grange, and mercantile over at Poison Springs. All of them ain't making a plum nickel, but the Prophets keep them running anyways."

"No one is that altruistic."

"What's that mean?"

"Unselfish. They have to be getting something in return."

R.C. grabbed her hand and walked her over to the edge of the mountain. He pointed his finger at the mountain range in the distance, which was on the other side of the valley. "All the land you can see, plus some you can't belongs to the Prophet family. This is their land and everything on it. What else they got to get?"

Chapter 30

When Poole arrived home from work, there was a message waiting for him from the sheriff. Eagleton had scheduled an important meeting and wanted everyone back in the office, immediately. Poole had just finished a double shift and was exhausted. He and another deputy had combed the foothills around McCain's farm for the last two days trying to find Belleshota, with no luck. The back of Poole's head still looked like a tumor had attached itself. The golf ball-size knot hadn't stopped hurting since waking up in the dirt alongside T.J.'s body. There was never a question in Poole's mind that he was going to lie about what really happened. If he had been on duty like he was supposed to be, instead of in Rose's bed, T.J. would still be alive, and Belleshota would be the one dead.

Poole got a beer from the cooler and went back to the car. He used the steering wheel to pop the cap off the bottle, and then guzzled the beer. The sun beat against his red neck as the temperature continued to climb above one hundred degrees—and the air conditioner didn't work. "Damn." He wiped his face with a towel.

It wasn't the heat that was really bothering him. It was the heated passion that erupted in him when he had made love to Rose. He felt her body, but he only saw Belleshota's face. The only way he knew to exorcise her from his memory was to kill her.

He wiped his face with a towel again and tossed it in the back seat with his jacket. His mind settled back on Rose. Something in him wanted to love her, but that would take too much out of the thrill of the sex. Besides, she had a brat, and he couldn't stand kids. As long as he had control of her daughter, he could control the mother. To keep his wife happy, he occasionally gave her gifts when she became suspicious of his long absences from home.

The last trinket he picked up for her was Belleshota's bracelet, which he had found in his Jeep. He reached into the back seat and got his deputy's jacket. He searched the pockets for the bracelet, but it was gone. He thought for a moment before realizing that he must have dropped it at the brothel. Poole cursed, and started the Jeep.

* * *

Poole was the last one to reach the office. He joined the other deputies crowded around Sheriff Eagleton's desk.

Eagleton's message was short and terse. "I want Belleshota in custody or dead by this time tomorrow. No excuses."

Poole made the mistake of being the first one to speak. "Some of us have already put in sixteen hours without a break. We need . . ."

"Shut the hell up, Elan. You've already lost your bonus pay for the year. Another crack from your fat mouth and it's your job." Eagleton's usually calm blue eyes were dark. "Anything else?"

Poole kept quiet.

"Effective immediately, everyone works around the clock until we get her. If you don't, you can also forget your bonuses and your jobs." The men groaned, but didn't say anything. "Listen to me you bunch of selfish ingrates. T.J. was not only my son, but also one of ours. I expect you all to do your jobs, no matter the costs. Now, I've spoken to the sheriff over in Weavilwood. His men will continue searching the area north of McCain's farm and the eastern quadrant of Hickcut Point. The rest of you will concentrate on the foothills."

One of the deputies worked up the courage to speak. "Sheriff, we're talking an area of over sixteen thousand acres to be covered by eighteen men. Can we get any more help?"

"No. A missing person's report has been filed on Belleshota in Seattle. As far as anyone else is concerned, she's just missing, and that's the way I want to keep it. The last thing we want is the state police coming around. Belleshota is on foot and she doesn't know her way around here. Someone has to be helping her."

"It's probably one of those crazy prospectors," a deputy said.

"That's why all of you are going to round up every one of them and bring them in. Someone knows where she is."

"What if she gets to a telephone and calls out?" Stephenson asked.

"All the telephones have been routed through our emergency switchboard. She won't get through without us knowing about it. Anymore questions?" The deputies mumbled as their eyes searched one another. Poole raised his hand to speak. Eagleton's eye bored down on him. "What do you want?"

"I just remembered something. McCain's dog was in the truck when I arrived, but when I woke up, he was gone. That crazy mutt was attached at the hip to Josh—wouldn't let anyone near him except a few of those prospectors."

"Which ones?"

"Bushnell, Gingham, Heifetz, and that pot-smoking Indian, Charlie Whitefingers."

"Okay—find Bushnell and Heifetz and see what they know. Contact the sheriff in Weavilwood and tell him to make sure his men check on Whitefingers and Gingham, on Hickcut." Poole felt redeemed. "Okay, you men have your assignments. After you call home, hit the road. The men rose from their chairs to leave. "Poole—stay, I want to see you." Eagleton sat down behind his desk. "Tell me how T.J. died.

"Boss, I told you what happened."

"Tell me again until it makes sense to me."

"I met T.J. out at McCain's just like you told me. We heard gunfire coming from around the barn, so we went to investigate where we found McCain's body. That Belleshota woman came running from the barn firing her gun at us like a crazy woman. One of her slugs hit T.J. and he fell next to me. She would have killed me, too, but she ran out of bullets. I had the drop on her until someone slugged me over the head from behind and the lights went out. The next thing I saw was Stephenson's face when he revived me."

The sheriff eyed him suspiciously. "When I spoke with you earlier that day, you said you were at Mary's Burgers, which puts you twenty-six miles from the farm. There is no way you could have gotten to the farm that fast."

Poole squirmed in his chair. "When you told me that T.J. needed backup, I jumped on the pedal. I took the shortcut through Rick Campbell's pastureland to the canyon highway and looped down to McCain's back gate. T.J. arrived a few minutes later." A bead of perspiration trickled down the back of Poole's ear, which he hoped Eagleton couldn't see.

The sheriff's eyes stay fixed on him. "Elan, my son is dead. If I find out he died because of your negligence or incompetence, you're going to lose more than your job."

Poole swallowed hard. He knew he had to be convincing. "Sheriff, you know how much we all loved T.J. He was like a brother to me. I wish I could have taken the bullet for him. I should have shot that bitch instead of trying to arrest her, but believe me, I won't make that mistake twice. Stephenson and I aren't going to rest until we drag her out of the mountains."

"You're not going anywhere, except Las Vegas," Eagleton said, turning his attention to the paperwork on his desk.

Poole was convinced he hadn't heard the sheriff right. "Las Vegas?"

"Samantha Prophet is flying in and you're going to pick her up at . . . ."

Poole leaned over. "Come on, Tom, send someone else. That woman has made a fool out of me twice. You got to give me a chance to square things—make things right."

Eagleton snatched the pile of papers off his desk and threw them in Poole's face. "You are a fool, and it didn't take a woman to convince me of that." He got up and came around the desk, hovering over him. "Do you really think I'm stupid?"

"I don't understand . . ."

"You know perfectly well what I'm talking about—that little whore you keep over at Gertie's. Did you really think you could keep something like that a secret? Everyone knows you spend more time out there than you do at home. You're an embarrassment to my office. If you learned to keep your hands to yourself, we wouldn't be in this predicament and my son would still be alive. I'm holding you personally responsible for this mess! Poole's face was flushed as the sheriff continued shouting. "I'd fire you right now if I didn't need every man. Now, I want you to get out of here and go pick up Samantha Prophet. Do you think you can handle that without screwing it up?"

"Yes, sir, I can do it," he said, rising clumsily out of the chair.

The sheriff turned his back to him. "Then get the hell out of here." Poole grunted and left the room.

Stephenson was waiting for him outside. "What did Eagleton want?"

"My head on a pole. He blames me for T.J.'s death."

Stephenson walked ahead of him. "You should have been there, Elan."

Poole pushed Stephenson against the building. "Hey, I don't need this crap from you too. It wouldn't have mattered if I had been there. That crazy bitch would have shot us both. Eagleton for some reason doesn't see that. He's got me running errands like some paperboy."

Stephenson swatted Poole's hand off his chest. "Sometimes the cards fall like that. If you want my advice, cut that filly loose you're shacking with at Gertie's. Ever since you've been with her, you haven't been worth a damn around here." Stephenson turned and went back into the office.

Poole thought about what Stephenson had said. As painful as it was to admit, Stephenson was right. He had to do something.

Hundreds of women had come through the valley over the years, but none more captivating than Rose. She had a special quality. He noticed it the first time he laid eyes on her. Her face was pale and weary from the long trip and she was seven months pregnant, but walked proudly like a woman twice her age, instead of the fifteen-year-old she was.

Poole was on duty that night and used his position to erase all traces of her existence. He hid her at the brothel and paid Gertie a generous sum each month for her silence. The Prophets paid handsomely so money was never a problem—until now. If he lost his job he would lose his pension. He had been a deputy for sixteen years, and he liked to think, the most likely successor to T.J.'s job after the sheriff retired. He could forget the promotion now, but it still wasn't too late to salvage his job. He walked toward his Jeep. The first thing he needed to do was to get rid of Rose. There would be other women.

Chapter 31

Sydney and R.C. reached the mesa by early evening. Dusk seemed to hang on the horizon like a shroud, forever. Sydney enjoyed the sunset as she swam in the refreshing hot springs, located in back of R.C.'s metal quanson hut. She thought about what R.C. had asked her earlier: *"What else they got to get?"* The words still resonated in her head. While it seemed perfectly natural to R.C. that the Prophets would subsidize the livelihood of two towns, Sydney knew better. She also knew something else. If the Prophets owned the towns they also owned the people.

R.C. sat in a nearby chair reading a magazine, occasionally distracted by Sydney bathing in the frothy water in a blue lace bra and panties. "You're the first woman I've had at my camp. Can't says I mind though. I ain't seen a woman in her skivvies since I chased some young girl around the room at Gertie's—ten or eleven years ago."

"You need to get out more," she said, swimming to the bank. In an effortless motion, she bounced out of the pool onto her feet. Gingham handed her a towel. When they got back to the hut, Sydney's lips were quivering. She found a blanket by the wood stove and wrapped it around her body.

R.C. threw another log on the fire. "Should have told you how fast the temperature drops around here. One minute it's hot as Hades and by nightfall, cold as my wife, Emily."

Sydney laughed. "I didn't know you were married."

"Was—back in '76'. It was a good day when she left. She wasn't nothin' but a pain in my rear. Nagged too much, wanted too much sex, and didn't give me a moment's peace. She run off one night with some marine or navy guy. Stupid bastard didn't know I'd have paid him to take her away. Now, if she looked anything like you, I might have put up a fight." He spit tobacco into a can, then wiped his mouth. "In the end it don't matter. I was born to live this life. Now, I got a question for you. What kind of kinfolk and man of yours would let you run all over the place and do the kind of work you do?"

Sydney fluffed her hair with her hands. "Believe me, this is the last place I want to be. I'm supposed to be in Baja enjoying myself about now." She slipped her slacks over her legs, and then sat down to put on her boots. "I guess I got the sun I prayed for, but not the fun I expected." She buttoned her blouse, put on her jacket, and slung her gun holster over her shoulder.

R.C. chewed his tobacco slowly as he kept staring at her.

"What?" she asked.

"Where's your man . . . your kinfolk? Why do they let you run around doing this crazy kind of work by yourself?"

She sighed. "I have no family and I'm not married. And even if I was, I wouldn't need their permission to live my life the way I choose."

He spit another trail of tobacco juice from his mouth. "Seems to me you should be listening to someone other than your fool self, or you wouldn't be on the run and stuck up here with a buzzard face like me."

"I told you, none of this was planned. I'm ready to go now," she said with a cold voice.

R.C. laughed as he reclined in the wooden chair. "And just where might you be going?"

"To a telephone. Someone on this mountain must have one."

"Ain't no telephones, I told you that. And even if there was, everyone that got one been notified by the sheriff about you. Only a silly-minded person would take up with you, which don't say much for me, I guess."

"No one will let me use their phone because they're scared of the sheriff? I can't believe that."

"Missy, you just don't get it. Maybe and if you had shot that worthless Elan Poole—that be one thing. He's breathin' air that someone else could be using. But you killed T.J. Eagleton, the

166

sheriff's only son, who most people around here love more than God."

Sydney rested a hand on her hips. "You mean to tell me that there is no way to communicate with the outside world?"

"Didn't say that," he said, stretching his arms out over the back of the chair. "Charlie Whitefingers got one of those tall towers up at his place."

"What?"

"You know—them radio towers. He uses it to talk to his kinfolk in North Dakota."

"You mean a shortwave radio?"

"Yes—suppose that's what it is alright."

"How far is it from here?"

"Up on the butte above. Takes about a day by mule. Faster if you hike."

"Can you take me there?"

"Who you gonna call?"

"I have some friends that will help me if I can contact them, so will you take me there?"

R.C. yawned. "Yeah, we can head out at sun break, but don't get your hopes up. Whitefingers ain't the friendliest person around here."

* * *

When Poole arrived at Gertie's he was in for a surprise. Rose wasn't there, and neither was Belleshota's bracelet. "What do you mean she's gone?" he asked the manager.

"One of the girls dropped her off in town to see her kid last night. She'll be back around 10:00, if you want to wait," said the man. Poole stormed out of the building. He didn't have an hour to wait. He was supposed to be in Las Vegas by midnight to pick up Samantha Prophet from the airport. The smoke of burning rubber filled the air as he squealed his car onto the highway and headed toward the Montgomery's house.

The Montgomery's lived out on Route 2, fourteen miles away. Timothy Montgomery worked the night shift at Nellis Air Force Base, and probably wouldn't be home. Margaret, his wife,

167

was a stay-at-home mom, raising six daughters and Rose's daughter, Marie. Rose wasn't to visit her daughter without his approval, which he kept to a minimum, because it was the only leverage he had for keeping her in line. She had tried sneaking off before and Poole made her pay for it. The last time she tried to run, she ended up in the clinic, and he didn't let her go near her daughter for three months. After tonight he wouldn't have to worry about her any more.

Poole saw an ambulance pulling away from the Montgomery's front door. He parked on the road and went to the house. Timothy Montgomery rushed past him on the steps.

"Hey, what's going on?" Poole asked.

"Margaret is sick—I gotta go to the hospital."

"Where's Rose?"

"Inside." Montgomery didn't have time to explain what happened and Poole didn't ask. Montgomery raced to his truck and chased after the ambulance. Poole opened the tattered screen door and entered the house. The Montgomery's oldest daughter had tears in her eyes as she tried consoling her siblings.

"What happened?" Poole asked.

"Mama had a seizure," she said. Poole didn't see Marie with the girls. "Where's Marie?"

The fourteen-year-old had her hands full trying to keep order. "She's in the kitchen with Rose." Poole stormed to the kitchen and found it empty. The back door was wide open.

* * *

Rose dragged her young daughter behind her as she made her way along the creek. Marie cried and struggled against the woman she barely knew. Rose heard Poole yelling her name. Marie's wails for help were leading him straight to them. Rose picked her daughter up in her arms and ran until Poole's voice was muted by the sound of the wind and brush. She dropped to her knees in the sand when she was far away from the house. She didn't know where she was, and at the moment didn't care. Her daughter slept in her arms clinging to her neck. Rose wept.

The chilly wind swept through the orchard. Rose found a large cactus to hide behind until morning. She didn't know where she going, but she was certain of one thing; Poole would have to kill her because she would never give up her daughter again. With the diamond bracelet in her pocket she was confident she'd find someone willing to help her.

* * *

At 4:00 a.m., a Chevrolet Avalanche pulled up in front of the Weavilwood Sheriff's office. A short black woman dressed in camouflage cargo pants, a sleeveless denim vest and sunglasses, walked into the office.

"May I help you?" asked the lone deputy, standing at the counter.

"I'm trying to find the White River Copper Mine."

"It's closed this time of night."

She gave him a weary smile. "Thank you, but I still need to know how to get there from here. I'd appreciate your help."

"Get back on the highway and head east. You'll see the sign just before you hit the junction."

"Thank you," she said politely.

As he watched her backing the truck out of the stall, he wondered what interest she had in going to the mine in the middle of the night. Her California license plate read *BLOODSTN*. The deputy checked the plates with Motor Vehicles and then called his boss at home.

Twenty minutes later, the Weavilwood Sheriff called Sheriff Eagleton over in Poison Springs. "You may have trouble heading your way."

Chapter 32

A purple and white Learjet bearing the corporate logo of
Cornerstone Global Insurance streaked across the Nevada sky.
Marcus sat in a cream-colored leather seat, his feet buried in plush
wool carpet, talking on the telephone. The jet suddenly banked
hard to the left. He slipped on his shoes, unbuckled the seatbelt,
and went to the cockpit. "What's going on—you fall asleep?" he
asked as he sat down in the co-pilot seat and strapped on the safety
buckle.

Doc pointed out the widow. "No, I almost missed our
spot."

Marcus strained to see through the dark clouds. Two barely
visible rows of bright flares illuminated a landing path on the
desert floor.

"Jordan must be joking. My jock strap is wider than that
piece of sand down there. This has got to be the wrong place,"
Marcus said.

Doc lowered the landing gear as he made his approach. The
jet's right wing dipped, but then straightened.

"Hey, you sure you can fly this plane?" Marcus asked.

"Relax, we're fine."

"Yeah, that's the same thing my brother-in-law said before
he buried the nose of his plane into the Atlantic."

Doc laughed. "Was that Benno you were talking to on the
phone?"

"Yeah. He ran down some information on Samantha
Prophet. She was an attorney in Santa Fe, where she was
implicated with two law partners in an illegal baby scam. The
partners got sent to jail, but Samantha and some others were
cleared. Even so, the incident left a sour taste in her mouth. She
gave up law and moved to Seattle to be with her sister. Now she
donates her time as a consultant to various adoption agencies.

Once a year, she and baby sister spend a couple of weeks visiting orphanages in Asia and Europe."

"How about their finances?"

"Solid. They're quite the philanthropists. They donate tons of money each year to children's charities."

"Philanthropists wouldn't hang around with people like Jai-Robson Priest. Any connection between the sisters and Priest?"

"Nothing yet."

"Priest wouldn't be here unless it was important business. He's in bed with the Prophets, metaphorically speaking. That can't be good."

Doc touched the jet down on the ground and followed the flares to a large hangar Jordan Bloodstone was pointing to. He guided the jet through the giant doors.

Marcus looked out the window. Jordan had a string of lanterns strung across the rafters for light. "What is this place?"

Doc cut the engines. "Don't know, but I told Jordan to find us something close to Poison Springs, but out of the way."

Marcus lowered the landing steps for Jordan to enter.

She met them with a grin. "High, Marcus, how was the trip?"

"Boring, considering the company. You look good, girl."

"Thanks." She saw Doc emerging from the cockpit. "Julian." She gave him a hug. "Did you have any trouble finding this place?"

"No, but where exactly are we?"

"About eight miles southeast from a town called Weavilwood, and thirty-plus miles from Poison Springs," she said as they left the plane. "There's nothing out here, except a mining company and an airfield over the hill about three miles from us."

"An airfield?" Doc asked.

"Yeah, it's an old Air Force landing strip that's being repaired."

"And this spot?" Marcus asked.

"A deserted maintenance warehouse, once owned by the air force. It's isolated, so I don't think anyone will be looking around here—especially the sheriff's office."

"The sheriff?" Marcus asked.

"Yeah, Syd's in a lot of trouble. She's wanted for the murders of the man she was here to see, and a deputy sheriff who just happened to be the sheriff's son."

"That's crazy. There has to be a mistake," Marcus said.

"No mistake. This valley is sewn up tighter than a drum." Jordan knelt down and drew an oval shape on the dirt floor with her finger. "We're outside Weavilwood, which is here," she said, marking the arc of the oval with an x. "The opposite side of the valley is Poison Springs. There are roads on each side of the valley connecting the towns together—and the only way in and out. Both have roadblocks set up. If Syd is here, there's no way she can get out."

Doc scratched his scalp. "Wait a minute. Marcus, didn't you say you notified the folks here of Sydney's disappearance?"

"Yeah, I spoke to a guy named Eagleton yesterday, and he didn't say a damn thing about any of this."

Jordan rose to her feet and dusted off her pants. "There's more. I spoke to a girl who works over at the convenience store in Poison Springs who spoke to Syd, twice. The first time was to get directions to Joshua McCain's house. The second was after her release from the Poison Springs jail, following an assault charge on one of the deputies."

"The same one that was killed?" Doc asked.

"No, another deputy named Elan Poole."

"The sheriff conveniently forgot to tell me that too," Marcus said.

"She was on her way to Weavilwood. Apparently she was still looking for Joshua McCain."

"How about Sydney's car?"

"I haven't had a chance to look for it yet."

"It can wait until sunrise," Doc said.

"Well, I can't. I want to see Sheriff Eagleton," Marcus said, as he headed to Jordan's truck.

Doc looked at his watch. "He's probably home asleep."

"Then we'll get him up," Marcus said.

Chapter 33

Poole sat at his desk, bored. All the other deputies were out on duty, while his job had been reduced to manning the office and playing personal valet to Samantha Prophet. She had barely spoken to him on their helicopter flight from Las Vegas to Poison Springs, for which he was thankful. Poole was a large man, but felt small in the presence of the taller woman whose deep-set eyes never seemed to blink. Although she visited often, Poole had never actually met her. Her arrivals were generally kept secret and she only met with the sheriff.

Poole heard her husky voice through the thin wall. She and the Sheriff had been in a closed meeting since her arrival, and judging by the tone of her voice, she was pretty upset with Eagleton about the airfield.

"I'll deal with Belleshota. Your job is to see that the field gets finished before my sister's plane arrives. I don't want any more excuses or distractions," Samantha said.

Poole leaned back from the wall. *Plane*? That could only mean one thing: Another shipment was coming in—and it must be large. Why else would they be working on the old airstrip that was seldom used? He leaned back to hear more.

The sound of the front door opening startled Poole. He lost his balance and the chair slipped from under him, crashing to the floor. He looked up and saw a light-skinned black man in a business suit laughing at him.

Embarrassed and angry, Poole shoved the broken chair out of the way and rose to his feet. "The office is closed," he snapped.

"Your doors are open and this place is lit up like its New Years," Marcus said.

"I don't care what it looks like, we're closed. If you need directions back to the main highway, I can help. Otherwise, you have to come back."

"We'd like to speak to Sheriff Eagleton," Doc said.

"Well, you can't. He's in a meeting."

"He's in a meeting at 4:30 in the morning?" Marcus asked.

"Yes he *is*." Poole leaned his frame over the counter. "You can talk to him when the office is open."

Doc noticed Poole's name badge. "Are you the officer that arrested Sydney Belleshota?"

A lump the size of coal formed in Poole's mouth. "You know her?"

"She's a friend of ours."

"And who are you?"

"Julian Sebasst."

Poole nodded his head. "Yeah, I know you. You're one of the names that popped up on the inquiry report we ran on her. Why are you here?"

"I would have thought that was obvious to you," Marcus said.

"Well, enlighten me," Poole sneered.

"Why was she arrested?" Doc asked.

"Trespassing—and resisting arrest."

Marcus snatched the toothpick he had been chewing on from his mouth. "Trespassing—what the hell do you have in this gopher town worth trespassing?"

"She was sleeping in a barn on property that is owned by the federal government. There are signs posted all around the property warning people to stay away, but she ignored them. We brought her in, kept her overnight, then let her go. The bitch repaid the favor by killing two men in cold blood."

"If she did, she damn well must have had a good reason," Marcus said. Poole's body froze, and his face looked like it was ready to explode.

"Were there any witnesses to the killings?" Doc asked.

"Yeah, me. The crazy bitch did this to my face before she escaped. Does that answer your question?"

Doc looked at Poole's puffy nose. "She's not crazy and she's not a bitch," he said with a cold stare. "How did you manage to escape from her?"

The question caught him off guard. "What . . . whaa . . ?" he stammered.

"If you were there, why didn't you stop her?"

Marcus could tell by the confused look on Poole's face that he was searching for a good lie to tell. Marcus used sign language and spoke slow. "What my . . . friend . . . is . . . asking you."

Poole slammed his fist on the counter. "Get the hell out of my office!" Marcus chuckle.

"We'll leave, but we'll be back to see the Sheriff," Doc said.

"Get the hell out, now!"

* * *

Jordan was waiting for them in the truck. "I heard someone screaming all the way out here. What's going on?"

"Marcus was trying to see how many ways he could get under Poole's skin," Doc said.

Marcus slammed the truck door as he got in the back. "He was lying through his yellow teeth about Sydney."

Doc looked back at him. "Of course he was, but now he knows we know he was lying, thanks to you. It's going to be tough getting a straight answer from anyone in this town."

"Well, if you're waiting for an apology, you're going to be waiting a long time. The minute I laid eyes on that fat bastard I didn't like him," Marcus said.

"Did you happen to smell the air in there?" Doc asked.

"Yeah, she must buy her perfume in bulk," Marcus said.

"Who are you talking about?" Jordan asked, as she backed out to the street.

"Samantha Prophet. She's in town," Marcus said.

* * *

Samantha closed the mini-blinds after the truck pulled away. She stormed out of the office to the main counter, where Poole was still in a state of shock. "What do you think you're doing?" she asked.

"They wanted to know . . ."

"I know what they wanted. Sheriff, I want this man out of here."

Poole gulped. "Ms. Prophet, I . . ."

"Shut up, Elan," Eagleton said. "Ms. Prophet, can I talk to you in private for a minute?" Samantha flung Eagleton's door open and went back inside.

"I know Poole is an idiot, but I need every experienced man we have right now. And Poole is the only one available to transport the shipment in from the mountain."

"Fine. Just make sure I never see him again."

"Are those the men that have the stones?"

"Yes," she said, through clinched teeth.

Eagleton's palms were sweating as he paced. "First we have Belleshota's business partner showing up over in Weavilwood asking questions, and now these men. I don't know if we have the resources to contain them."

Samantha spun around. "Contain them? This is our town, don't you forget that. They can't do anything here unless we let them."

"Suppose they find Belleshota?"

Samantha was rigid as a board with her arms folded. "How do you suppose they can accomplish that, if we can't?"

"I think we need to pull in more men from the mine to help us—just in case," he replied.

"No! We need every available man working on that airfield. I don't want Jai-Robson Priest's airplane here one minute more than it takes to conduct their business. Your job is to make sure everything runs smooth. How many deputies do you have on duty?"

"All of them. Four on the roadblocks, one at the airfield, and the rest are searching the foothills for Belleshota."

Samantha grabbed her jacket off the chair and walked toward the door. "Pull two back; I need them."

"Ms. Prophet, I can't do that. I'm already short."

"Do it. Belleshota is my responsibility." Samantha breezed past Poole like he was invisible as she left the office. The sheriff sat at his desk with a drink in his hand, and a worried look on his face.

Poole stepped into the office. "How'd it go?"

"How do you think it went? We've got visitors coming to town tomorrow, a crazy woman is on the loose, and her friends searching for her."

"You want me to take care of them?"

"No! You've caused enough of a mess. What I want you to do is go home, take a catnap, and then go over to the Roadster Inn. St. John and his friends are probably staying there. I don't want you to let them out of your sight. If they start fishing around in areas they shouldn't be, I want you to call me immediately and let me know."

* * *

On their way back to Weavilwood, Jordan took the highway cutoff at Route 17. She drove south fourteen miles in pitch darkness on a gravel road before stopping in front of a gate, dangling on rusty hinges.

Marcus turned on the overhead light and looked at the map. "You sure this is McCain's place?"

Jordan checked the coordinates on the GPS. "This is it. According to the printout, Sydney's Land Rover should be straight ahead, about a hundred or so yards."

Doc opened the window to the smell of hayfields. He used his flashlight to read the EPA warning posted on the fence. "Let's go."

Jordan drove through the gate. When they reached the farmhouse, Doc saw something off to the right. He turned the flashlight on and saw two vehicles parked in front of a barn.

Sydney's vehicle lay dormant in the sand alongside McCain's truck. Shotgun casings were on the ground.

"I guess the sheriff is in no hurry to secure the crime scene," Doc said, as he leaned over and picked up a shell casing.

Marcus grabbed another flashlight from the glove box. "I'll check the barn."

Jordan inspected Sydney's vehicle, and unlocked the hidden safe under the passenger seat. "Nothing here—and her security box is empty."

Doc found more shells on the other side of the truck. He knelt on the ground and examined the dark spot in the sand.

Marcus came out the barn, holding a cell phone and water bottle. "I found these and some blood by the door. The phone is Sydney's."

Doc came around the side of the Land Rover. "There's more blood in front of the truck, and someone took out Sydney's tires, which means that if she's alive, she's most likely on foot. Let's take a look in the house."

The century old farmhouse was empty, and the moon was visible through the corroded tin roof barely being supported on rotten beams.

Marcus felt something scurry across his foot. "Damn, Doc, there's nothing in this hole except rats and sand." Doc took another look around and agreed. If there was ever anything here, it was gone now.

Chapter 34

The sun was high in the sky by the time R.C. and Sydney reached the top of Hickcut Point. Charlie Whitefinger's house was an old forest station lookout tower, located at the top of the ridge. The three-story wooden structure was covered in aluminum and supported on a rock foundation. The square tower had an observation deck with glass windows extending around the building.

Sydney climbed the last few feet up the fire trail, before stopping to look at the tower. "Somebody actually lives up there?"

R.C. pulled himself up and joined her as they caught their breaths. "I told you he's not quite right in the head. Been that way ever since Iraq, I suppose." They began the slow climb up the decrepit steps to the observation deck. Several steps were missing.

"Isn't there another way into this place?" Sydney asked.

"Nope. Charlie covered the other entrance in sheet goods. He's got this bug about protection. He don't trust nobody. That's why he hides up here in this fort he calls home. This place was forest property back in '41' until some bright boy realized there weren't no wild land to protect. Folks used it during WW2 to watch for the Japanese coming to bomb us, but I reckon' the bright boy that come up with that idea was the same one that built it in the first place. Charlie picked it up for near nothing, and the town folks was glad to see him go."

Sydney noticed the quietness. The only sounds she heard were the birds and rustling of trees being blown by the humid air. "I don't hear anything. You sure he's here?"

R.C. choked as his lungs fought for more air. He stopped again to rest. "Oh, he's here, missy. Probably had his eye on us the whole way up the trail." He started up the steps again. Sydney's footsteps mirrored his as they made their way to the top.

Charlie Whitefingers was sitting on the observation deck, reading a newspaper in army boots and torn jeans, and no shirt. An assault rifle rested on his lap.

"Hey, Charlie—how you doing?" R.C. asked.

The half-Indian's face was expressionless. Whitefingers didn't look anything like what Sydney imagined. He had the gangly frame and jaunting jaw of Abraham Lincoln, but was the color of an Ethiopian, with the straight hair of a Shoshone. Whitefingers folded the paper.

"This here lady is Missy . . .?" R.C. had forgotten her name.

"Belleshota," Whitefingers answered, looking at her with the brooding chocolate eyes of an eagle.

"How do you know my name?" Sydney asked. He remained silent. She looked to R.C. for help.

"Charlie, she needs to use the radio. Them bastards in town are after her."

Whitefingers rose from the chair. "I know what she's done; it's all over the bandwidth. Why'd you bring her here?"

"She needs to use the radio to call . . ."

"No," Whitefingers said.

R.C. had warned her that Whitefingers could be difficult, but this was ridiculous. "Why?" Sydney asked.

"Because I don't know you and I'm not willing to risk my life to help you."

"All I'm guilty of is defending myself against a crazy deputy trying to kill me."

"Doesn't matter. You're not welcomed here."

Sydney's mouth sprang open, but no words came out. She threw her arms up in frustration as she tried controlling her anger. Whitefingers walked indoors. Sydney caught up with him and swung him around by the arm. "I didn't hike all these miles in this damn heat for nothing. I'm sorry I had to invade your little sanctuary here, but I need to use your radio."

Whitefingers pried her fingers off his arm. "Woman or not, I'll bounce you off this tower if you're not on the way down those steps when I blink again."

R.C. stepped in between them. "Charlie, settle down. This woman ain't done nothin', but be in the wrong place at the wrong

181

time. You know how the sheriff is always pressing folks. He hates us and anybody else that ain't like them. You don't help her, then she's as good as dead. You know that."

"She's already dead, and so are we if we interfere. They're coming after her," he said, pointing at the window behind them.

R.C. went over to the window. "I don't see nothin'."

Sydney went out onto the deck. All she saw were rocks, trees and mountains. "There's nothing down there."

Whitefingers stood behind her. He picked her hand off the rail and used it as a pointer. "Two men—a mile and a half below the saddle in the trees. They've been on your tail for the last two hours."

Chapter 35

Two horses snorted as they struggled and fought to make it to the top of the slope. One of the Weavilwood deputies dismounted.

Whitefingers watched as the deputy removed his cowboy hat and used a kerchief to wipe his bald head. The deputy saw the black Indian on the observation deck. "You must be Charlie Whitefingers."

"What do you want?" Whitefingers asked.

"We want to talk with R.C. Gingham."

R.C. came out to the rail. "I'm Gingham; I do something wrong?"

"That depends. We're hunting a woman fugitive wanted for murder."

"Ain't seen anyone for a couple of days, except Charlie here. I come to bring him some supplies."

"You came by yourself?" the deputy asked.

"Yup," R.C. said, as he chewed tobacco.

"Then you don't mind if we take a look up inside?"

R.C. gave Whitefingers a worried look.

"You step one foot on my property, I'll shoot you," Whitefingers said.

The deputy on the horse eased his rifle from the saddle sleeve.

His partner removed his mirrored sunglasses. "Now, Whitefingers, we don't want any trouble with you. We know Gingham didn't come up here alone. We've been following two sets of tracks all day, and they led us here. Now, that Belleshota woman is here and we're taking her back to town with us. The best thing you can do is step aside and let us do our jobs before someone gets hurt."

"You have a search warrant?" Whitefingers asked.

The deputy exhaled. "Yeah, we got a warrant. Show it to him, Marsh." Marsh whipped the rifle around and fired.

Whitefingers groaned, buckled his knees, and fell through the railing. A second shot sent R.C. stumbling back through the doorway.

* * *.

The deputy hovered over R.C. "Where's the woman, Gingham?" When R.C. didn't answer, the deputy grabbed him by the hair and slammed his head against the floor. "Talk!"

Marsh searched the tower but didn't find Sydney. "She couldn't have gotten far." He used his rifle butt and smashed the shortwave radio equipment.

"What did you do that for?" his partner asked.

"Just a precaution in case she tries to double back."

* * *

Sydney was hidden behind a secret wall in the closet where Whitefingers had pushed her. She stumbled around in total darkness until her face hit a cord suspended from the ceiling. When she pulled the cord, a battery powered light flickered on. The small bunker had a bed in the corner, food, and a cache of small arms and rifles mounted on the wall. There was a trap door in the floor with a rope attached, which she used to lower herself down to the hidden door in the foundation.

She crept around to the front of the house. Charlie Whitefingers lay face down in the dirt by the steps. Two gunshots rang out from the tower. Sydney bit down on her lip. They had killed R.C. She stroked the nervous mare as she slowly reached up and removed the rifle from the deputy's saddle.

* * *

Marsh leaned over the deck rail. "She must be in the woods." He signaled his partner that it was time to go. Midway down the steps, his foot sank through rotten timber. His partner grabbed his arm and pulled him free. When they turned around, they found themselves blinded by the reflection from a riflescope. Sydney fired twice.

* * *

Sydney kissed Gingham goodbye and lowered a blanket over his body. This was the second time he had saved her life, but this time it was at the expense of his life and his friend, Charlie Whitefingers. She was alone with no idea of how to get off the mountain in one piece. Next to the shattered shortwave, she saw a map tacked on a bulletin board, hanging from the wall. It was an outdated forest service map with red-penciled markings that appeared to be trails leading from the mountain. Sydney didn't know which one to take. She couldn't risk going back the way she came, and there was no way she was taking the trail that headed in the opposite direction from where she needed to go. That left the "forest service trail," which led down the mountain to a place called "Deception Pass." The pass led to the desert and eventually a military reservation.

Sydney packed some food and water in the saddle, then swung her body up on the horse. According to the map, it was over thirty miles to the desert floor, and another eighteen miles to the military reservation. Nellis Air Force Base and the federal government owned millions of acres of land in Nevada. Hopefully this was one of their reservations.

She jammed the rifle in the saddle and took another look at the map before tucking it into her waist. Deception Pass was just a dot on the map and she prayed it actually existed. She guided the horse to the edge of the slope and gently coaxed him down.

Chapter 36

Holloway didn't think things could get any worse for him, but he was wrong. The botched attempt to kill St. John ended up costing him more than just a sleepless night of agonizing pain.

After digging St. John's bullet from his arm and spending the rest of the evening popping pain pills, he wasn't in any shape to go anywhere. By the time the drugs wore off and he could drive, it was too late. The hotel clerk at the Legend told him that St. John and Sebasst had checked out of their rooms and left town. Holloway went straight to the bar.

Everything had gone wrong. St. John was gone, his career was in the toilet, and the only tangible reward he had for his effort was the $15,000 he'd received from Jai-Robson Priest. In hindsight, even the cash had been a mistake. He hadn't asked for enough. He should have squeezed Priest for more money, but it was too late for that too. If Priest had any sense, he'd leave town before the cops discovered that the burned corpses on the mountain road were his men.

Holloway spent the next two hours in the bar drinking. Finally, when he was tired of his own pity-party, he knew he had to find a way to benefit from his misfortune. By the time he finished his sixth drink, he had a plan.

He had seen and heard enough over the last four days to know that Cassandra Prophet was not the patron saint she pretended to be. She and her criminal associates were up to something big—and he thought he knew what it was.

It had to do with the stones and the gold mine in Nevada that he had overheard the U.W. professor talking about with Sebasst. St. John was in possession of a map that Cassandra wanted. What wasn't clear was why that was so important to her. If he could figure that out, she would pay him to keep his mouth shut. Maybe even make him a partner.

Holloway paid his tab and went outside. His legs were a little wobbly, but he felt good enough to drive. He started the truck and headed to Cassandra Prophet's estate.

* * *

After lunch, Cassandra received a telephone call from Jai-Robson Priest. She took the call in her bedroom. She came out angry and went straight to the greenhouse to see Kane.

"Get the car ready, we're going to the office," she said.

"I thought the cleaners were scheduled to work today."

"Elias, just do as I said!" She stormed off, slamming the greenhouse door behind her. Kane dropped the dead foliage from his hand into the trash, and put on his coat. Something was wrong. He went to the garage and brought the Mercedes around to the front door. Twenty minutes later, Cassandra came out in jeans and flip-flops and got in the front seat with Kane. Her face was paler than usual.

"We're not taking Hanna with us?" he asked.

"I left her with the maid until Clair arrives."

"I thought you gave her the day off since we were staying home."

"Well, obviously we aren't going to be home. Now start the car."

Kane opened the electronic gate and turned out onto the street. As he drove up the hill, he noticed an unfamiliar white pickup following behind.

"Drop me off at the office and then go pick up Clair. She's expecting you. When you get back to the house, pack. I'm going on a short trip with Priest and you're coming with me," Cassandra said.

"How long will we be gone?"

"I don't know. Is Priest's manuscript in the vault or my safe?"

"The vault."

"I'll get it. After he and I conclude our business, you can give it to him. Not a minute before." She turned and looked out the window, and didn't speak for the rest of the trip.

187

Kane dropped her off at the garage elevator, then drove back up the ramp to the 5th Avenue exit. While he waited for the traffic to let him in, he looked for the white truck. He found it parked at the corner intersection. Kane eased out into traffic and headed to the freeway.

He took the bridge to West Seattle. The pickup maintained a safe distance behind, changing lanes often to avoid being detected. He wasn't doing a good job. Kane didn't know who was following him and it didn't matter. It further complicated an already complicated situation for him. He had spent four years of his life for an opportunity to travel with Cassandra to Nevada, and nothing short of him being killed was going to stop him now. He planned to be on that flight with Cassandra, and Hanna needed to be with him. He just needed a way to persuade Cassandra.

Kane exited at Alkai Beach and pulled into an alley in back of a cream-colored house. The back door was locked.

He pulled a small file from his pocket, picked the lock, and entered through the utility room. The first floor was empty. He quietly went up the stairs to the hallway. The elderly nanny was in the bathroom with her back to him, combing her hair. She didn't see or hear him until it was too late. He grabbed her from behind, snapped her neck, and eased her plump body to the floor.

* * *

What the hell is taking him so long? Holloway was sitting in his truck across the street, impatiently waiting for Kane to come out of the house. He had been watching the house for the last hour, but hadn't seen any activity since Kane had entered. Kane's car was still parked in the alley. Holloway realized he was wasting his time following Kane. If he really wanted to know what Cassandra was up to, he needed to be at her office where she was. Yet, the more he sat and watched the more curious he was about what Kane was doing. He tossed his binoculars on the seat and started the truck.

Holloway angled the truck into the alley and parked alongside the garage next to Kane's car, but was hidden from the house. He waited until he was sure the alley was empty before

188

getting out with his camera. He crept along the side of the house and looked in the window. There wasn't anyone in the living room. He moved to the next window, but still didn't see anyone.

He must be upstairs.

Holloway jimmied the window open and climbed in. He walked to the stairs and stopped. It was too quiet. He got scared and went back out the window, closing it behind him. When he reached the alley, Kane's car was gone.

* * *

On his way home, Holloway's truck swerved across the centerline, twice. He took another drink and tossed the empty bottle out of the window. He couldn't think rationally. He was still trying to figure out how Kane managed to get past him. He had thought about going to Cassandra's office, but decided it was pointless. It would be easier to search her office tonight after the building was empty.

Holloway stopped at his favorite tavern and picked up pizza for dinner. When he got to his house, a message from his attorney was waiting for him on his answering machine. The Board of Inquiry would be rendering their decision on his case tomorrow morning. Holloway cursed as he deleted the message. He knew what the finding would be and he had no intention on attending. He had been humiliated enough.

He rubbed his arm. With all the liquor he had consumed, it hadn't done anything to dull the pain. He went to the kitchen to get his pills, but found them scattered across the floor.

"Shit," he said, bending down to pick them up. He heard a noise and looked up. Kane was standing behind him.

Chapter 37

Cassandra sat at Kane's desk, staring at the maroon walls filled with Remington paintings. The western art reminded her of how much she missed Santa Fe. It was home, the place her parents were buried. But it was also the place of bad memories for her sister. They had moved to Seattle for a new start. The thought that they might have to relocate again was a distinct possibility, particularly if she was right about Priest.

The telephone on Kane's desk rang. Cassandra didn't bother to answer it. Instead, she reached across the desk and yanked the phone line from the wall.

She was in a foul mood, brought on by the telephone conversation she had earlier with Priest. He called to say he was leaving the country and he wouldn't be back. The reason: Sebasst could cause him problems and he didn't need the attention, especially from the State Department. Cassandra knew it was a lie, but she couldn't change his mind—even when she told him he would forfeit his two million dollar deposit.

Priest was impulsive and unpredictable, but he wasn't the kind of man to throw away two million dollars, and he wasn't easily scared. She believed he was running because he had done something stupid. Her first instinct was to let him go. Give him his scroll, keep his money, and cut her losses. That's what she wanted to do, but she couldn't. She had more than one million dollars already invested, and would lose a lot more if she allowed him to walk away.

* * *

For six years Cassandra had been supplying Priest with everything from weapons to women. But thirteen months ago he contacted her for something special.

"This is a joke, right?" she asked.

Priest flashed his white teeth. "This is no joke, Cassie. I have many clients willing to pay me vast sums of money to provide them with the youthful treasures you can provide."

"Sixty girls?"

He laughed. "Many men desire the warmth of a youthful woman. The great Solomon once said, 'the joints of thy thighs are like jewels, the work of the hands of a cunning workman.'"

Cassandra knew he was a pedophile, but she didn't let that bother her. What she did care about was how she was going to find and move that much product in one shipment. Moving pregnant teens and babies was risky business, but finding and transporting blue-eyed blonde girls, between the ages of nine and twelve would be almost impossible.

Her overseas supplier had been murdered in Kiev, four months earlier. Without him, Cassandra had to work outside of her usual network to get the girls. She spent months searching Eastern Europe for just the right ones, and paid hundreds of thousands of dollars in bribes, fees, and forged documents. But the biggest expense and challenge was solving the security and logistical nightmare of transporting and smuggling sixty girls across the globe to the United States.

The risks were enormous and the costs were high, but the payoff was huge. If she pulled it off, Priest was primed to pay her twenty million dollars once the girls were delivered to Poison Springs.

After her distressing conversation with him this morning, Cassandra had to call Eagleton and tell him about the change in plans. Eagleton assured her the airstrip would be ready for their arrival and that security would be tight. Even so, she felt anxious. Something could still go wrong.

* * *

Cassandra rose from behind Kane's desk and went to the vault. Kane had sealed Priest's scroll in an airtight shipping container. She tucked it under her arm and closed the vault door behind her.

She stood in the doorway watching the workers move her furniture back in place. One of the men accidentally brushed against the bookshelf, knocking a silver-plated frame from the shelf. He caught it before it hit the floor and gently placed it back on the display holder.

The Daguerreotype photo was of a dour face man with a kaiser moustache. It was the only picture Cassandra had of her ancestor, Alpaca Uriah Prophet.

Cassandra remembered her father's stories about their great-great grandfather. He was an Englishman who had come to America with nothing more than a strong work ethic and strong back. The only legacy he left was an old cowhide map to his gold mine in the Nevada desert.

Her father kept the worthless map preserved between the pages of his favorite bible, which Cassandra inherited. She threw away the bible, but used the map to find the mine. While the mine had been stripped of its gold, Cassandra found it valuable. It was ideal for her base of operations, and she did everything to protect its location.

Years of mixing fiction with fact along with a little folklore, kept fortune hunters busy looking for the mine in the mountains instead of the desert. That changed eleven months ago when Dr. Trevor Constantine knocked on Cassandra's door.

He told her that he was searching for a series of hand-carved stones made by her great-great grandfather with the directions to the gold mine.

Cassandra had heard rumors about the stones, but never believed the stories. Constantine showed her his research papers on a Belgian anthropologist named Brogo.

Brogo discovered the stones in 1921 on the Gushuite Indian Reservation, where he was researching the oral history of the Western Shoshone. After his death, the stones and his other possessions were shipped to his family in Belgium and sold to an auction house in 1953.

Constantine had searched for the person that purchased the stones. He eventually traced them to a deceased woman, whose family lived in Cape Town, South Africa. Constantine spent the last two summers traveling to Europe pursuing leads, and was confident he was close to finding the stones. So confident, that his friends were taking one-year sabbaticals from their respective universities to travel with him to South Africa to continue the search. But of course that required a lot of money—money Constantine didn't have. He wanted Cassandra to underwrite the cost, in exchange for whatever they found in the mine. Constantine's only interest was in acquiring the stones, which he felt were of immense historical value.

Cassandra politely rejected his offer, telling him that she didn't invest in speculative ventures—especially "fortune hunting," which was extremely risky and offered no guarantee of a return. Constantine had left her house disappointed, but not discouraged.

From the day he and his associates arrived in Cape Town, Cassandra had Erik Roth keeping an eye on them. Since then, she had tried everything to get the stones. Now that they were in St. John's possession, and he was in Poison Springs, Cassandra had reason to be worried.

* * *

A janitor pulled the steam cleaner into the hall. "You can use your office now, miss."

Cassandra crushed the empty soda can in her hands and dropped it in the trash. Just as she was going into the office, the elevator door opened. Kane stepped off with Hanna holding his hand.

"What's she doing with you?" Cassandra asked.

"Clair wasn't home. Are you sure she knew I was coming to get her?"

"Of course she knew. I spoke to her just before we left. I can't believe she did this. Give me your phone!" Kane handed her the cell phone.

She called the nanny's house, but there was no answer. "What am I suppose to do now? It's too late to try and find someone to watch her. I can't believe Clair did this . . ."

Kane placed a hand on her shoulder as she started crying. "It'll be okay. We can take her with us. I'll watch her."

Chapter 38

Poole found himself staring at a mountain of pink hair rollers attached to his snoring wife. He slipped out of bed and got dressed. She rolled over on her stomach and farted. If this was all he had to look forward to, he'd rather put a bullet in his head now. He thought about Rose. She and her brat had probably hitched a ride out of the valley and were hundreds of miles away by now. He took comfort in knowing that she would keep her mouth shut, because the only thing she feared more than him was being deported.

Poole made some sandwiches and coffee. He had a long day ahead of him. Things had dramatically changed in the last three hours.

The Sheriff had called to tell him that Cassandra Prophet would be arriving late this afternoon. Everyone had been redeployed to ensure the airfield would be ready. Eagleton had pulled back the deputies to provide security, while the miners were finishing the airstrip. That left Samantha Prophet and two deputies out searching for Belleshota.

The manpower shortage worked to Poole's advantage. The sheriff had assigned him to watch Sebasst and St. John. As Poole saw it, Sebasst and St. John were smart and had just as good a chance of finding her as anyone. Their odds would improve dramatically if she knew they were in town. All he had to do was stick close to them and wait to see if she'd make contact.

When he arrived at the Roadside Inn, the manager was waiting for him outside.

"They're not here," the manager said.

"What do you mean they're not here?"

"The black woman booked their rooms last night, but they never showed up. I figured they must have left town."

"Why the hell didn't you call and tell me this?" Poole yelled.

"Hey, I just found out myself."

Poole went inside the motel. He grabbed the telephone book and called the motels in Weavilwood. No one had seen them. He went back to the Jeep. *Where are they?*

* * *

The beep from the telephone woke Doc. He reached up on the consol and picked up the receiver. "Hello," he whispered.

"Julian, where are you?" asked Alexia Davidovich.

"Good morning to you, too," he said, as he turned the cabin light on.

"Sorry for the early call. Mr. Rood gave me this number. Are you okay?"

"Yeah, I'm fine. Just a little groggy."

"You slept on the airplane?"

Doc yawned. "It's a long story, but the U.S. Marshall doesn't care about my room accommodations. What's up?"

"I ran Elias Kane's photo through our facial recognition software and came up with some interesting and rather disturbing information. Whoever he is, he's not Elias Kane. The real Elias Kane died in 1953 in Ogden, Utah."

"So his passport records are fake?" Doc asked.

"Everything about him is a fake. There is nothing to indicate that he lived in the United States prior to coming to work for Cassandra Prophet."

"You think he's a foreign national?"

"I don't know, but if he's American, he certainly has been busy overseas. The Russian have an international warrant issued for him in the murder of a retired Russians general, and Scotland Yard wants to talk to him about the death of one of his previous employers in Manchester."

"Who was he?"

"Not a he—a she. She was a Ukrainian doctor who the authorities discovered later was operating an illegal baby adoption service."

Doc sat up straight and rubbed his eyes. "Any connection between the doctor and the Russian general?"

"More than likely, but nothing confirmed. He was in charge of regulating Russia's state-supported orphanages."

"Russia and England. Kane does get around."

"That's not the half of it. The French, Croatians, and Saudis also want him for a string of suspicious murders in their countries."

"And you still can't identify him?"

"We have no idea who he is. Flight records under his alias shows he spent time in Buenos Aires as a pilot working with an Argentinean businesswoman named Perguree, who controls the second largest arms cartel south of Mexico. He also spent time in Lebanon with Omar Abazullan, better known as *The Lebanese*—a wealthy Arab, whose family is heavily involved in arms dealing. Both Abazullan and Perguree were with Jai-Robson Priest at Cassandra Prophet's house. All three are suspected of being members of a larger group of a loose confederation of criminals who share resources and services."

"Then Cassandra Prophet is probably involved."

"More than you know. Detective Holloway's attorney found him dead, yesterday at his home, with a gunshot to his head."

Doc's head was spinning in confusion. "And you think it was Cassandra Prophet?"

"She or Kane. The police found video and audio tapes in Holloway's truck. One of the recordings showed Kane entertaining Priest, Abazullan, and Perguree at Cassandra's house the night of her charity benefit. The police went to pick up Kane this morning, but he's gone—and so are the Prophets."

"Gone where?"

"According to the maid—on a business trip to Germany."

"I don't think Cassandra is going anywhere without her big sister. Samantha Prophet is here in Poison Springs."

"What is she doing there?"

"I haven't figured that out yet."

* * *

Jordan Bloodstone finished washing her face and got dressed. When she came out of the lavatory, Doc was still on the

196

telephone with Alexia and Marcus was sprawled across the other divan, asleep.

Marcus heard the hatch door opening. He opened his eyes to see Jordan dressed in khaki shorts, military boots, and baseball cap. Even with boots, she looked small. With a boy-cut hairstyle and youthful face, she couldn't convince anyone she was forty years-old.

"Where are you going?" he asked.

"Out to get some fresh air."

"Be careful—and remember not to get too close to that mine or airfield you were telling us about."

Jordan rolled the hangar door open and hot air hit her face like a blast from a furnace. The desert was as foreboding as it was last night, with miles of sand and an occasional outcropping of rocks and cactus. The large hill to the south separated the desert from the White River Copper Mine and airfield.

Jordan headed north. As her body acclimated to the heat, she picked up the pace and was soon running at normal speed. It wasn't long before her mind was more focused on Sydney than on the direction she was running.

She and Sydney were business partners, but also close friends, although it hadn't always been that way. When Sydney and Jordan worked for Marcus, the women didn't like each other. Over time, they learned to respect each other and their differences. Jordan was methodical and patient, while Sydney was impulsive and relied on instincts. It was those traits, and her mental toughness and determination that Jordan hoped would keep Sydney alive.

Jordan ran for thirty minutes and stopped when she reached a sand dune and realized she might be lost. Running in sand in the middle of the desert had not been one of her better ideas. Her cap was drenched in sweat, and she was exhausted. She re-tied her boot laces and was about to leave, when a yellow Jeep suddenly appeared from over the dune. Two Weavilwood deputies got out.

"Hey—stop!" a voice said. Jordan cursed under her breath. One of the men approached her. "What are you doing out here?"

"Jogging," she said, in between breaths.

"This sector is off limits to civilians."

"Sorry, I didn't know that." She turned to leave.

The deputy caught her by the elbow. "Not so fast. We need to see some identification."

"Why?"

The deputy was caught off guard. "Ma'am, I don't want to argue with you, just let me see some I.D."

"Okay." She removed a passport wallet from her shorts and handed it to him. The other deputy kept his eyes glued to her as his partner flipped through the wallet. He looked at the driver's license, and then turned to her military identification. His eyes lingered on her photo for an uncomfortable twenty seconds, before he finally gave it back.

"You're a Marine colonel?" he asked.

"Was," she said.

"Then you of all people should understand the need to keep civilians off a military reservation."

"As I said, I'm sorry. I wasn't paying attention to where I was going. If you tell me how to get out of here, I'll be glad to leave."

"A person just doesn't accidentally wind up in the middle of this place unless they're after something or looking for something. Which one are you?"

"I told you what I was doing."

"Well, I don't believe you. I'm going to ask you one more time; what are you doing on this reservation?" He stared at her, while his hand rested on his gun holster.

"That's your choice, but it's the truth," she replied. Jordan knew she had been made. There was no way they were going to let her go, and she was tired of playing their game. "The Air Force hasn't owned this property for over sixteen years, so I could just as well ask you the same question."

The deputy withdrew his radio off his hip. "We better call this . . ."

198

Before the next words left his mouth, Jordan crippled him with a kick to the groin, snatched the radio from his hand, and slammed it against the other man's skull. They both dropped to the ground, and she finished them off with knee kicks to the jaw.

She cuffed the men together, shoved them into the back of the Blazer, and closed the hatch. As she went to get in the vehicle, she thought she heard someone crying. She looked around, but didn't see anything.

Jordan started the engine and disengaged the brakes. Then she heard the sound again. She grabbed one of the handguns on the seat and got out of the truck. She walked to the back of the Blazer and followed the muted sound to a cluster of sage bushes rooted by a dried waterhole. The bushes stirred. Jordan carefully circled around the bushes and came up from behind. She found herself staring at a terrified woman holding a hand across the mouth of a frightened toddler. The other hand was trying to get her to accept Sydney's bracelet.

Chapter 39

Jai-Robson Priest's plane was as large and ostentatious as his ego. The re-tooled 747 airliner had gold-plated accoutrements and space enough to comfortably seat 400 passengers, even though he rarely traveled with more than his entourage, three pilots, and occasional guests, like Cassandra Prophet.

Cassandra sat in mid-cabin typing on her notebook while talking with Eagleton on the phone. "And my sister, any word from her?"

"No. She's up on Hickcut Point checking on a pair of deputies from Weavilwood who haven't reported in. It's impossible to get any kind of radio reception until she reaches the peak."

"Notify me when she contacts you." She snapped the phone shut and turned her attention back to her notebook. Kane sat beside her playing cards on the lap tray. Hanna was stretched out on the seat in front of them playing with toys.

One of Priest's men approached Cassandra. "The minister wishes to see you." Cassandra looked up and saw Priest sitting in the galley. He motioned for her to join him. Cassandra sighed and closed the computer.

Kane stopped shuffling the cards. "You want me to come with you?"

"No, stay with Hanna." She slipped on her shoes and climbed up the spiral staircase. Priest was stretched out on the couch in his white army uniform. He pushed his giant bible off the couch to make room for her.

"Come, Cassie; sit beside me." Instead, she sat in the seat across from him. She wiped away the imaginary lint on her pants, and nervously twisted a button on her blouse.

Priest laughed. "You are afraid of me; I cannot believe this."

She crossed her legs. "Fear has nothing to do with it. This is business—until I receive the rest of the money you owe me."

"Cassie, Cassie . . ." he said, leaning over and grabbing a large cigar off the table. "We are friends. Have I ever given you reason to doubt me or not trust me? Do not worry, you will be paid all that I owe once I see and approve what I am paying for."

"Have I ever given you reason not to trust me?" she asked.

Priest blew a large smoke ring at the ceiling and laughed. "You are a remarkable woman, Cassie. You must reconsider my proposal and unite with me. Together we could do mighty things."

Cassandra fanned the smoke away with her hand. "You know I work alone."

"But in my country, you would be under my protection and be free to conduct business uninterrupted by meddling fools who frown on such things here in America.

"I have all the protection I need, thank you," she said, glancing down at Kane.

"Your manservant, Kane? He is small and only one man. I have armies at my disposal."

"A wise person would not underestimate Elias's abilities, and you are a wise man."

"Indeed I am," he smiled.

Kane kept his eyes on them as he pulled a handgun from inside his coat and placed it on the seat next to him. He didn't expect any trouble on an airplane, but he wasn't taking any chances. When no one was watching, he reached under his seat and pulled out Hanna's toy bag, placing it on the tray in front of him.

Hanna strained to see over the back of the seat. "Uncle, what are you doing?"

Kane's hands remained hidden in the bag, working. "I'm just putting away my cards."

"Will you play with me?"

"When the airplane lands. Now sit down and buckle your seat belt real tight like a big girl. The airplane will be landing very soon."

"I want to sit next to you."

"No, you need to stay where you are. If you scoot over to the window you can see the sand below." Hanna's brown eyes lit up like Christmas. She bounced over to the window seat and pressed her forehead against the glass.

"Uncle, I see small cars!"

Kane looked off the left wing and saw a row of jeeps lined up along the runway. While she was riveted to the window, he cinched the toy bag closed and pushed it back under the seat. Kane grabbed the transport tube that contained the scroll and slipped the shoulder strap over his head. He put his gun away and waited for the airplane to land.

* * *

Samantha Prophet was stepping over dead bodies at Charlie Whitefinger's house when she saw Priest's jetliner passing over Hickcut Point. R.C. Gingham lay sprawled in a pool of blood on the floor, and two deputies were dead on the outdoor stairs—one dangling upside down with his foot wedged between the rotten steps.

"Get him down," Samantha said to the deputy.

Deputy Stephenson came in off the observation deck. "Belleshota's not here, if she ever was."

"She was here. Who else would shoot them with their own rifle?" Samantha asked, as she inspected the .50 caliber bullet hole in one of the deputies. From the stairs, she saw fresh hoof marks leading down the hill and disappearing into the trees. "Belleshota is headed toward the mission. She jumped over the handrail and landed on the ground. "Let's go."

The deputies hated Samantha Prophet. She was relentless. Nothing slowed her down. Not the heat, not fatigue, and certainly not their complaints. She had driven them hard to Gingham's hut, where they found Belleshota's leather jacket and McCain's dog. Then, she drove them nonstop for seven hours until they reached Whitefingers' house.

"Miss Prophet, the horses need watering and rest," Stephenson said.

Samantha flung herself in the saddle. "We are not stopping until we catch this bitch. When she's dead, then you can rest." She yanked the horse's reign and he started trotting down the slope.

Chapter 40

No wonder they call it Deception Pass. Sydney dragged the reins of her horse while walking along the stream of jagged rocks. For two hours she had searched, unsuccessfully, for the entrance to the pass marked on her map. The pass was the only route leading through the mountain to the desert. All she found so far was a wall of rock. She stopped to rest the horse. She was tired too, but the fatigue was mental, not physical. Sydney was constantly looking over her shoulder to see who was chasing her. Although she never saw anyone, her instincts told her she was being tracked, and they weren't far behind.

Sydney knelt down at the stream and splashed cold water on her face. She sat back against the rocks and thought about her situation. It almost seemed pointless to continue running, because she really didn't know where she was going or what she would do once she got there. The one thing she did know was she didn't want to end up dead like R.C. and Whitefingers. She pulled Constantine's rumpled letter from her pocket and read it again:

Joshua

I write you this letter in hope that it will find its way to you. By now you should have received the telephone message I left on your answering machine. I have found the stones, which I entrusted to Mr. Marcus St. John of the Cornerstone Global Insurance Company in Seattle. In the event something should happen to me, he has been instructed to give you the stones, once you tell him my father's gravesite. I only ask one favor. When you are through with the stones, please give them to Leicester for me. The treasure is of no consequence to me (you have always known this, but they represent a marvelous period of our American West and must be preserved.)

Trevor

Sydney folded the letter and put it back in her pocket. She traveled downstream for six miles and found a brook streaming down the face of the mountain. She followed the trail of water over the rocks until she reached an opening in the mountain. The cave was dark, wet, and barely large enough for the horse to squeeze through. Sydney coaxed the animal down a muddy trail that ended in front of a waterfall. She jumped back on the horse and guided him under the falls to the other side and deception pass.

The pass was a one-horse trail surrounded in canyon cliffs. Travel was slow and difficult across the rocky terrain, but eventually the rocks gave way to shrub grass, then sand. The trail meandered down to a draw of more brush and trees. On the other side of the draw was a road. The dirt road looked like it hadn't seen a tire in months. A nineteenth century Spanish mission sat abandoned off the road.

Sydney pried the crisscrossed planks off the stucco siding and kicked the doors open. A flock of birds shot over her head and out the doors. The dilapidated mission turned out to be nothing more than an anthropological relic filled with broken pews and a sanctuary for rats. Sydney stumbled out of the building, gagging for fresh air.

She pulled Whitefingers' map from her pocket and stretched it out against the post beam. As near as she could tell, the road she was on ran along the foothills and connected to the main highway. The alternative route was through the desert. According to the map, the reservation was only eight miles away as the crow flies. But experience had shown there was no direct route to any place in this valley.

Sydney flinched when a desert lizard slither across her boot—the same time that a .50 caliber bullet shattered the post near her hand.

"Shit." Sydney saw a cloud of dust and horses flying down the mountain trail. She ran along the side of the mission as bullets tore at the stucco above her head. Leaping on her horse, she pulled the reins—spinning him around one hundred and eight degrees,

205

then dug her heels into his flanks. The stallion shot north into the desert.

Chapter 41

Marcus was in the lavatory shaving when the floor began vibrating, and turbo engines rattled the windows. A can of shaving cream shimmied across the counter and dropped in the sink.

He ran outside with shaving cream still on his face and a towel draped over his shoulder. "What was that?"

"An airplane. It just flew over that hill. It must be landing at the airfield."

"It sounded like it was dropping on top of us."

Suddenly, a Chevy Blazer bounced over the hill, speeding toward them leaving a cloud of sand behind. They slid the doors open to let Jordan in. Marcus peered into the tinted windows and saw two bound deputies in the back. In the front was a half-conscious woman clutching a sleeping child.

He opened the passenger door. The woman was sunburned and dehydrated. "She looks half-dead. Who is she?" he asked as he touched the little girl's head.

Rose's eyes sprung open. She screamed and attacked Marcus with her nails.

He caught her arms. "Hey, lady, take it easy. I'm only trying to help. . ." Rose fainted in his arms. He laid her back on the seat. "What the hell is wrong with her?" Jordan wiped a finger across his cheek, showing him that his face was still lathered in cream.

Doc opened the hatch door to get the deputies. "What happened?"

Jordan helped him drag the men out. "I ran into some trouble over by the copper mine. I didn't have any choice but to bring them back with me."

The woman and child were hiding in the desert. Her name is Tatiana."

"Russian?" Doc asked.

"Armenian."

207

"What in the world is she doing here?" Marcus asked.

Jordan lifted the child in her arms. "She and her brother fled to nearby Russia during her country's war with Azerbaijan. They separated and she ended up pregnant in an orphanage in the Republic of Georgia. Her boyfriend introduced her to an adoption broker—a Ukrainian woman working in the former Soviet states. The woman promised her a job and transportation to the United States, in exchange for her baby. She agreed, and the woman paid the orphanage $2,000 for her freedom. She was put on a ship along with several other young women and sent to England. From there she was flown to Mexico and bused into the United States. Deputy Poole had her stashed in a brothel in Weavilwood."

"That's messed up. What happened to the others that were with her?" Marcus asked.

"She never saw them again."

"What was she doing in the desert?"

"Running away from Poole . . ." Jordan pulled Sydney's bracelet from her pocket. "And looking for someone willing to help her."

"That's Sydney's. Where did she get it?" Marcus asked.

"Poole had it."

"How did she get to Poison Springs?" Doc asked.

"That's the strange part. She says she was transported by boat."

"Boat?" Doc asked.

"Yes."

"That's crazy. I have seen more water in a teacup than I have seen around here," Marcus said. Doc turned and went to the jet. Marcus looked at Jordan. "What's he doing?"

* * *

Doc spread the map out on the table. "We know that Poison Springs was built over the mining camp, Crazy Flats, and that the Alpaca map shows a body of water flowing east and west, through the camp and beyond. If the water source is still there, it could explain how Tatiana got here."

Marcus studied the map. "According to this, the White River is the nearest body of water from here, but it's at least two hundred miles away."

"Yeah, but remember what Professor Shengatti said. It could be an offshoot of the Colorado River."

"That's even further away. Besides, even if it is, I haven't seen as much as a mud hole around here."

Doc thought for a moment. "It could be underground. Crazy Flats was a mining camp and mining camps have tunnels. What if there's a tributary flowing though the tunnels?"

Marcus stroked his chin. "That they're using to smuggle girls into Poison Springs?"

Doc saw the doubt on his face. "Why not?"

Marcus arched an eyebrow. "Because an underground river of any size in this desert wasteland would have made the cover of the National Geographic, if it existed."

"Is that right. How many people do you think have even heard of Crazy Flats, much less know it's buried under Poison Springs? While you're chewing on that, also think about this: the Prophets aren't trying to get their hands on the stones so they can find the gold mine. I think they know exactly where it's at. So, that makes me wonder why they would kill to keep its location a secret. The only conclusion that makes sense to me is that they're doing something there they don't want anyone to see."

"Smuggling?" Marcus said.

"Could be," Doc said.

"If you're right, the access point is probably well concealed. It would be difficult to find," Jordan said.

"We'll take another look around Joshua McCain's farmhouse. Two men died there and it was the last place Sydney was seen. I'd say that's a good place to start looking," Doc said.

* * *

Poole left the Roadster Inn and went to the office, fully expecting to being told to clear out his desk. He had no idea where St. John and Sebasst were.

Instead of being fired, the sheriff told him he was making the trip to White Pine Mountains. Poole almost fainted. He hadn't been allowed to go to Cattail Falls in three years. But now he was on the security detail assigned to escort the girls, who were arriving from Mexico. He didn't know who the buyer was, but he was already envious. Cassandra Prophet had excellent taste in selecting women. As he drove east toward the mountains, he formatted a plan on how to steal another Rose.

* * *

Cattail Falls Wilderness was located on forty acres of wetlands in the foothills. Two school buses wobbled over soggy road and stopped at the gate. Poole checked underneath the buses for anything suspicious. Satisfied, he stood and slowly walked around the second bus, dragging his fingers along the side as he went. He stood on his toes, trying to peer through the black tinted windows, but he couldn't see anything.

He tapped his flashlight on the bus door. The driver opened the door. "How many have you got in this shipment?"

"Sixty," said the driver.

"You sure?"

"Of course I'm sure. You can recount them if you like."

Poole stepped up on the platform. "Yeah, I might just do that. Any trouble?"

"No, a few of them started wailing a ways back when we put on their hoods, but no big deal."

Pooled strolled the aisle looking left then right at the identically dressed teenage girls, in black blazers, white blouses, and plaid skirts. He removed the hood from one of the girls, then another. Despite the fear on their faces, they were pretty, and blonde. "They're all blondes?"

"Every one of them," said the driver. "They're gonna make someone mighty happy."

"Uh huh," Poole said, staring at the willowy frame of a tall girl sitting by the window. He reached over and lifted the hem of her skirt with his flashlight. She squirmed and pushed his hand away. He laughed.

"Knock it off, Poole. These girls are bought and paid for," said the miner sitting in the back of the bus. I'm here to see that *all* the girls arrive *safely*."

Embarrassed, Poole left and got back in the Jeep. He signaled the guard to open the gate.

The buses followed Poole's vehicle along the marsh road, passing acres of sword-shaped cattails and grass sledge. The road dipped through a pool of shallow water, then climbed a half-mile to the entrance of the preserve.

Cattail Falls didn't look any different than the two dozen ghost towns on the mountain, except this one was owned by Cassandra Prophet and was off limits to the public. The only standing buildings were a two-hundred-year-old corncrib and mill.

The town's mill once powered the water wheel, which was used to grind corn into meal and to provide residents with an endless supply of water. So much water in fact, that eventually the runoff from the mountain saturated the town, making it uninhabitable.

* * *

Poole led the girls down the stairway to the elevator at the bottom of the mill. From there, they travelled 750 feet underground where they heard the rushing water. One of the girls managed to get the hood off her head. Her eyes confirmed what her heart already knew. The promise of a good life in America had been a lie. She was the first one pulled onto the military amphibious boat.

Chapter 42

Doc and Marcus searched the farmhouse for nearly an hour, with no luck.

Marcus struck the top of the well cap with a tire iron. "This is solid cement, Doc, just like the other one. If there is water on this farm I don't know how we're going to get to it. Anyway, we've been out here too long, already. We're wasting time. We need to find Sydney."

Doc re-read the warning sign posted over the barn door. "And how do you propose we go about doing that considering we have no idea where to look?"

"We know Poole had her bracelet, which tells me he's got a pretty good idea of where she's at. I say we go after him."

Doc walked over to the other well. "You can't just waltz into the Sheriff's office and kidnap him."

"Okay, we find out where he lives and go to his house."

"That would be a pretty stupid thing to do," Doc said, inspecting the well head.

Marcus slammed the tire iron against the well. "It's better than nothing and it sure beats the hell out of turning up the desert sand out here looking for water. You got a better idea?"

Doc headed toward the barn. "We keep looking here until we find the source that feeds these wells."

"What makes you think there's still water under this place?"

"I don't know much about contaminants, but it seems a little excessive to me that the EPA or any other agency would go to the extreme of capping wells—especially out here in the middle of the desert. Come on, let's try the barn again."

Marcus climbed up the ladder to the hayloft, while Doc searched below.

"There's nothing up here," Marcus yelled.

"Nothing here either," Doc said, tossing a bale of hay out of his way. "I'm coming up." He stepped on the first rung of the ladder and felt something odd. It was ever so subtle, ever so slight, but it was there; a cool wisp of air against his naked ankle. Doc swept away the straw and dirt from under the ladder, exposing a seam in the floor. He tried pushing the ladder out of the way, but it didn't budge. It was anchored to the floor. Doc pulled up on the ladder, which popped it loose from the floor, revealing a hole with stairs.

"I've got something," he said.

Marcus jumped down off the loft.

The short steps led down to a storage cellar and a trapdoor in the floor. Doc tugged on the handle, but it didn't move. Marcus grabbed hold and they pulled together, but the door still didn't open.

"It feels like it's locked," Doc said.

"Locked, why would it be locked from underneath?"

"We're going to find out. Hand me your tire iron." Doc pried away one of the planks around the door, then the second and third. He pulled the flashlight from his pocket and looked underneath the trapdoor, where he saw a lock attached to the latch. He worked the tire iron under the latch, broke it off, then lifted the door open.

Marcus shined the flashlight on yet another series of steps. "Damn, this is ridiculous." They entered the black hole and followed the stairs into what looked like a mining tunnel.

The cavern was pitch black. They moved slowly, following the flashlight beam at their feet. Each step sank them deeper in groundwater.

Marcus's $700 shoes were covered in mud. "I'm going to beat your ass if I come up with some kind of cancer messing with you down here."

Doc heard the rush of water from behind the wall of hand-sewn timbers. "There is nothing wrong with this water. Give me a hand with this." Marcus helped him kick a hole in the side of the rotten boards until the hole was large enough for them to crawl through.

On the other side, they found a body of clear water flowing downward and disappearing into a cave. Doc took off his loafers.

"What are you doing?" Marcus asked.

"I'm going to follow the water and see where it goes."

"The hell you are. I'm not letting you go in there alone."

"You can join me," Doc said, peeling off his shirt and tossing it on the ground.

The thought of stripping off his clothes and jumping into the black hole of water was a challenge Marcus could live without. "You know I don't do water."

Doc smiled. He knew Marcus couldn't swim. "So wait for me, I won't be long."

Marcus couldn't say or do anything to stop him. "You better be back here in twenty minutes or I'm coming in after you."

Doc stepped down into the cold water, which rose quickly to his neck. The current moved him to the cave entrance, then his head suddenly disappeared under the water.

"Doc?" Marcus yelled.

"I'm okay," he shouted back.

"Famous last words." Marcus mumbled to himself and sat down on a rock to wait.

* * *

Sheriff Eagleton was waiting for Cassandra when she stepped off the airplane. She and Kane rode in the lead Jeep with Eagleton, while Priest and his men followed them as they made the short trip to the White River Copper Mine.

Five deputies stood at the gate as the vehicles passed through and parked next to the two shuttle buses in front of the office.

Cassandra entered the job shack, then Priest, who had to duck his head under the doorframe.

The foreman stared at the giant African dressed in a mink coat. It took a moment before he noticed Cassandra standing next to him. "Ms. Prophet . . . welcome back home," he said.

She gave him a perfunctory handshake. "Have the girls arrived?"

"They just entered the channel. It will take them about an hour to get through the mine. Will these other gentlemen be joining us?"

"Only the Minister and his people."

Kane took a seat on the bench by the window with Hanna. "I forgot Hanna's toy bag on the plane and I'd like to go back and get it."

Hanna played on the floor, drawing circles in the dust. Her white dress was ruined.

Cassandra cast angry eyes at her daughter. "Do whatever you want, just make sure you're back here in an hour." Eagleton tossed him the keys to the Jeep.

"Thanks," Kane said.

Cassandra and Priest followed the sheriff and his men out the back door to the mine pit behind the shack. They took an elevator down to the waiting mantrip, which was a five-foot high rail car made of iron and cage with passenger compartments at each end. The foreman passed around hard hats and told them to hold on to the safety handles as the cart began its slow descent into the mine.

Kane waited ten minutes before making his move. He looked out the windows. There were deputies out front, but the back was clear.

"Remember what I told you, Hanna. If you stay here and play real quiet until I get back, I'll give you a surprise."

"A big surprise?" she blurted as her blue eyes lit up.

"Yes, but remember, you must be very quiet until I return." Kane slung the document tube over his shoulder and snuck out the back door. The guard in the tower was out of position and didn't see him run into the mine.

The elevator shaft was just inside the entrance. He looked down the dark hole, but couldn't hear anything. He swung the metal tube off his shoulder and knelt on the ground. Flipping the tube upside down, he carefully unscrewed the bottom cap, revealing a digital keypad. He entered a six-digit code, set the timer, and wedged the tube in a space above the head frame.

When he returned to the office, Hanna was sitting like a little lady on the bench. Kane picked her up.

"I was quiet, uncle."

He smiled and kissed her. "I know—you're such a good girl," he said, hugging her.

"Do I get my surprise?"

"Yes, but we have to leave here first."

* * *

Doc didn't know how far he had swum, but it felt like miles. He lost his flashlight in the last tunnel, and was guided by the illumination of the rock crystals imbedded in the cavern walls. The water was getting colder with every stroke he took. His arms and legs felt like logs, but he refused to turn back. He flipped over on his back to rest and tried to avoid thinking about the razor-sharp stalactites suspended over his head. This tunnel was much larger than the last one. Suddenly, Doc felt his body drifting faster as if being drawn by a magnet. He rolled off his back and treaded water, but he couldn't stop. Struggling against the water was useless. He was in the middle of a strong current, and had no choice but to relax and let the water carry him. He came to a fork in the rocks where he saw a small channel branching off to his right.

He fought his way across the current and made it into shallower water. The water was still over his head, but soon his feet touched bottom and he walked out to dry land. Several yards into the mine, he found a pile of debris on the ground covered in years of cobweb and dust. Underneath was an old sluice trough, once used for washing placer gold. A few yards further was a large section of a flume, which miners used to carry water.

Doc ended up at an airshaft that angled upward through the rocks. The opening was barely large enough for him to squeeze through. He used his arms and legs to inch forward. He ended up in another cavern, but this one had deep tread marks in the earth.

Doc knelt down and inspected the wet clumps of mud. He followed the tracks and heard the echo of what sounded like a

216

waterfall. He moved cautiously toward the opening he saw up ahead.

Seventy yards in front of him was a mining shack elevated on pier posts, enclosed in a one-hundred-foot high cave. The lean-to was surrounded in a bank of river rocks, which protected it against the water gushing from the mouth of the cave. Two amphibious boats sat beached on the rocks in front of the shack. He looked around to make sure he was alone, and then slid into the water.

Halfway across, two deputies came out of the door-less shack. Doc ducked underneath the water until the men passed. The men walked to the back of the shack and took the stairs up to the mantrip platform. Doc surfaced, caught a lung full of fresh air, and then went back underwater.

* * *

Doc hid behind the boats, then ran for the shack when the men weren't looking. He peeked in, saw that the room was empty, and entered.

Against the wall was an assay counter and pigeonhole organizer on the wall. A set of rusty scales sat on top, next to a row of small bottles covered in century-old dust. Doc picked up one of the bottles and read the faded label.

Jai-Robson Priest's voice boomed through the thin wall. Doc carefully placed the chemical bottle back on the shelf. Against the opposite wall was a roll-top desk with a backpack and notebook computer.

Doc turned the computer on and placed his ear against the wall to listen to what was going on in the inner room. A few minutes later, he had heard and read enough. He closed the computer.

The sound of the mantrip could be heard making its way through the cave. Doc went outside and eased back into the water. The trip back was more difficult, because he had to keep Cassandra's computer dry, by holding it above his head. When he reached land, two men surprised him from behind. Doc broke free, until someone tackled him and smashed a rifle butt against his head.

Chapter 43

Poole threw a bucket of water on Doc's face and dropped the bucket on the ground.

"Sit him up over here," Cassandra said. Two burley men lifted him off the floor and pushed him down on the chair. "How did you get in here?"

Doc had a migraine-size headache and cobweb vision. One thing he could see was Jai-Robson's menacing smile as he sat at the table cradling a bottle of champagne.

"How did you find this mine?" Cassandra shouted.

Doc sat motionless.

Poole handed Cassandra her computer. "He had this on him." The blood drained from her face.

Eagleton walked in. "He's alone—he must have come down the south tunnel from McCain's barn."

Cassandra's body was trembling. "Where's St. John?" Doc still didn't answer her. She turned his head with a hard slap to his face.

Doc grimaced. "If I were you, I would be more concerned about what you're going to tell the FBI."

Eagleton gave her a concerned look.

"He's bluffing," Cassandra said, trying to convey confidence in her voice. "Whatever you think you've discovered, certainly has no relevance for anyone, least of all you."

"You're using this mine as a way station," Doc said.

"I don't know what . . ."

"You know exactly what I'm talking about. You're buying and selling women and babies. You smuggle them in from Europe and keep them imprisoned here until you find a buyer."

"That's absurd. I work with a lot of orphanages overseas, none of which would allow me to do what you're accusing me of. I am a legitimate businesswoman, and you would be hard pressed to prove otherwise."

"Not really. According to what I read in that little computer of yours, I'd say half the people in this valley are working for you in some capacity. If you think a legitimate businesswoman is someone who creates a cottage industry on the backs of the young woman you've exploited, then I guess you are. But even you have to admit, you've sunken to a real low."

"What are you talking about?" she asked.

"You just purchased sixty young girls from the Republic of Georgia and the Ukraine, so you can sell them to pimps and pedophiles like your friend over there." Priest dropped his glass of champagne. "You got these girls from adoption agencies that believed you really cared about the welfare of children. But all you're about is getting paid. You don't give a damn about the life of misery, loss of innocence, and death you've consigned these girls to. You're pathetic and so is everyone that's in this with you."

Cassandra lashed out at him with her fists as she spewed obscenities at him. Doc pushed her off him, and she stumbled to the floor. Before Doc knew what happened, Priest picked the chair up with him in it and tossed it against the wall. Doc struggled to his feet, and was met by Priest's fist. Two men pinned Doc against the wall while Priest beat him.

Cassandra fixed her hair and straightened her jacket. "That's enough. Sit him back in the chair."

Priest put another fist in his face, before lifting and dropping him back in the chair. Doc slumped over. Poole smiled.

Cassandra lifted Doc's chin with her finger so she could see his bloodied face. "I just want you to know that your friends are going to die just like you." She flung his chin from her hand and he fell to the floor. "Drag him out of here and get rid of him."

There was hesitation in Eagleton's voice. "Ms. Prophet, I don't know about . . ."

"Just do it!"

Priest pushed the sheriff aside. "You cowardly fool, I will gladly do this," he said, motioning his men to pick Doc up. "I will take this man out to the desert and do this for you. This is how much I value our friendship and care for you Cassandra." He clasped her hands.

Instead of being repulsed, she felt curiously comforted—a feeling she had never experienced before. For the first time, she thought about what would happen to her if she ended up in prison.

She walked out of the office with Priest. "Mr. Minister, is that offer you made me still open? I'm afraid that if Sebasst is right and the authorities know about my business operations, I will not be able to return home."

Jai-Robson's arm swallowed her waist as he pulled her to him. "Of course, Cassie, you are most welcome in my home. Of course, I shall provide and protect you." He drew her nearer.

She pushed back. "And Sam?"

"Yes, of course, your sister may also join us."

Chapter 44

Marcus knew he had waited too long for Doc to return. He stood to his feet and moved to the mouth of the cave. "Doc . . . Doc, you hear me?" he yelled, but of course there was no answer. There hadn't been one for over an hour.

Marcus ripped one of the rotten timbers from the wall, intending to make a raft. He dropped the large plank in the water and watched it sink. "Damn!" *Brilliant idea, Marcus. Suppose Doc was right about these tunnels running for miles underneath the valley. He could be anywhere.* He needed another plan, because waiting wasn't working.

He went back through the wall to the storage bin and up the steps to the barn. When he went outside, two deputies were waiting for him.

"You're Marcus St. John," said the middle-aged one who was built like a refrigerator.

"Is that a question?" Marcus asked.

The big deputy pulled his gun out. His young partner stood by nervously watching.

Marcus raised his hands.

"Where's the woman?" the deputy asked.

"Which woman are you talking about?"

"Don't get smart with me. You know who I'm talking about—Jordan Bloodstone."

"She left last night."

"Sure, just like your friend, Julian Sebasst did." The deputy stepped closer, raising the gun. "Move." Marcus started walking toward their vehicle. "You're headed in the wrong direction," the deputy said, spinning him around and pushing him toward the barn.

Marcus knew they planned to kill him. He figured Doc had already been caught or worse—killed. He kept walking with the deputies directly behind him. He needed an edge, a distraction—something to separate the two men.

"You know how much money I have?" Marcus asked as he moved closer toward the barn door.

"Shut up, we're not interested."

"Hey, I'm just saying why waste away in the bush country when you both could retire in the Caribbean with a million dollars in your pockets," Marcus said, as his fingers touched the door.

The young deputy stopped in his tracks. "A million doll . . ." Marcus swung the door back into the man's face. The blow knocked both deputies on the ground. The young deputy was unconscious, but his partner was only dazed. He scrambled for his gun, but when he looked up, Marcus was gone.

* * *

The deputy was still trying to clear his head when he entered the barn. He saw the opening in the floorboards under the loft. He leaned over, looked down, as Marcus came up from behind and hit him over the head with a tire iron. The man fell into the hole.

"Idiot." Marcus dropped the iron on top of the deputy's body and closed the trapdoor. He went outside and stirred the other deputy awake.

"What's your name, kid?"

"John Aris."

"You married—have a family?"

"Yes . . . a wife." He saw his gun in Marcus's hand."

"That's good. Now, this is what you're going to do. You're going to tell me everything you know, including where my friend is." Marcus placed the gun barrel on the man's throat. "You can start talking now."

* * *

Jordan opened the hangar door for Marcus.

"Where's Doc?" she asked as he jumped out of the truck.

"Cassandra Prophet is holding him at the copper mine, along with a bunch of girls she's smuggling into the country."

223

He hurried past the bound deputies strapped to the support beam and ran up the steps into the jet. Rose and her daughter were watching television.

"Hello," she said, with an appreciative smile on her face.

Marcus nodded, then quickly made his way to the cabin closet. "How's she doing?" he whispered to Jordan, as he peeled out of his sweat-drenched shirt.

"Much better. I told her she was safe with us, and that we would help her when we get back home."

Marcus pulled a spandex tee shirt off the shelf. "Well, if you want to keep that promise we better get moving. Hand me my shoulder strap," he said as he pulled the shirt over his head and tucked it in. He reached in the overhead compartment and retrieved two automatics and a box of clips. "You packing anything heavier than your handgun?"

"There's a pump shotgun in the back of the truck."

"Good, you'll need it. There are five deputies, the sheriff, some armed miners, and Priest's people."

"What's your plan?"

"We go in and get Doc, and get out; that's the plan."

An explosion shook the building. Rose clutched her daughter as the Learjet swayed.

Outside, they saw a mushroom cloud billowing over the hill. "That was the biggest damn explosion I've ever heard," Marcus said.

"It came from the mine," Jordan said.

Marcus shoved the extra gun clip in his waistband and ran for the vehicle.

* * *

The explosion tossed Cassandra over the top of the Jeep. She managed to crawl underneath seconds before tons of rock and metal rained down from the sky. She staggered to her feet choking on black smoke, and wiping grit and sand from her eyes. For a brief moment she thought she was dreaming. The opening to the mine had imploded under tons of limestone rock and sand. The office, job shack, and supply house lay wasted in the sand like

224

pieces of discarded cardboard. Cassandra, Eagleton, and a few others were the lucky ones. Several others were dead or trapped in the rubble.

Eagleton's bloody hand grabbed her shoulder. "Ms. Prophet, this was no accident. Someone set off that explosion. We need to get you out of here!" Cassandra stood in shock watching the black smoke rising from the crater in the earth. The mine, the tunnels, and everything she had worked for were gone.

"Ms. Prophet?" Eagleton asked. She didn't hear him. Eagleton guided her to the nearest vehicle and pushed her in. He pulled one of his men aside. "Get her to the airplane. We'll follow behind with the girls."

* * *

Pool had no idea of what just happened. He was just glad to be alive. He maneuvered the lead bus around a pile of rocks and fell in behind the small motorcade of Jeeps waiting to take them to the airstrip. Suddenly, the electric gate starting closing and gunfire erupted from the guard tower. Poole looked up and saw a truck speeding down the canyon road.

* * *

Jordan rammed the truck through the gate, saw Poole in the bus, and headed straight for him. Hysteria broke out on the bus when the girls realized the truck was not going to stop. Poole fumbled to unlatch his gun strap.

Jordan headed for the rubble of debris in front of the bus. When the tires hit the plywood siding, she punched the accelerator and the truck went airborne. Poole screamed and covered his face.

The truck smashed through the accordion doors, with the nose coming to rest on the bus platform. Jordan jumped out of the truck, scooted over the hood, and kicked the rest of the door off the hinge. Poole lay wedged in the seat, with a broken steering column speared in his chest.

The driver of the other bus ran when he saw Jordan dragging Poole's dead body off the bus.

Deputies swarmed from their vehicles, but were met with gunfire from Marcus, who had used the diversion to sneak past the guard tower. Eagleton and his men fanned out and boxed him in.

Chapter 45

Sydney knew that the woman pursuing her was gaining ground, but at least the deputies with her were nowhere in sight. Sydney was too tired to keep running. It was time to make a stand and fight. When she reached a draw at the base of a hill, she pulled up on the reins of her horse and skidded to a stop. She jumped off and scrambled up the rocks looking for a good place to hide. A series of boulders near the rim of the hill offered her the best protection. She squeezed her body between two of the large rocks and waited.

Samantha dug her heels into the flanks of her horse trying to coax him up the forty-five degree grade. The horse resisted, bucked, snorted, and finally collapsed in the sand from exhaustion. Samantha pulled a rifle from the saddle and ran up the hill.

Sydney saw her coming and knew the best chance for stopping her was before she reached the clump of bushes forty feet below. She moved to the other side of the rock to get a clear shot. That's when she heard the sound of an airplane engine.

She scampered to the top of the hill and saw the jumbo jet on the desert runway. Several feet from the plane were four men huddled in the middle of the desert. Sydney raised the riflescope to her eye. The image was blurry—too much swirling sand from the engines. She scooted along the ridge until she found a better vantage point, where she rested the rifle barrel on a rock to steady her view. Three men stood in a circle beating a bare-chested black man whose hands were bound in front of him. She adjusted her scope. The men released him and he sank to his knees. A big black man stood over him, holding a gun to his side. Sydney zeroed in on the man's intended victim. "Julian?" She couldn't believe her eyes. She looked again. It was him and he was about to be executed. She didn't have the angle or distance to shoot the man holding the gun.

If she didn't try, Doc would certainly die, but if she did, she'd be an easy target for the woman.

Sydney heard the bushes rustle below as the woman inched closer. Sydney reached up and quietly pulled her rifle off the rock. She backed up against the boulder trying to think, but she didn't have time. Doc would be dead if she didn't act now. She would only get one shot and she had to make it count. Sydney gripped the rifle, sprang to her feet, and fired. Seconds later, another shot rang out, and Sydney fell off the boulder.

* * *

Sydney's bullet tore through the side of Priest's coat, landing harmlessly in the sand. His two aids looked to the hills, but they couldn't see the invisible sniper. They panicked and ran toward the jet. Priest turned around and shot them in the back. "I will not have cowards working for me!"

Doc lunged from his crouched position, hitting Priest's body like a football player tackling a dummy. The gun flew out of his hand.

Priest scratched at the sand trying to reach the gun, but Doc looped his bound wrists over Priest's neck and pulled him back. Priest pounded the ground, fighting for air, as Doc choked him with all his strength. Priest rolled over onto his side, but that made matters worse. Doc grabbed the mink coat by the collar, pulled the coat over Priest's head, and shoved his face into the sand.

"That's enough; let him go," said the voice standing over them. Doc ignored the warning, and continued pushing Priest's face deeper into the sand. Doc felt the touch of a gun against his neck.

"I have no desire to kill you, but I will if you don't release him—now!" Kane said.

Doc let go. The African struggled to his feet, coughing and spitting sand and blood from his mouth.

"Minister, Ms. Prophet is waiting for you on your airplane. The military will be here in a few minutes. I will finish things here," Kane said.

228

Priest caught his breath, thanked Kane, and lumbered toward his jet.

Doc fell over on his back, exhausted. He looked up at Kane. "Who are you?"

Chapter 46

Samantha made her way over to the spot where Sydney had fallen. She worked her way along the ridge and back again, but still couldn't find her in the ravine.

Sydney watched the skinny woman searching the bushes. "I'm sorry, but you're looking in the wrong place."

Samantha spun around and saw Sydney standing on top of a boulder, holding a handgun. Blood trickled down the side of her face.

"Where's the letter?" Samantha asked.

"Is that the only question you people know to ask?"

Samantha tightened her hand on the rifle. "I want that letter."

"And I want world peace, but we can't always get what we want. Drop the rifle." Sydney could tell by her eyes that the woman had too much pride to give up. "I know what you're thinking, but . . ."

Samantha screamed and raised her rifle. Sydney shot her twice, and she fell into the ravine.

* * *

Doc stumbled aimlessly in the open desert not sure of which way to go. The roar of the jet taxiing down the airstrip pointed the way. He stood watching as it rocketed past him with Cassandra Prophet and Jai-Robson Priest on board. Just as it lifted off the ground, a bomb ripped the fuselage apart and the jetliner disintegrated in the air. The force of the blast knocked Doc off his feet. He sat up and looked at the burning debris in the sand. Beyond the smoke he saw a woman with red hair running toward him. She was covered in sand and sunburned, but he'd recognize her anywhere. He tried to stand, but stumbled.

Sydney helped him to his feet. "Julian, how did you find me?"

"I was going to ask you the same question," he said, giving her a feeble hug. His face was covered in blood. Sydney tore the sleeve from her blouse and gently wiped his face. His nose was broken, and an eye was completely closed.

"Damn, Julian, how the hell did you let this happen to you?"

"Messing with the wrong woman," he grinned. "But I don't think I have to worry about her anymore," he said, pointing to the plane wreckage.

"What happened here?"

"A disgruntled employee didn't like the business she was in or her friends. I guess he thought blowing them out of the sky was a reasonable solution to the problem."

"Who was she?"

"Cassandra Prophet."

"She doesn't by chance have any relatives around here—a tall crazy woman resembling a tadpole?"

"That would be the sister. Your paths have crossed?"

"Yeah, on the other side of the hill over there." Doc stood erect, and looked around.

"What's wrong?" Sydney asked.

"The airfield is empty. Where is everyone?"

* * *

The sheriff had Marcus penned behind the rubble that was once the supply shack. Jordan pulled the first girl from the seat and guided her out. The rest followed. "Run," she shouted, pushing them out of the door. Three miners fired on the bus, but Jordan's shotgun blasts stopped two of them.

Marcus saw deputies trying to outflank him, while the guard in the watchtower kept him cornered with no place to go. Marcus released his spent clips and slid in fresh ones as he pondered his situation. The man in the tower would certainly pick him off if he tried to move. On the other hand, he couldn't wait around for the deputies to sneak up behind him. He peeked to see where Jordan was. A bullet ricocheted off the metal flashing next to his head.

231

Jordan and the girls were safe behind the bus, which was fifty feet away. He could make it that far, but first he would have to deal with the guard in the tower. He knelt on one knee, leaned his body around the stack of wood so he could see around the corner. The guard moved across the walk ramp trying to get a better shot at him. Marcus waited.

When the guard came into view, Marcus fired both guns. The man collapsed against the guardrail and fell over the side. Gunfire erupted again. Marcus ran full speed toward the bus firing as he went. His bullets hit the gas tank of a jeep and the explosion sent the deputies ducking for cover.

Marcus heard the sound of the helicopters before he saw them hovering over the charred remains of the copper mine. Eagleton and his men dropped their weapons. One of the Air Force gunners had a machine gun trained on them. Another helicopter landed next to him.

"Are you Sebasst?" shouted the airman.

"No, but we need to find him," Marcus said.

* * *

Marcus spotted Doc and Sydney walking along the road leading from the airport. "There . . . down there!" he said, pointing from the helicopter. The helicopter landed and Marcus jumped out and ran over to Doc.

"I was beginning to worry about you," Marcus said, as he helped Sydney carry Doc to the waiting medic in the helicopter.

"I'll be okay. Just let me rest a bit."

"Give me a minute with him," the medic said.

Marcus went over to the other helicopter where Sydney and Jordan were. He gave Sydney a hug. "I don't think we should let you out by yourself, again."

Sydney sat in the helicopter drinking a bottle of water. "You won't get any arguments from me," she said with a smile.

The medic stitched the cut over Doc's eye. "When you get back home have your doctor look at it."

"Okay, thanks."

The lieutenant boarded his helicopter. "The state police will be here shortly. You and your friends have a way out of here?"

"Yeah—we'll be okay, thanks," Marcus said.

"Okay. We're going to want to ask you more questions when you're feeling better."

"How did you know we were here?" Marcus asked.

"We got an anonymous telephone tip on the base."

"It must have been from Kane," Doc said.

"Kane? Yeah—I forgot about him. What happened to him?"

* **

The last of the state troopers left the airfield after midnight. Kane came out of hiding, carrying Hanna who was asleep on his shoulder. He walked over to the sheriff's helicopter and gently strapped Hanna into the seat. They would be in Las Vegas by morning where a plane would be waiting for them. Cassandra's network and infrastructure were gone. But more importantly, so were the primary people who had been responsible for much of the abductions and plundering of women and babies from his country.

Now that his job was done, he could finally go home to the Republic of Georgia. He would take a few months off to find Hanna a good home. After that he'd report to the Bureau of Special Intelligence to receive his next assignment.

Thank you for purchasing my book. Please turn the page to
see a preview of the next Julian Sebasst novel

VIPERS NEST

Another Julian Sebasst Novel
Vipers Nest

By
D.M. EDWARDS

A young black woman stood alone in the mirrored elevator hoping it would get stuck so she wouldn't have to get off. She tried unsuccessfully to rearrange the unruly curls that hovered over her round-framed eyeglasses, and then smoothed her hand over her suit. She stopped once she realized her personal appearance was the last thing Marcus St. John would be concerned with. Still, when the elevator door opened on the fourteenth floor, Nikki tugged one last time at the hem of her jacket before exiting.

The long walk along the empty hallway atop the St. John Towers felt like a death march as she tried to ignore the sound of her high heels clicking against the hardwood floor. The twin office complex stood in the heart of San Francisco near Union Square Park, serving as the iconic corporate headquarters of the St. John Group and its affiliated flagship, the St. John-Sebasst Security Force.

At the office door, she paused before knocking. Marcus was not the kind of man that handled bad news well and what she had to tell him was worse than bad. She was expecting to be fired. She sucked up a lung full of air and rapped softly against the twelve-foot high mahogany door. Marcus told her to enter.

Nikki had never been in his office before, but she had heard about it. Even so, she wasn't prepared for what she saw. The Afro-centric suite was filled with Moroccan burl wood furniture, and polished European chrome, with Brazilian bamboo flooring. Contemporary African art paintings hung on the wall. Marcus smiled and motioned her to take a seat while he sat behind his desk, talking on the telephone. Nikki was thankful to see that he was in a good mood. Instead of sitting in the chair by his desk, though she chose the conference table in the middle of the room.

Marcus St. John looked bigger than life sitting in the high-backed leather chair, like it was a throne facing a twenty-foot tropical aquarium embedded in a wall of black acrylic. Prominently displayed on the wall above his head was a treasured pair of mint condition 1847 Walker revolvers, given to him by his childhood friend and business partner, Julian "Doc" Sebasst.

Nikki placed her brown portfolio case on the table, then moved it to her lap to help keep her knees from trembling.

* * *

Marcus swiveled his chair to face away from Nikki and gaze across the San Francisco skyline. He roared with laughter into the telephone. "Doc, you can't say I didn't warn you. If God wanted you swimming with the sharks he would have made you a whale. You're too damn old to be tempting fate because of some stupid bucket-list wish."

"There's nothing wrong with scuba diving. I'll be more careful next time. I just thank God that El wasn't with me."

"You got that right. My godson shouldn't have to suffer because of his daddy's poor judgment. You've gotten soft living down there on your little island you think is paradise. Maybe you'd regain your senses if you moved back home."

"St. Thomas suits me and my family just fine. Besides, if that meant having to put up with you again, I'd rather go back to the lagoon and let the sharks gnaw my leg off."

"That was cold, Doc."

"You earned it. Tell me something. If you hate the tropics so much, why are you investing three hundred million dollars in a hotel in the Caymans?"

Marcus thought that was a stupid question. "Uhh . . . because the Caymanians have one of the highest standards of living in the world, a GDP of $2 billion, and a financial haven for greedy bastards like you who want to shelter their dirty money from their wives or the government. I don't have to be in love with a place to know that I can make a boatload of money there. And for the record, it's five hundred million, not three hundred million."

"Ouch. How'd that happen?"

"Hell, if I knew that, I wouldn't have sent Max down there to find out," Marcus said with a hint of sarcasm and a sharper tone than he intended. "Sorry, man, I'm just frustrated over the delays. I've spent half a billion dollars and all I've got to show for it is a giant metal erector set sitting in a hole the size of New Jersey."

"I thought Max retired."

"He did, but I needed him after Thornton damn near destroyed the company. I'm still trying to figure out how much damage he caused."

"How bad is it?"

"Nothing I can't handle," he said.

"Good, so tell me how bad?"

"What?"

Marcus paused, not wanting to answer the question. He was thankful when he heard something hit the floor. Nikki had dropped a folder. Her mouth twitched when she attempted to smile. She placed the brown portfolio case on the table. Marcus thought he saw her knees trembling. He frowned.

"Marcus, are you still there?" Doc asked.

"Yeah."

"Tell me what's going on?"

Marcus sighed. "I'm still up to my neck in these bogus lawsuits that may cost us our future grandkid's inheritance, and of course my own little personal black hole in the Grand Caymans that's costing me a ton of money every day it sits idle. And to top it off this morning I get to work at five, turn on my computer, and find the screen is black as your ugly mug. My IT people tell me we've got a bug in the system, and meantime I've got five hundred thirty-seven people here with nothing to do but take pictures of their asses on my copy machines."

"What's the status of Masterson's case?"

Marcus paused before answering. When he did it was somber. "I can deal with all the shit being thrown at me, except this." Another pause. "I've been jammed in a corner a lot of times, and I've always been able to fight my way out. But this . . . I can't find a workaround. Her lawyers are willing to settle out of court for five million dollars."

"That's ridiculous. Don't pay her a dime. You didn't do anything."

Marcus gave a cynical but nervous laugh. "She's almost got me convinced that I did. She has depositions from people I don't know, swearing that I slept with her at hotels I've never been to—on dates that I can't prove otherwise. I tell you one thing I've learned from all this. My next personal assistant will not have access to my personal calendar, and she'll be a gap-toothed grandmother from Guatemala."

"What's the board saying?"

"Stallworth and a few of the other board members are urging me to take the deal, even though it would seriously violate my ethics clause; the same one I voluntarily agreed to put in place as a condition for taking the company public. Ironic, huh? If I don't take Masterson's deal, this thing will go on forever and in the end I would probably still lose. If I take it, I risk losing my company to once loyal board members that are looking at me sideways. Hell of a choice, don't you think?"

"You do know Masterson set you up. You can't give in to her attorneys."

"Knowing and proving it are two different things. Between Rachael Masterson's allegations, the lawsuits caused by Thornton's incompetence, and the hotel, I don't have time to breathe."

"What does Caitlin want you to do?"

"No surrender, no retreat. You know how she is."

"That's good advice, so listen to her. I'm catching a flight up there tomorrow."

Marcus spun his chair around to face Nikki, who sat patiently waiting for him at the table. "I appreciate the support,

Doc, but there's nothing you can do. Hell, there's nothing I can do. In order to fix the leaky pipe you have to know where it's leaking. I have no idea who is doing this or why."

"Let me talk to the board. This is the time they should be rallying around to support you, not looking at the easy way out."

"It's not entirely their fault. They have the welfare of the stockholders to consider."

"The stockholder's interests are best served by the board of directors supporting you and not questioning your integrity."

Marcus knew Doc was right, but the board was too fractured to listen to reason—even from him. Marcus had long since regretted taking the company public. His second mistake was giving up his controlling share of the corporation in order to finance the expansion of SJS. But his biggest regret was not having Doc on the board. Doc could always be counted on to watch his back.

"Look, Doc, maybe I could use your help, after all. I know the Caymanians are purposely delaying construction on the hotel, I just don't know why. I think Max could use your help dealing with them."

"Sure, where's he staying?"

"At his beach house in Nassau with Lorne."

* * *

When Marcus hung up the telephone, he picked his half-smoked cigar out of the ashtray, stuck it into his mouth, and got up from the chair. He looked taller than his official six-foot-two. His French-cuffed shirt lie sculptured to his lean frame, and his wine-and-chocolate tie complemented his caramel-colored skin. Beneath the graying temples and salt-and-pepper mustache was a boyish face with a rakish smile that seemed permanently etched on his face.

He went to the table and sat down, crossing his legs. "Nikki, sorry to keep you waiting. I hope you're here to tell me our network is up and functioning again." He saw the answer in her eyes before she opened her mouth.

"I wish I could, but I can't, sir. I'm afraid we have a much bigger problem on our hands. Our entire system is infected, including Cornerstone Insurance Recovery in Seattle."

Marcus's teeth clutched the cigar. "How is that possible?"

"We think it was a malicious worm sent via e-mail to one of our computers. From there, it replicated itself, invaded our system, and copied our computer protocols."

"Give me that in English," he said, lighting his cigar.

"Someone managed to hack into our financial records and bank accounts, including your personal account."

Marcus bit through his cigar and spit it from his mouth. "How the hell could something like this happen, Nikki?" he yelled.

Her body shuddered. "We don't know . . . yet, sir. Our forensic people are checking for answers. Until we have some additional safeguards in place, the server will stay shut down."

Marcus swore as he jumped up from the table and flung the chair halfway across the room. Nikki continued looking at the floor, afraid to breathe. Marcus saw the portfolio on her lap move up and down as she nervously tapped her foot. He straightened his tie and composed himself. Hovering over her shoulder, he asked, "how bad did we get hit?"

She swallowed hard and opened the case.

He placed his hand on her shoulder for her to stop. "I don't need the details . . . just the bottom line, Nikki."

She cleared her throat and rested her clasped hands on her lap. "Six hundred thousand dollars from SJS, one point two million from Cornerstone Pension Investments and—" She couldn't bring herself to look at his face. "You lost the twenty-five million you had just transferred into escrow for the hotel. They also stole confidential data, including social security numbers from our insurance files at Cornerstone."

Marcus felt numb. "How many files were accessed?"

"All of them."

The gravity of the crime warranted her outright firing, but what she got instead was twenty seconds of stunned silence. Marcus sat back down at the table.

When he spoke, it was soft, but firm. "Where was the money transferred?"

"To a bank in New Mexico, then to New York and Miami. We lost track after that—"

He looked at her. "How do we get it back?"

She thought for a moment. "We would need to find out who stole it, the bank it's in, the account—" She didn't need to finish.

Marcus buried his head in his hands.

* * *

ABOUT THE AUTHOR

D.M. Edwards lives in the Pacific Northwest with his wife, where he works as a housing manager for county government. He is currently working on his fifth Julian Sebasst novel. Mr. Edwards may be contacted at dmedwardsauthor@gmail.com.

5

13373697R00129

Made in the USA
Charleston, SC
05 July 2012